DRY BONES IN THE VALLEY

DRY BONES IN THE VALLEY

William MacLeod Raine

GUNSMOKE

First published in the UK by Hodder and Stoughton

This hardback edition 2010
by BBC Audiobooks Ltd
by arrangement with
Golden West Literary Agency

ISBN 978 1 408 46273 7

British Library Cataloguing in Publication Data available.

Printed and bound in Great Britain by
CPI Antony Rowe, Chippenham and Eastbourne

DRY BONES IN THE VALLEY

1   THE DAY WAS YOUNG. FROM A
    crotch in the far Sierras rays of the early sun
    streamed across the greasewood and the prickly
pear. A thick dust filled the air, stirred by the milling cowponies as the Quarter Circle F Y riders roped and saddled.
Rufe Rogers was tightening the girth on his paint horse
when Kurt Barlow, the ranch foreman, swung around beside him. Kurt was a big rangy crook-nosed man, short-
tempered and overbearing, his coffee-colored face tough as
weathered leather.

"The old man wants to see you," he snapped.

Rufe was surprised and disturbed. He had been with the
outfit two weeks and the boss had not spoken a dozen
words to him. His guess was that news of his trouble had
drifted up from Texas.

"What for?" he asked.

"How the hell would I know?" Barlow demanded irritably. He was annoyed because Fen Yont had not told him
him why he wished to see the new rider. The ranch owner
was full of tricks like that, always keeping his motives under cover. He did not trust his own foreman.

"Must want to cuss me out or tie a can to me," Rufe
suggested.

Barlow ignored this. He yelped a question at the group
waiting to start riding circle. "Everybody up?" His glance
fell on a dilatory puncher cinching the saddle on his nervous mount. "Why in blazes are you always last, Arkansas?"
he rasped, and turned his horse to jiggle from the yard at a
road gait.

The young Texan watched the riders follow. He would
have liked to be one of them, carefree and undisturbed in

mind. A month earlier he had not known what it was to worry.

After turning his horse into the corral, Rogers walked to the big sprawling house and along the wide porch to the end room known as Yont's Give-'Em-Hell quarters. It was here that he cut his employees down to size when they angered him. More than once this had taken the form of a personal thrashing which had left the victim battered and helpless for a week.

Yont did not look up when Rogers came through the doorway. With the stub of a pencil he was writing a letter and he finished it before paying any attention to the cowboy. He was a big bull-necked man with cold protruding eyes, hard as topaz, set in a long-jawed craggy face. His shoulders and body were heavy and powerful. Fifty years on the sun-and-windswept desert had thickened but not softened them. Across his stomach a steel band of muscle stretched. Though he had money enough to burn a wet mule, as one of his riders had put it, the old clothes he wore would have been scorned by a tramp.

Fendrick Yont leaned back in his chair and silently scrutinized his employee. Rufe gripped his big hat nervously in both hands, but his eyes did not waver from the searching ones that gimleted into him. Yet under the pressure of them he was the first to speak.

"Kurt told me to report to you," he said.

The ranchman took his time to answer. "You left Texas three weeks ago two jumps ahead of a sheriff's posse out to capture you for robbing a Fort Worth bank and killing a teller," he accused harshly.

Rufe was half-expecting that charge. His eyes narrowed warily. "News to me," he replied. "I've been a heap of things but never a bank robber."

Yont tossed a folded newspaper across the table. The young man stared down at a picture of himself beneath which was a caption, *Five hundred dollars reward offered for the arrest of this bandit, Rufus Rogers.*

"Looks kinda like me—and like a heap of other fellows I know," the Texan said. "But the name is wrong. They call me Jim Dillard."

The big man's barking laugh was skeptical. "Since

2

when?" He reached a hand across the table. "Lemme see your hat."

This is pay day, Rufe thought, and passed the hat to Yont.

On the sweat pad were inked the initials R. R.

"You're a poor liar," the ranch boss told him scornfully. "Can you give me any reason why I shouldn't arrest and send you back?"

Rufe shifted his defense. "All right. I'm Rogers. But that doesn't make me guilty. I hadn't a thing to do with that robbery."

"That's your story, but not the way the paper tells it. You are guilty as sin. You had been palling around with the bandits. Fifteen minutes before the holdup, you were seen with them. Before you could be arrested, you lit out hell-for-leather. Nobody puts out a five-hundred-dollar reward for an innocent man."

"Listen, Mr. Yont. I was a puncher on the chuck line. The way of it was that I had come up with a herd from Lampasas headed for Dodge, and after the boss had sold the beef stuff, I lit out for home. At Fort Worth I got in a poker game and blew my wad. That's when I met those birds from Trinidad and played around with them two-three days. How was I to know they were outlaws just because they asked me to hold their horses while they went into the bank to cash a check?"

Rogers put his case quietly with neither excitement nor panic in his voice. There was nothing shifty in his direct gaze. That it was an unlikely story he knew, and he did not expect it to be believed.

"Our prisons are full of convicted men who cry innocent," Yont said, watching his man with searching wary eyes. "Why should I believe you?"

He did not care a rap whether the Texan was innocent or guilty. He had a use for this man, but first he had to let the fellow see he was completely in his power, as helpless as a snake beneath a forked stick, and he had to find out of what malleable or indomitable stuff Rufe Rogers was made. The owner of the Quarter Circle F Y could see that this youngster was physically lithe and tough, and that, in spite of his manner of assurance, he was not old or experi-

3

enced enough to be entirely sure of himself. He would probably go a long way to save his life, though he might need careful handling.

Yont flung a question at him. "How old are you?"

"Twenty-two come November."

That age suited Yont very well, but he gave no sign of it. He rubbed his unshaven chin thoughtfully, not for an instant lifting his probing eyes from the youth. Just as well let the kid sweat awhile. It would do him good to realize fully that he had his tail in a crack and could not wiggle loose.

He said, as if thinking aloud: "In Fort Worth they are all set to lynch you. So the paper says. According to its story, killing that bank clerk wasn't necessary at all. Well, that's your funeral, not mine. As a law-abiding citizen it is my duty to notify the officers you are here."

If Yont expected to break down the Texan and make him beg for mercy, he was mistaken. Rogers had made his plea and let it ride at that. He stood tall and straight, his shoulders squared.

"And get the five hundred dollars reward," he reminded the ranchman. "Don't forget that."

"That kind of talk won't get you anywhere," Yont snarled. "You're too brash with your betters. I've a mind to pack you back to Fort Worth where there is a rope waiting for you."

It came to Rogers that this old fox had some plan in his brain that had not yet reached the stage of words. There would be no profit in rousing his ire. It would be wise to talk softly until Yont had declared himself.

"I wouldn't like that, Mr. Yont," Rogers said. "I reckon I'll let you do the talking."

"I ought to turn you in," Yont said, and drummed with his fingertips on the table. "No two ways about that. But you are young and I hate to see you strung up or even sent to the penitentiary for twenty years. Maybe I could keep you on the spread—if you're smart enough to take orders, obey them exactly, and keep your mouth pad-locked."

"Kurt Barlow can tell you I'm a good waddy."

4

"The orders will come from me, not Kurt. And you'll jump to carry them out. Understand?"

"Yes, sir."

"I've got the whiphand. Never forget that. When you hear the lash crack, you move fast. You're my man."

It was not so much what Yont said as the way he said it that sent a scunner through Rufe. He spoke from lips that were a thin cruel slit in the ugly lupine face. Already the Texan had heard a good deal of guarded talk about this man. He had come up the hard way, trampling down those who stood in his path. The drive of an arrogant and restless will had carried him to success—from a thirty-dollar a month puncher to the ownership of the Quarter Circle F Y, the biggest spread in the district. Rumor had it that he had been ruthless in his method of building it up. Homesteaders had been driven out, by threats, by arson, by different forms of violence. The underground whisper told stories of two obstinate nesters who had not been known to leave the country, but had disappeared without disposing of their stock or household goods. Drygulched at the order of Fen Yont, was the opinion of their neighbors.

Rufe did not like the situation at all. This old wolf was still on the make, extending his holdings a bit here and a bit there at the expense of others. To pledge himself to blind obedience was something he could not stomach, but if he should be taken back to Fort Worth now, he was lost. He had no doubt that half the town would be hot for summary vengeance on the callous murder of the bank clerk.

Young Rogers sparred for time. "If you know I'm wanted by the law, probably others here know it too or soon will. Unless I keep on the move I'll be arrested."

Yont shook his head. "Very little chance of that. I take the Fort Worth paper for the cattle market quotations, but nobody else in the county sees it. This nook in the woods is full of refugees from the law. Nobody pays any attention to them. Why would anybody think Jim Dillard was Rufus Rogers? You're safe enough—if I want it that way."

It is neck meat or nothing, Rufe thought. *I've got to throw in with this old devil and run out on him later if he crowds me too much.*

5

"We can do business, Mr. Yont, I reckon," he answered.

"Thought you would see it that way," the older man said grimly. "When you joined up with bandits you forfeited your right to an option."

"Have it your way. I can't persuade you different." The young man lifted his shoulders in a shrug. "I don't reckon you would ask me to do anything wrong."

A shutter dropped over the eyes of Yont, a film that left them opaque and blank. "Get it straight. I'll be the judge of what's right and what's wrong. You don't do any thinking. When I give an order, you carry it out."

Rufus Rogers' gorge rose in resentment. He could barely keep from telling this old slavedriver to go to blazes, but a picture rose to his mind of a rope flung over the limb of a cottonwood and tightened around his throat, a howling mob surrounding him. He had no illusions about that. If he was taken to Fort Worth while the town was in its present temper, it would be the end of the road for him. Nor could he see any third way out. Any break to escape now would be futile. Before he had traveled a dozen miles, he would be picked up.

"Looks like you've got the deadwood on me, Mr. Yont," he said.

The cowman's grating voice snapped advice. "Remember that twenty-four hours of the day, young fellow." He added with a thin smile, "You'll get along fine if you do."

Rogers said bitterly, "The way a Negro slave used to do, owned body and soul."

Yont was willing to let that idea sink into him, but he replied with some words that might help to palliate the sting of it. "Men guided by me have plenty of money to spend."

Rufe had been brought up in a borderland of violence and insecurity. Bad men had poured into Texas from half a dozen states to escape the penalty of their misdeeds. They formed bandit gangs and preyed on honest settlers. The cattle trail end towns roared with young insurgent life. Always in that raw frontier there had been a struggle between good men and the ruffians who infested the towns and the brush country. But the law and order party was gaining the upper hand. The riffraff were drifting westward—to the mining camps of Tombstone and Bisbee, to the gulches and pockets of the Dragoons, Huachucas, and the White Mountains that offered a hundred convenient gorges to shelter men on the dodge. Into that new refuge for criminals Rufe Rogers had been driven by the whip of circumstance. It had been his own fault. The spirit of the lawless frontier translated liberty into license and the wild surge of youth had taken his reckless feet on forbidden trails. But in him was the blood of decent God-fearing pioneers and he had never crossed the line beyond which lies a morass of evil from which there is no escape.

"You can start earning it right now," Yont continued. "The first job I'm giving you is legal. You don't have to break any laws, except that you had better make out you have lived here a year." He unrolled a section map and spread it on the table in front of him, pinning down the edges with an ink bottle, a spur, a pair of scissors, and his pocket knife. His pencil jabbed at a quarter section defined by a red line enclosing it. "You will ride in to Rifle today and file on that piece of land. It is open to homestead entry. Make your application under the name Jim Dillard." He flung a sharp question at Rufe. "Nobody knows you at Rifle—you've never been there?"

"No."

"Fine. Get your story straight. You've been working for me here a year. You're twenty-two years old, and you want to get hold of a homestead claim. There won't be any trouble about it. The registrar Hagen has done business with me. I'll give you the entry fee."

Rogers knew the pattern of this method of evading the law. Hundreds of cowboys all over the West had taken up land ostensibly for their own use, and as soon as it was patented, had turned the homestead over to the owner of the spread. The practice was so common that rarely was the legality of the transfer questioned. Most ranchmen considered it a legitimate transaction. They felt they had a priority right of use.

There was a catch in this somewhere, Rufe guessed. The map showed that Dead Cow Creek ran a winding course across the quarter section.

7

"Looks as if a watered claim like this would have been taken up long ago," he said.

"Smart, aren't you? Maybe somebody blundered. You don't have to worry about that. By tonight it will be your claim, and next year it will be mine. Keep your mouth shut and don't do any talking. Just go into the land office and file."

"Sure. I reckon I'll have to live on it, won't I?"

"Yeah. Build a shack—do some fencing—fiddle around making improvements."

"Anybody claim this hundred and sixty now?"

The eyes of the cattleman half-shuttered and looked at Rogers empty of expression. "What claim can anybody else have on land upon which you will have made lawful entry?" he inquired.

Yont might as well have said in blunt words that he was using the Texan to jump the claim of somebody who had made a defective entry.

The old scoundrel is making me a cat's-paw to pull his chestnuts out of the fire, Rogers thought. *I'm the guy who is liable to be rubbed out for starting trouble and he knows it, but I have to play along with him.*

"How far is Rifle?" the Texan wanted to know.

"About twenty-six miles. You had better start right away." Yont handed him the letter he had been writing. "Give this to Hagen himself, not to his clerk."

The ranchman drew some dirty ragged bills from his pocket to pay the expenses.

"Might have known he would not have clean money," Rogers murmured irritably as he stood on the porch and shoved the greenbacks into his jeans.

2 RUFUS ROGERS WOUND IN AND OUT of the arroyos between the cowbacked hills. He was following a trail that would save him three or four miles. It led him across a divide from which he looked down on the desert below. From this height all detail was blurred. To the eye the floor of the plain showed a gray-brown stretch level as a carpet, but he knew that when he reached it he would find a rolling surface pockmarked with washes, sandy wastes, and hillocks sown by nature to greasewood and cholla and palo verde.

He eased his body in the saddle, letting part of the weight rest on one stirruped foot. Normally he was a gay and carefree youth, but now his mind was troubled. Circumstances were projecting his life into a crooked channel from which he could see no way out. He recalled Yont's harsh words, *When you hear the lash crack, you'll jump. You're my man.* Rogers had the strong urge that outdoor Westerners have to control their own destiny. Even when his wildness had been uncurbed, he had felt this was because he wanted it so, that whenever he wished to pull up and change course, he could. But now this old wolf had him bitted and bridled. He had lost the freedom of action that now meant so much to him. His birthright he had sold for safety, and this filled him with a sense of cheapness.

It was difficult for the young Texan to understand the urges that moved a man like Yont. His inordinate greed and ruthless ambition had broken up his own family. The lash of his domineering will had driven the daughter to run away with a young cowboy with whom she was in love. He had never seen or heard of her since that midnight

9

flight. In one of his rages he had horsewhipped his only son, a boy of eighteen, and the lad had left within the hour to go his separate way. A current rumor was that the grief-stricken mother had faded out of a life Yont had made unendurable. To the world the man had shown no sign of sorrow at any of these losses. In the intervening years he had grown more grasping and intolerant.

Rufe gathered the loose reins and set the pinto to the steep descent into the basin below. By the time he reached it, the sun was high in the heavens and its rays set heat waves dancing in front of him. A dry gully led him out of the foothills to strike the main road again. It meandered along the edge of the rise taking the line of least resistance. Circling a detour around a bluff known locally as Sentinel Point, he came unexpectedly on Rifle nestling against the rock walls behind it.

Rufe had seen a score of Western towns on the same pattern. One main street with wooden sidewalks flanking a road the bed of which was churned to dust by hundreds of shod hoofs. Frame buildings with false fronts, every other one a saloon or gambling hall. Cowponies at hitch racks drowsing in the sun, their tails occasionally flicking flies from the flanks. A barefoot Mexican asleep in the sun with a big sombrero over his face. Two loungers in chaps squatted in the shade against an adobe wall. A whisky bottle in the gutter and a litter of soiled cards scattered in front of the Acme Palace. These made a picture familiar as the face of a silver dollar, a drab and squalid one common to the cattle country.

For a brief period that picture vanished. Two riders wheeled into the road from a side lane and came toward him. His glance flashed over one and took no note of him except that he was boyishly slim. It rested on the other, a girl, darkly vivid, with soft dark hair slightly disordered by the wind. She was wearing a riding costume and sat the saddle with easy grace, flat back erect, elbows close to the slender body, foot firm in the stirrup. Her head was turned to the lad beside her. They were sharing a moment of amusement; the Texan could see mirth rippling over her mobile face. He thought that this wild frontier was a strange place to see a lady so obviously used to the refinements of civilization.

Rogers dismounted and tied in front of the Legal Tender saloon. He sauntered in and bellied up to the bar.

"What'll it be?" a baldheaded man in a white apron asked. He wore no coat, and embroidered red rubber supporters held up his sleeves.

Rufe said, "A beer—cold," and nursed the drink while he took stock of those present. Three cowboys were playing pitch and another was lying on a bench set against the wall. A fat man was dealing himself a hand of solitaire.

"Know Mr. Hagen, the land agent?" Rogers inquired casually.

"Sure I know him." The bartender nodded toward the solitaire player. "That's him."

Rogers finished his beer and walked across the room to watch the play of Hagen. "Jack goes on that red queen," he volunteered.

Hagen looked over his shoulder and snapped, "I'm playin' this game."

Rufe put Yont's letter on the table in front of the land agent. The fat man read the letter.

"You Jim Dillard?" he asked.

"That's right." Rogers decided that since he was to be Jim Dillard, he had better begin forgetting his real name.

"Let's go." Hagen hoisted himself heavily from the chair to his feet and waddled to the door. He was not only fat but huge. Because he was a squat man his terrific girth was more noticeable. His short legs supported two hundred fifty pounds of fat.

"Stranger, ain't you?" Hagen asked. "I haven't seen you around."

The man who was now Jim Dillard slid a grin at him. "If I'm taking up land, I have to be a resident here, don't I?"

"Sure," the government man jeered. "Likely you were born in this town and I just never happened to notice you."

Dillard did not answer that dig. A couple had just come out of a store and were moving down the sidewalk. They were the two who had passed him on horseback a few minutes earlier. From the striking resemblance they had to each other he guessed them brother and sister. In the girl's movements was a buoyant animal vigor suggesting that she loved life and found it good. A light wind whipped down the street and the long skirt clung to and modeled the smooth rounded thighs. She had an arresting face, with lovely planes and dark long-lashed eyes. Again he wondered how beauty such as this, tempered like a fine blade, could come out of such a parched land and grace a town so rough and colorless.

The fat man swept off his hat with exaggerated gallantry and bowed. "Howdy, Miss June—Cape," he greeted them, voice and smile unctuous.

Dillard thought her answer was a little on the frosty side. Her glance swept indifferently the face of the Texan. *To her, he told himself, I am just a piece of the scenery like a hundred other punchers she has seen and never expects to meet again.*

Hagen led the way into the land office and seated himself in a big chair back of a desk, his wide spread overflowing from it. Dillard asked him quite casually who the young people were that they had just met.

"Interested in the boy or the young lady?" Hagen tee-heed. "Seems as if an oldtimer like you ought to have met him. He and another brother and his sister own the Flying W ranch. Seeing as you'll be neighbors, you're certainly going to get acquainted soon." The chuckle in the man's fat throat held ribald sarcasm. "Miss June is sure enough going to love you."

"We'll leave the lady out of this," the man who called himself Jim Dillard answered coldly. "I'm here on business. We'll stick to that."

"You bet." The registrar's belly shook with malicious laughter. "Fen Yont's business. I reckon you're his errand boy."

"You and I both," the young man replied. "He pulls the string and we jump to do his dirty work."

Hagen flushed angrily. Though he knew it was true, he did not like to admit even to himself that he was Yont's bought man. He preferred to put it that, since he had been put in his position through the influence of the big cattleman, he respected a political obligation.

"You can't talk to me that way, you young whipper-snapper," he retorted. "I won't stand for it."

"Suits me fine," Dillard agreed. "We'll quit paying each other left-handed compliments and talk turkey. If you have a map I would like to see the piece of land I'm homesteading." He had seen the plat earlier in the day, but he wanted to get information from the registrar.

Hagen produced a book of plats and pointed out a quarter section divided by a bend of Dead Cow Creek.

"Who owns the land adjacent to this?" the Texan asked.

"Fellow name of Balcom took up the hundred and sixty to the right. His range riders filed on these others and deeded them over to him after they had proved up."

"Funny he didn't have one of his boys pick up this quarter. With the creek running through it I would think it a choice location."

"The fellow who made the survey for him did not know his business. Quite a few of the early claims got the wrong boundaries."

"Balcom won't like my filing on it," Dillard suggested.

"He won't mind," Hagen said. "There won't be any objection from him." The registrar did not mention that Balcom was dead and the spread was now held by his heirs. It was in his mind that this brash cowpuncher would be moving into a situation where he would be in trouble up to his neck. This pleased Hagen. He resented being told that he was a crook. The young Texan had made an enemy, for no reason except that he was annoyed at his own conduct and was taking his resentment out on the first man available. He had enjoyed pricking the bubble of Hagen's smugness.

A quarter of an hour later he walked out of the land office with a paper in his pocket certifying he had made homestead entry on the Southeast Quarter of Section 12, Township 8, Range 6 West.

3 AS THE NEW HOMESTEADER START-
ed to free his pinto from the hitch rack, a
gay voice yelled, "Hi yi, Tex." A young fellow
on the sidewalk grinned at him. The stranger was tall, lank,
redheaded and long-legged. He wore levis thrust into the
tops of high-heeled dusty cowboy boots, a checked cotton
shirt, a flat-topped black hat that had seen better days, an
unbuttoned vest and no coat.

Rufe knew that the double cinch on the saddle had been
the means of identifying him as a Texan. It was likely that
the friendly lad who had hailed him came from the same
state.

"Right first crack," Rogers admitted, and sauntered to
the sidewalk. "Makes two of us from there."

"You bet. Call me Charley Runyon."

"Rufe——" Rogers chopped off the last name in time.
"Jim Dillard," he corrected.

Charley laughed, no offense in his manner. "Most made
a mistake, didn't you? Better practice it, fellow."

"That's right. You have your new one down pat, I notice."

Runyon slapped a hand on his thigh and flung out a
cloud of dust. "How wrong you are, Rufe-Jim," he laughed.
"Let's go wet our whistles in baptism of your new name."
He tucked an arm under the elbow of his fellow Texan.

Around the bend of the road a stage swung, the four
horses bringing it in at a gallop. The driver, Cad Wallop,
always finished his run with a flourish. From the Concord
descended a drummer representing a whisky firm, a small
girl promptly claimed by her parents, a preacher dressed in
black, and a middle-aged, heavy-set man who carried a Win-

14

chester and wore a belt from which dangled a holster that held a Colt's forty-five.

The Texans passed through the swing doors into the Wagon Wheel and ordered beer. Jim Dillard—to use the name he had chosen—stood at the far end of the bar and faced the door. He was not easy in his mind about the heavy-set man who had got off the stage. He was a law officer of some sort, a ranger, a sheriff, or a United States marshal, and it was within the possibilities that he had come to pick up a wanted bank robber by the name of Rufus Rogers. There were a dozen saloons in town and three or four general stores. If this lawman was searching for a fugitive, he would go into some of them to pick up information. As soon as he did so, Jim Dillard meant to slip out to the tie rack, fork the pinto, and get away from Rifle.

After taking a pull at his beer, Charley Runyon laid the glass on the bar, tilted an eyebrow at his companion, and murmured, "The gent sure is garnished with hardware."

Dillard nodded. "Looks like he's on the prod."

"Not lookin' for me," Runyon said. "I ain't that important."

The other Texan was afraid he was. It had been a mistake for him not to have got rid of the pinto. All along the way from Fort Worth, settlers would remember that a man on a paint horse had traveled westward. And that cowpony was now tied to the rack not thirty yards from the Wagon Wheel.

"Reckon I'll be driftin'," Dillard said, his voice indifferent. "I got quite a way to ride before night."

He threw a dollar on the bar, got his change, and turned to go.

A man pushed open the swing doors and stood at the entrance. His eyes swept the room, picked up two grizzled freighters at a table, the bartender, and came to rest on the Texans. He carried a rifle in his left hand. The other arm hung at his side, not far from the handle of the revolver. It was in his mind that one of these two young cowboys might be the man he had come to arrest. He was not at all sure of that. There were a good many pintos on the frontier. The one in front might be owned by an honest

15

rancher. The brand was unknown to him and had told him nothing.

"That paint horse in the street belong to either of you?" he asked.

Runyon shook his head. "What paint hoss? I didn't notice any."

"Seems to me I saw one at the Legal Tender hitch rack," Dillard said. His stomach muscles had tightened, but his casual voice was cool and easy.

"My name is Folsom," the officer said, his frosty eyes shuttling from one to the other. "I've come here to arrest Rufus Rogers for murder and bank robbery. I'll take yore names."

"You are an officer?" Runyon asked.

"A deputy United States marshal. I'll ask the questions."

Charley Runyon knew that the young Texan he had just met must be Rufus Rogers, but he did not betray that knowledge by even a look in his direction. He leaned against the bar, his elbows resting on the top of it and one heel hooked negligently over the rail. "Sure. You gotta get yore man. I haven't seen this bandit Rogers far as I know. What does the guy look like?"

Folsom reached into his pocket, drew out a printed folder, and handed it to Runyon. "Read it, both of you. But first I'll listen to yore names."

"Me, I'm Charley Runyon and my friend is Jim Dillard, both of us from Trinidad, Colorado. A couple of waddies on the loose, you might say."

"Any proof of that—letters from yore folks or anything?" the marshal asked harshly.

Runyon's smile was bland and engaging. "We didn't leave an address. Jim and me are kinda black sheep, the way our folks feel."

"How black?" demanded the officer. "Is one of you a bank robber?"

"Not unless we robbed one in our sleep," Dillard replied. "Where at was this bank robbed?"

His new friend Runyon looked up from the paper he was reading. "Fort Worth, Texas," he answered. "Listen, Jim. 'Five hundred dollars will be paid for information leading to the arrest of Rufus Rogers, one of the bandits who held up the Fort Worth Cattlemen's Bank, on March 25th, and murdered a teller, Jeremiah Grace. Rogers is about 23, weighs around 165 pounds, height six feet, eyes blue, well-muscled, scar on right arm below elbow. Has pleasant friendly manners, but is considered a desperate character and will probably resist arrest.' Might be either of us, Jim, or any of a dozen other guys in town." Runyon turned his grin on the officer. "Would you say my manners grade up to the recommendation here, Mr. Marshal?"

"Something funny about this ad," Dillard said, after he had glanced over the paper. "If there were several of these bandits, why doesn't this reward offer cover the others too?"

Folsom's face was grim as that of a hanging judge. "The others were caught and their hash settled. The sheriff never got them to jail. A mob took the fellows and strung them up to a telegraph pole."

The shock of this news sent a hideous crawling up Dillard's spine. These men had been genial companions. One of them had lent him ten dollars he could never repay, though they had also done him a great injustice by using him as an accomplice. If he had been three minutes later in his getaway he would have been captured and lynched within the hour.

"Seems kinda final," Runyon suggested. "You aimin' to take this Rogers back to decorate another telegraph pole?"

"No mob takes a prisoner from me without somebody getting hurt," the marshal answered. There was pride in the man's quiet voice. He was not bragging but stating a fact.

Those present accepted this at face value. That Folsom was both obstinate and fearless one could read in the resolute eyes and steel-trap jaw.

"If we run across this guy Rogers and turn him over to you, do we get the reward?" Dillard asked.

"You get it." The officer's level gaze challenged him. There was in the sheriff's office at Fort Worth a picture of Rogers, a tintype of him for which he had sat with the captured bandits two days before the robbery, but the likeness was so blurred that an identification from it would be difficult. The marshal thought that either of these two might be Rogers.

"Are you holding back on me?" Folsom asked sharply. "Do you know where this fellow is?"

Runyon said nothing. He let his narrowed eyes rest on the other Texan, as if by chance.

"If I did know, I'd sure talk," Dillard told the officer. "That five hundred split two ways is more *dinero* than Charley and I get in a year chousing longhorns outa the brush."

"Just for the record I reckon you boys would have no objection to rolling up the sleeves of your right arms to show you have no scar below the elbow."

Dillard's impassive face did not betray the fact that a cold wind was blowing through him. "Why, sure," he began, and started to take off his coat. Midway he stopped. "No, I'll be damned if I do," he said with heat. "I'm no bandit and I won't be treated like one.

Runyon thought, *If this guy is holding a busted flush, he is making a good bluff. I'll go along with him a ways.*

He said, gently, "Why pick on us, Mr. Marshal? This country is full of buckaroos six feet tall with blue eyes. You've got it in yore nut that one of us is a holdup man and you can't make up yore mind which. Why don't you flip a dollar? Heads it's Jim, tails it's me."

"Uncover your right arms to the elbow and I'll make up my mind," Folsom said.

"I don't reckon either of us is in a mood to do that, not unless you have some evidence against us," Dillard said with a grin. "We Texans are a little touchy."

The marshal laid his hand on the butt of his revolver. "I've got a little persuader with me. You said you were from Colorado not Texas."

Dillard reproved him with gentle sarcasm. "Do we look like pilgrims new out from the states? Just for the cod of it, pull your forty-five and see how far you get. You can't go around shooting up on suspicion all the blue-eyed cowboys you meet. About coming from Colorado, we had drifted there from Texas."

That Dillard had challenged on safe ground Folsom knew. His threat had been a foolish one. He tried another approach. "Assuming you are good citizens, don't you think it is your duty to support the law?"

"You bet," Dillard answered heartily. "If you need a posse to help you arrest this fellow after you have found him, count us in."

"When I find him I won't need a posse," the marshal told him curtly.

"I expect you're right about that," he agreed, and turned to Runyon. "We might as well drift, Charley."

They walked out of the saloon to the sidewalk.

Jim said in a low voice, "Much obliged, fellow."

Runyon set cold hard eyes on him. "I don't know why I fronted for a cold-blooded killer. You're Rufus Rogers. I knew that all the time. From what I've heard, this bank teller didn't have a chance for his white alley. Get out of this burg before I change my mind and sic' this Folsom on you."

He turned his back on Dillard and went down the sidewalk, spurs jingling. When he reached the land office, he walked into it.

"What can I do for you?" Hagen asked.

"Fellow who calls himself Jim Dillard was in here a while ago. I saw him come out. What did he want?"

The fat man turned on him suspicious eyes. "That any of yore business, young fellow?" he wheezed.

"I dunno yet," Runyon replied cautiously. He had not made up his mind what he meant to do about Dillard, if anything. It annoyed him that he had vouched for the man, who was undoubtedly a bandit. He had come through for the fugitive because they were both Texans and for the added reason that the law was just now at a discount in his regard. There was a matter of brand-blotting in Bexar County for which he was himself wanted. Moreover, he had liked Dillard's clean-cut appearance and his easy friendliness. They did not fit a hardened criminal. In his mind was a reluctance to believe his new acquaintance guilty of murder.

"When you find out, let me know," Hagen told him with heavy sarcasm.

"Sure." Runyon tried again. "I'd like some information about him. Seeing as he was in talking with you, I thought you might know him."

19

"Never saw him before and never want to see him again," the government man flung out.

"He just came in to tell you it was a nice day," Runyon suggested.

"I can tell you one thing. He's a smart aleck, not the only one I've met in the last hour."

Runyon grinned. He had asked for that. "Fact is, I've got a notion he might be a guy who had hit his saddle sudden for a getaway from a sheriff."

"Any evidence?" Hagen's eyes showed a malicious interest. If this cowpuncher meant trouble for Dillard, it would suit him very well.

"He acted kinda funny when a marshal got off the stage. Well, so long." Runyon flung up a hand in farewell and turned to go.

"Wait a minute. He came in and filed on a quarter section along Dead Cow Creek."

The cowboy was surprised. If this man was Rufus Rogers with the law hot on his heels, what in heck was he doing filing on land? Staying on one spot was something you would not expect him to consider. He must be ready to light out at a moment's notice.

"Fixin' to homestead, is he? I reckon I'm barkin' up the wrong tree. On Dead Cow Creek, you say. Didn't know there was any free land there."

Hagen said, with his falsetto giggle, "Somebody is going to be surprised."

"Who?" Runyon asked.

It occurred to Hagen that he had said enough, perhaps too much. Fen Yont would not want any talk about this until his man was settled on the quarter. "Wait and see," he answered with decision.

The young man left the office with the feeling that there was something queer about this. He had been convinced this Dillard was the fugitive bandit Rufe Rogers. The man had made a slip and given himself away. There could not be two men with the first name Rufus recently arrived on pinto horses. But this business of settling on a homestead just did not fit into the picture of an outlaw riding hell-for-leather to escape the law.

4. WHEN JIM DILLARD REACHED THE Quarter Circle F Y, it was close to midnight. Both at the Big House and the men's bunk building all lights were out. He unsaddled, turned the pinto into the home pasture, and tiptoed into the long sleeping shack. Five minutes later he was asleep.

The sound of the breakfast gong awakened him. Already the men were charging through the door to answer the call that always brought them hurrying. Jim flung on his clothes and washed swiftly at the pump in the yard. He was hungrier than the rest of the ranch riders, since he had left Rifle on an urgent impulse without waiting to eat supper. In an incredibly short time he slid into his place on a bench at the long table.

From the head of the table Kurt Barlow tossed a question at him sharply. "Why didn't you join us yesterday?"

"The boss sent me to town on an errand," Jim explained.

"Hmp! Teacher's pet." The foreman's snarling voice held a bullying tone.

Jim laughed amiably. "Not the way I look at it. Give me my choice and I'll ride with the boys."

"A two-bit cow-tailer not dry behind the ears," Barlow sneered, and dropped the subject.

After the foreman had left the table, the bandy-legged youngster with red hair who was seated next to Dillard made comment. "Kurt is sore because he thinks the old man has took a smile to you."

"Then he has it wrong, Red," replied Dillard. "Yont doesn't give a tinker's damn for me."

Dillard found Yont driving a rivet through the broken

21

leather of a stirrup. The man's bad teeth showed in a ruthless grin. "So you didn't make a run for it," he taunted.

"Would it have been any use?" the cowboy asked.

"Not a bit. You wouldn't have got twenty miles. You would have been shot down or dragged back."

"I was of that opinion and didn't try," Dillard said. He added dryly: "I may not be here long."

Yont's brutal eyes narrowed. "That's what you think."

"I'm not the only one thinks it. At Rifle I ran into a deputy United States marshal looking for Rufe Rogers. He'll probably be along one of these days."

"Did he see you?"

"Saw me—talked with me—wasn't dead sure whether I was his man and wanted me to turn up my shirtsleeve to find out if I had a scar on my arm."

"Which you didn't do, I judge."

"Correct. I played the honest citizen insulted at being taken for a bandit. He had to let it ride that way. But he's still loaded to the hocks with suspicion."

"Unfortunate. But I reckon I can cover for you."

"Wouldn't it be less trouble to turn me in and collect the five hundred bucks?" Jim fleered.

Choleric blood rose beneath the tan of the big man's harsh face. "You'll talk yourself into a noose yet," he exploded. Yont liked to prod barbs into others, but his arrogance resented receiving any. "Any more back talk from you and I'll beat you into a rag doll."

"Why get on the prod, Mr. Yont?" asked Dillard. "I'm taking orders from you, but I don't have to like it."

The ranchman hammered a heavy fist on the floor of the porch. "I don't give a damn whether you like it, but you'll keep your big mouth shut and take it." He brushed his employee's incipient rebellion aside and came to the business of the meeting. "Did you file on that one hundred and sixty?"

Dillard flung across the table the receipt signed by Hagen. "Before I start living on this land, don't you think you had better wise me about who the real owner of it is?" he suggested.

"It has never been filed on before. You're the owner, for the moment. When I think best I'll give you any more information you need. The boys will help you build a shack on it tonight."

"Quick work," the new homesteader said.

"I'm tearing down a line cabin I can get along without. We'll wagon the lumber across to the creek and knock you up a shanty. Red will pack food to your claim. Before morning you'll be all fixed." With his malign grin he tacked on a rider—"Snug as a bug in a rug."

"With every card in the deck stacked against me," the schemer's victim said bitterly.

"I wouldn't say that. A buckaroo with Fen Yont behind him holds one big ace as a kicker."

"I had forgotten I have one dear friend," Dillard amended, his thin smile sardonic. "Of course nobody will dare touch me."

During supper that evening, Kurt Barlow announced sulkily that the day's work was not ended. They were going to spend the night building a house. The complaints of the tired riders were loud and profane. What house? they wanted to know. And why couldn't it be built next day?

"Don't ask me," snarled the foreman. "I don't know a thing about it. If you've got any kick coming, go to the old man."

One man present could have answered their question, but Dillard continued to eat without comment. It seemed wise to postpone making himself the object of their resentment. They would be in a better humor when they found out a day or two later.

With two wagons following them, the riders cut across country to the line cabin, taking a zigzag course through the cactus and mesquite. What annoyed the ranch hands was that they were not hired for hammer and saw work. They were cowpunchers and would have ridden out a stampede or a blizzard from dark till morning without a murmur, but they had a feeling the boss had no right to take them out of their saddles to do a hoeman's tasks.

At the line shack they lit a fire of dead wood and lounged around it until the wagons arrived with the tools. It took less than half an hour to knock the flimsy building to pieces and load the wagons for transportation.

Barlow chose a site for the new location on an open knoll

a dozen yards from the creek. It was easy for him to guess what Yont had in mind. This was Flying W terrain and had been in the possession of that ranch for more than twenty years. *The old blister aims to set up a counterclaim,* the foreman thought. *He is going to put this kid Dillard on it and hell will break loose in Georgia.*

Beneath a full moon the Quarter Circle F Y men hammered and sawed. The frame of the hut went up quickly. Long before daylight the job was finished and the workmen gone. They left with Dillard food and blankets. He lay on the floor and slept. Next day he would have plenty of time to make a cot out of the unused planks.

It was long after sunup when he awoke. For breakfast he had black coffee, bacon, and corn bread, after which he went out to take a look at his newly acquired holding. His claim lay in a grassy park through which the creek ran lazily. Under other circumstances he would have been pleased to take up this quarter section. It was a nice spread of fairly level land, well watered, with grass fetlock deep. A young fellow starting a herd could not have asked for a better location. But he was no honest settler. He had been put here to do the dirty work of a scoundrel who was blackmailing him into this.

Yet, when his eyes fell on a ten-year-old mossyhorn steer all skin and bone tied to a young tree, a boyish grin lit his face. Red had brought it here back of the supply wagon. Yont had sent it with his compliments, moved by some ironic humor, as a gift to the new homesteader, a base from which he was to start his herd. The animal was re-branded. Red had guessed that the brand was meant to be TT. Dillard knew better than that. The brand was the Double Cross. It carried to him a harsh and contemptuous warning.

BRINGING THE RANCH MAIL FROM the Four Corners box where it was left once a week, June Crawford on her way home across country splashed through Dead Cow Creek and rode into the small park formed by the bend in the stream. What she saw astonished her, a frame shack close to the bank that had not been there when she passed by a few days earlier, in front of it a picketed horse. From back of the cabin came the sound of somebody hammering. This ceased, and presently a young man appeared carrying a saw.

He stopped, staring at her. "Hello!" he said, and smiled. "My first visitor."

"Who are you?" she demanded sharply. "And what are you doing here?"

"Jim Dillard," he answered. "Fixing up a place to live in. You must be Miss June Crawford. I saw you yesterday at Rifle."

"Who told you that you could live here?"

"I have just homesteaded on this quarter section," he explained. "It's a pleasant surprise that you are my neighbor."

"Homesteaded," she repeated, anger in her voice. "We've owned it twenty years. Saddle your horse and get off our land."

"There seems to be some mistake. The land office man at Rifle told me it was open for entry. I think you'll find that to be the case."

He spoke in a reasonable tone, but he was uncomfortably aware that nothing he could say would appease her resentment. He was an interloper and had no business here.

In that he agreed with her, but he had no intention of admitting it.

"Hagen told you that? He is a fat-headed fool." She looked down at him, arrogance in the slim rigid figure and the biting words. "We don't allow floating riffraff to jump land that belongs to us. Clear out *pronto*."

Her scorn irritated him and stirred his obstinacy. "I advise you to look up the land record, Miss Crawford," he said. "I think you are due for a surprise."

"If you stay here you'll be asking for trouble and you'll get it," she flung out stormily. "You had better realize that this is a hard tough country where settlers don't put up with any shenanigans from gentry of your sort."

He met her threat with eyes steady and unwavering. "I'm a little tough myself. You might pass it on to any of these settlers you meet that I aim to stick around and hold my claim."

"You've had your warning!" she cried, and reined her horse away.

Dillard watched her ride over the crest of a hillock and disappear. He was troubled at this development. It was one thing for him to take land away from people he had never met and who meant nothing to him. It seemed more flagrant to rob this girl with whom he would like to be friendly. To be an ally of the scoundrel Yont in so discreditable a scheme filled him with disgust. But he was caught in a tight from which he could see no other escape. If he tried a bolt into the mountains, he would be caught and dragged back. Folsom had alerted the country and news that he was in the neighborhood would be carried to every pocket in the hills. For the five hundred dollars reward somebody would be sure to betray him.

June Crawford's anger was still simmering when she rode into the yard of the Flying W. She drew up at the mounting block in front of the house, slipped from the saddle, and flung the bag with the mail on the porch. A seventeen-year-old boy took the horse to the stable. The girl's glance settled on her brother Peter shoeing a mare at the open-air blacksmith shop. Picking up her trailing skirt, she walked across the dusty yard to him.

26

"Any letter from that cattle buyer Gregg?" he asked.

"Yes. It's in the bag. I have some news you won't like."

He lowered the animal's hoof. "Spill it," he said.

"There's a squatter on that quarter section at the bend of the creek. He has built a shack there."

Peter Crawford was a big barrel-chested man, solid on his feet. Hard-packed flesh clothed his bones. Tight levis outlined the curve of his heavy muscular legs. Frosty gray eyes, a thin-lipped mouth, and a jutting jaw suggested both arrogance and temper.

"A squatter. D'you know him?"

"No. Says his name is Dillard. A young fellow. Sassy."

Blood beat up under the tan of his face. "Was he impudent to you?"

She shook her head. "No-o. All the hard words used were from me. I told him we wouldn't put up with trespassing by trash like him."

"No back talk from him?"

"Only to say he meant to stay there."

"He'd better not tell me that." Peter dropped the hammer. "I'll go down there right now."

"Something queer about it," his sister said. "Claimed he was at Rifle yesterday, that Hagen told him that quarter section was open to entry, and that he filed on it."

"Must be a lie. Hagen couldn't have told him anything of the sort."

June was not quite satisfied with that explanation. "He sounded as if he was telling the truth. You know how slippery Hagen is. You don't think Fen Yont could be back of this, do you?"

"No." He qualified his answer. "Hagen is Yont's man. No doubt of that. When Yont cracks the whip, he jumps through the hoop. Maybe this *is* some of that old devil's work."

"Hadn't you better talk with Hagen?"

"I'll do that, but I'll see the land-jumper first. Probably he was throwing a bluff. I'll show him that won't go with me."

He walked beside his sister to the house. From the wall of his bedroom he took down a belt with a holstered Colt's forty-five. He was buckling it around his waist when he came back to the porch.

June said, "You're not going to use that gun, Pete?"

"I won't need it to deal with a fellow like that," her brother answered, contempt in his voice. "But for him to see me carrying it won't do any harm. His kind need fear flung into them."

The girl had a feeling that this squatter would not frighten easily. It might be that this was not the way to handle the situation.

"He didn't look to me like a quitter. If Yont is just using him to make trouble, it might be a good idea to move carefully."

"I'll handle that," Pete told her shortly.

He was a stubborn man, dour at times, yet he recognized the wisdom of her suggestion. Below his arrogance was a stratum of good sense. He did not mean to make any false move that might backfire on him. Before he went too far he wanted to find out if Yont was in this.

Even in the days of their uncle Nate Balcom there had been bad blood between the Quarter Circle F Y and the Flying W. This was born chiefly because of Yont's insatiable greed and ambition. It irked him that another sizable ranch should have a spread on the creek so near his. That Balcom had taken up land before he did had no effect on his feeling of resentment. The Flying W was one of the best grass spreads in the district. It cut off his stock from feed and easy water. On the upper range in the wide stretch leading to the foothills there was constant conflict where the grazing herds intermingled. The Crawfords were confident that Yont's riders branded calves following Flying W cows. On the two or three occasions when they had been able to prove this, Fen Yont pleaded with a jeering grin a mistake. Ever since the Crawfords had succeeded Balcom, they had been annoyed, nagged, and infuriated by the sly outrages of their unfriendly neighbor. Fences had been cut, haystacks burned, and twice cattle found shot. Plainly Yont wanted trouble. Among his riders were half a dozen hard characters with bad reputations as gunmen. They would back any play he made.

The impression grew on Pete Crawford as he rode to

the bend that this was another of Yont's schemes. If he could get hold of this quarter section by hook or crook, it would make a wide roadway to the creek through the heart of the Flying W holdings. Cattle pouring down it would spread to right and left all over the Crawford range. War would be bound to come of it.

When Pete rode into the park formed by the creek bend and saw the cabin, he felt sure that Yont had done this to them. The house had been built since he had ridden over this ground two days before. No lone squatter had brought the lumber here and put up the building. One man could not do it.

Jim Dillard stood in the doorway and watched Crawford ride forward and dismount. Pete grounded the reins. He stood beside the horse, his hard hot eyes fastened on the homesteader.

"What made you think you could squat on our land and get away with it?" he demanded harshly.

"I'm not a squatter but a homesteader," Dillard explained.

"On land we have owned for twenty years. Don't pull that stuff on me."

"The land map doesn't show that. This quarter section was open for entry when I took it."

"That's a lie. You're one of Yont's two-bit riding scalawags. You can't tell me different. I've stood a lot from him, but I won't stand by and let him rob me of my land. Get this in yore noggin. The scoundrel is using you for a cat's-paw. He doesn't give a tinker's damn for what will happen to you. He knows if you carry on with this, you'll go out in smoke."

"Sounds like a threat," Dillard said, his steady gaze fixed on the other man.

"Call it what you like," Pete retorted. "No man alive can rob me and make it stick. Tell that to Yont. If he wants this to be a showdown, he can have it that way."

"I took up the land, not Yont. I'm within the law. It's not my fault your uncle had his rider file on the wrong piece. I stand on my rights."

"You haven't any rights," Crawford told him brutally.

"You are just a two-spot in Yont's game he is sacrificing to be rubbed out in making us trouble."

Dillard had already guessed this, but he gave no sign of it. "There is only one point for you to consider, Mr. Crawford, if that is your name. Have I a legal right to be here? Better check up on that. I understand that I have, and as long as I think so I'll be rooted here holding my claim. I don't scare easy."

Peter Crawford was exasperated. He did not like this situation any better than the Texan did. Though he had the hard toughness of fiber outdoor life on the raw frontier brings to its settlers, he was no callous killer. He would fight for his property if he was forced to do so, but he did not want to play Yont's game by destroying this dummy the Quarter Circle F Y owner had set up for him. In doing this he would forfeit the good will of many who were at present unfriendly toward Yont.

"I'll give you twenty-four hours to get off my land," he ordered. "Think this over, kid. Yont won't lift a finger to save you even if he could. I've got nothing against you personally, but I don't aim to sit on my behind and watch you rob me."

He swung to the saddle and rode away, anger burning in him. Crawford did not quite know why he had not beaten up this insolent squatter. It had not been because of fear. The ranchman was not afraid of anybody on earth. But there had been a quiet force in the fellow's lean strongly boned face that differentiated him from the average drifting cowboy. He did not look like the kind of rascal who would submit to having a quirt wound around his legs. There was in him a personal dignity that demanded respect.

6 OUT OF A WIDE EXPERIENCE MARshal Folsom had learned that the best way to get information about a fugitive lurking in a district was to question many people. Eventually some one of them would give him the tip he needed. The second morning after his arrival at Rifle, he dropped in to see Hagen.

"I reckon you know why I am here," he said after they had exchanged greetings. "I want this bandit Rufus Rogers. He left a trail as far as the San Simon and was last seen heading this way. Have you noticed any stranger here who might fit this description?" The officer handed to the land office man the reward poster.

Hagen read not only the itemized detail of the appearance of the wanted man, but also the amount of the reward. The five hundred dollars mentioned stirred his greed. He believed Dillard was the fugitive.

"I think I have met yore man, Mr. Folsom. Naturally I would want a cut of the reward if I help you." He wanted that last made clear.

The marshal satisfied him on that point, and Hagen told him that a young man who called himself Jim Dillard had been in to file on a quarter section of land. It could be he was on it right now. The man had worked for the Quarter Circle F Y for a few days. The foreman of that ranch happened to be in town. He might know where Dillard was. In his opinion this homesteader fitted to a T the description of the man Rogers.

Outside the land office Folsom met Charley Runyon. That young man asked him with a grin if he had yet found his bandit.

"I found you lied to me," the marshal told him grimly. "You did not come here from Colorado with Dillard. You got here six months before he did. The bartender at the Wagon Wheel is convinced you two had never met before that afternoon when you went in there for a beer."

"Since I have been here six months I am innocent as you are of that Fort Worth bank holdup," Runyon evaded. "I'm kinda glad to find out I wasn't in it."

Folsom resented his cheerful effrontery. "Perhaps you will be glad to know that in aiding a criminal to escape, you have made yourself an accessory after the fact."

"Golly! I'm certainly in a fix—if you can prove I knew this guy was a criminal. That will take some doing."

"Be careful, young man," Folsom advised, and brushed past him.

Runyon watched him stride straight-back down the sidewalk. The cowboy rubbed his stubby chin thoughtfully.

"Maybe I had better do something about this," he murmured to himself.

The marshal ran into Kurt Barlow in the Legal Tender. The man admitted in his usual sulky way that he was the foreman of the Quarter Circle F Y ranch. Folsom explained that he wanted information about a man who called himself Jim Dillard.

"Why come to me?" Barlow demanded, the hard eyes in the weathered face suspiciously on the officer.

"I understand he worked for you."

"What if he did?"

"I'm here looking for an outlaw who helped to rob a Fort Worth bank. I think Dillard is the man."

"That so?" Barlow sneered. "Me, I haven't lost any bandits."

Folsom sized the man up correctly. "Would you be interested in a share of a five-hundred-dollar reward?"

"That's different. Maybe I would." The foreman considered this silently. He had never liked Yont, and of late this feeling had grown into hatred. The boss had frequently let him know that he considered a foreman of no consequence. Also, he had a grudge against young Dillard for having been a party to his humiliation. "What you want to know about him?" he growled.

"Just two things. How long has he worked at the Quarter Circle F Y? And if he has left there, where is he now?"

"How much of this reward do I get?" Barlow asked, a glitter in his eyes.

The amount would have to be divided among two or three parties, the marshal explained. Barlow grumbled that this would leave him just small change, but he answered the questions. Dillard had been one of his riders only about two weeks and he was now located on a homestead claim at the Dead Cow Creek bend.

Kurt Barlow finished his drink and walked out of the Legal Tender with the marshal. The two stood talking on the sidewalk. The foreman gave the officer instructions how to reach the claim and exacted a promise that his name would not be used in connection with the arrest. He had, he said, private reasons why this would be embarrassing to him. His boss was lined up with this young bandit in getting him on the land.

Sunning himself indolently against an adobe wall, Charley Runyon watched the two men with interest. From their manner he thought they were discussing something important to them. Barlow stooped and made in the dusty road some sort of pattern with a stick he had picked up.

The guy is drawing a map, the cowboy guessed. *The lawman aims to take a ride. Kid Dillard's goose is cooked—unless someone tips him off.*

Runyon moved up the street to the rack where his pony was hitched. This was none of his business. He had got in as deep as he meant to go. If Dillard had gone bad, he was not to blame. A fellow had to play his own hand. He would be a fool not to take the warning Folsom had just given him. Very likely this Dillard was a cold-blooded killer as reported.

He untied the horse and swung to the saddle, though he had not made up his mind where he was going. To his mind there flashed a picture of Jim Dillard—his lithe clean body, the friendly smile, the frank honesty of his direct eyes. The guy was from Texas, his own state, and he was in a sure-enough tight. Runyon could not quite believe him guilty.

"Which way do we go, Two Bits?" he asked the pony, facing the other side of the street. "I'll leave it to you."

There may have been a faint pressure of the rein on the animal's neck. It turned to the left. "You've done made yore choice, Two Bits," Charley said. "I been hearin' about horse sense all my life and you don't know any better than to head for hell and high water. I'm a lunkhead for letting you take me into this jam, but I always was a sucker for trouble."

Runyon jogged out of town at a road gait. Now that he had made up his mind, he felt quite cheerful about it. He broke into unmelodious song:

> "Oh, Eve, where is Adam,
> Oh, Eve, where is Adam,
> Oh, Eve, where is Adam?
> Adam in de garden pickin' up leaves."

When his memory failed, he improvised and his version of the spiritual grew slightly ribald, but there was no irreverance in his mind. The words meant no more than an expression of high-hearted youth in the saddle. It was his way of saying that God was in His heaven and the world was all right. The day was wonderful, and the soft blue haze on the faraway mountains called for a response from the sense of beauty that lay deep in him. Like many young unlettered people, he was an inarticulate poet.

Jim Dillard was fashioning a table out of some odds and ends of lumber when Runyon appeared in silhouette against the sky on the summit of a small hill. The homesteader watched him intently as he descended to the creek. Any stranger might prove a danger to him. It was a relief to recognize the young Texan.

Runyon flung a leg over the horn of the saddle and sat at ease.

"Nice to see a reformed bandit settle down and saw wood for his breakfast," he said. "No more hellin' around, no more skulduggery."

Dillard wondered what had brought Runyon here, but he did not put his surprise into a question. He would find out if he waited.

"I'll have to get me a plow and start being a hoeman any day now," Jim mentioned. "A fiddlefooted fellow like you can't understand the pleasure a man gets from being a solid citizen who owns his own land."

"Do you reckon you'll like it better than the bank business?"

Dillard shook his head. "I'm from the brush country where we didn't have banks. It may surprise you to know that I've never in my life been inside one. The two-three times I had checks I cashed them in stores."

Runyon dropped his foolery. "Fellow, come clean. What about that Forth Worth bank robbery?"

Jim's unblinking eyes met his steadily. "I'm as innocent of that as you are, Charley." He told his version of the unfortunate circumstances that had implicated him.

The other young Texan listened and half-believed him.

"What's the idea of you taking up land? A man on the lam hasn't any use for a homestead."

They could hear the sound of a horse splashing through the creek and scrambling up the bank. A rider appeared. He turned toward the cabin.

"That idea came from the gent heading this way," Dillard said. "If you want my opinion, he is a black-hearted scoundrel."

Fen Yont drew up beside them. He said, with a chuckle: "Well—well, I see you've been right busy fixing up your little ranch, Mr. Dillard. That's fine. Keep busy. They say the devil finds mischief for idle hands to do." He looked at Runyon. "Won't you introduce me to your friend, Jim?"

"Mr. Yont—Mr. Runyon," Jim said stiffly after a moment's hesitation.

Charley's gaze rested with interest on the bull-necked stranger with the hard bulging eyes. He had heard a lot about this man and none of it good. That the ranchman was putting pressure on Dillard to help him in some dirty scheme he did not doubt.

"Glad to meet any friend of Jim." There was a sneer of mockery in Yont's face and voice. "A young fellow like you could do worse than follow his example and take up a nice spread of land."

"Why not?" There was a flavor of contempt in Runyon's voice. "Have you a good layout you can recommend, Mr. Yont?"

"No. You may be a fiddlefooted fool for all I know." Yont flung out a question sharply. "How long have you two known each other?"

He was suspicious of this visitor. The fugitive had told him he knew nobody in Arizona. Runyon might run to Folsom and betray Dillard for the reward.

Charley ignored the inquiry. "This is certainly a nice quarter section you have put Jim on," he said.

"Who told you I put him on it?" Yont snapped.

"Why, nobody. I just kinda got the idea."

"Don't get ideas about me, young fellow."

"And me learning in my history book at school that this is a free country," Runyon murmured, apparently to nobody in particular.

"If you are through with your business here, nobody is keeping you from leaving," Yont told him angrily.

"I'm not quite through." Charley turned to Dillard. "Like to see you a minute alone, Jim."

"Sure." Dillard walked with him down the creek thirty or forty yards.

Yont's gaze followed them, rage smoldering in his eyes. He resented the cool way this young stranger had asserted himself and was now excluding him from what he wanted to say. It might be something prejudicial to him or it might not. He did not want anything to interfere with his hold on Dillard.

When they were beyond the ranchman's hearing, Runyon stopped.

"Has that fellow got something on you, Jim?" he asked.

"He knows I'm Rufe Rogers. I took up this land to turn over to him and he keeps quiet about who I am."

"You can tell him to go soak his head. What he knows is common property now. Hagen knows it and Kurt Barlow and the bartender at the Wagon Wheel. I came to tell you that Folsom is on his way here to arrest you."

"I'm obliged, Charley."

"I daresay I'm a dadblamed fool," Runyon replied sourly. "You may be guilty as hell."

"But you don't believe I am, and you're right." Dillard

36

grinned ruefully. "For a run of the range cowherd I'm becoming right important. A lot of people in Fort Worth want to hang me. Uncle Sam wants to send me to the pen. The Crawfords of the Flying W have served notice on me to light out or get riddled with lead. And Yont insists I stay put here. I don't much like any of their plans for me."

"I have another one for you. Saddle yore bronc and light a shuck for parts far and unknown."

"I like that one best," Jim agreed. "Maybe I won't get far, but I can try." His glance shifted to the ranchman glaring at them. "Mr. Yont isn't going to be pleased. That is going to break my heart."

Dillard sauntered across to the place where his picketed horse was grazing and brought the pinto to the house in front of which his saddle lay.

"Where do you think you're going?" demanded Yont.

"I'm going to take a ride." In Jim's eyes there was a mocking reckless light. "I've got bad news for you. The worm has turned. I won't be here to jump next time you crack that whip."

Dark blood ran into Yont's scowling face. "Try to run out on me and I'll put a rope round your neck," he warned.

Dillard fastened a cinch before he answered. "You don't quite get it, Mr. Slavedriver. You no longer have anything to sell the law. It is no secret now that my real name is Rufe Rogers. Half the people in Rifle know it by this time, including United States Marshal Folsom. You might give him a message from me when he arrives. Tell him I couldn't wait on account of a pressing engagement elsewhere."

Yont's fingers clutched the butt of the revolver at his side. "I'll show you what I've got to sell, you damned bandit—and that's you!" he cried. "You're staying right where you are at. I don't aim to stand by and let a bandit ride away. Come out from back of that horse."

The hands of the Texan fell from the saddle, the right one to hover close to the forty-five resting in its holster. "Don't make a mistake," he said.

"Get your hands up or I'll riddle you," Yont ordered, and crossed in front of the pony to cover Rogers better. He had drawn his gun.

"Don't get on the prod," Runyon cut in. "I'm siding Jim."

The big man half-turned and glared at him. "Are you a blasted fool? There's a reward out for this bank robber. Interfere with me and you'll get ten years in the penitentiary."

"He's right, Charley. Keep out of this." Rogers' narrowed eyes were fastened on the Quarter Circle F Y owner. "If he tries to stop me, I'll handle it."

"You heard me," Runyon said. "I'm in this."

It was in Rogers' mind that to kill Yont, even if he could, would blacken the case against him as a desperate criminal. Yet he did not intend to surrender tamely. Was there any other way to escape? If so, it must be now while the rancher's attention was partly diverted toward Runyon. His body tensed and he plunged forward, diving at the man's thighs.

Yont's weapon roared. A bolt of lightning stabbed the Texan in the side, but did not stop him. His arms closed around the thick legs and the drive of the charge flung Yont from his feet. They plowed into the ground together, a tangle of arms and legs, both of them jarred by the shock of the fall.

Runyon came into action fast. The blue barrel of his revolver crashed against the head of the ranchman. It rose and fell again. Yont's great body slumped and his arms dropped slackly. Rogers lay on top of him, too weak and shaken to rise.

Charley helped him to his feet. "You're wounded," he cried.

Rogers swayed dizzily. The ground went up and down like sea waves. He clung to Runyon to steady himself. Supported by his companion, he reached the table and leaned against it.

"I'm sick," he said.

"Hang on to the table while I get Yont's pistol," Runyon told him.

The redhead laid the weapon on the table. "Lemme have a look at that wound, boy," he said.

"Not now." Rufe edged along the table slowly toward his horse. "I've got to get away from here."

The worried eyes of Runyon took in the red stain spreading on the shirt of the wounded man. "Stay there. I'll bring the horse." After Charley had brought it, he was still in anxious doubt. "Can you make out to ride?"

"Once I'm in the saddle." Rogers held fast to the horn, waves of faintness running through him.

Runyon doubted it. The man could hardly keep his feet. But it was in the code of the frontier that in an emergency a man must make his own choice. If he did not get into hiding, Folsom would arrest him when he arrived.

At the third try he managed to heave Rufe into the saddle. On the way to his own horse he picked up the revolver on the table. Yont lay on the ground, just beginning to show signs of life.

They traveled slowly, Runyon watching the wounded man uneasily. Rufe was leaning forward, both hands clamped to the horn. He was plainly a very sick person. His body swayed in the hull. Tortured eyes looked out of a haggard face. White teeth were shut tight. Only an iron will kept the torso from collapsing.

The path they followed took them upstream. It was brush country and the sharp claws of cholla and prickly pear clutched at them as they moved. Runyon was sure his companion could not go far. There was a limit to the punishment a stubborn will could inflict on its weak and flagging body. Runyon dismounted and walked beside the pinto, one hand steadying the rider and the other pushing aside the thorny vegetation. He spoke encouraging words the pain-wracked man scarcely heard.

"You're doing fine . . . Better rest here. I'll help you down and see to the wound."

Rogers did not wait to be helped. He fainted and slid down into the arms of his friend. Runyon laid him on the ground and with his knife cut away the wet soggy shirt from his side. In his hat he brought water from the creek and washed the wound using the bandanna that had been around his own neck. The bullet had struck a rib, been deflected by it, and had torn a way out of the body at an angle. After he had bathed the head of the unconscious man and covered the injured side with the wet kerchief, there was nothing else he could do. He must get help for Rufe soon or it would be too late.

The Flying W home buildings could be seen through the brush less than a mile distant. The owners of it were not friendly to Rogers, but he could not let that prevent him from appealing to them. They had a better reputation than Yont had, and no doubt would give aid to an injured man even if later they gave him up to the law. Charley swung to the saddle and galloped along the trail ripping a way through the brush.

A man bridling a bronco stared at him as he raced into the yard. He was Cape Crawford.

"What's the matter?" he asked.

"Fen Yont shot a man. He's back there on the trail—badly wounded, maybe dead. I came for help."

"How far from here?"

"A mile, I guess."

"We'll take the light wagon and carry him from the trail to the road." Cape called to a man in the corral. "There's a man been shot, Rod. Hitch up the light wagon and put some hay in the bed. Tell Pink to saddle and burn the wind for Rifle. We want Doc Burgess in a hurry." He turned to Runyon. "I'll let Sis know, so she can have a bed ready for him when we get here."

They met June coming out of the house and her brother explained the situation.

"I'll be ready for him," she said, and asked Runyon if the hurt man was anybody they knew.

"It's the man who took up your land," he told her.

Her instant fear was that somebody connected with the Flying W had shot him. White-faced, she turned on her brother. "Who did this? Was it . . . one of us?"

"Fen Yont did it, Miss," Runyon answered. "He's just a boy. I don't think he's bad. Yont was responsible for his taking up your land. Lemme tell you about it later."

She said, "The wagon is ready for you," and walked back into the house.

7 PETE CRAWFORD CAME IN FROM riding the line to discover an astonishing situation. The man he had given twenty-four hours to get off his land was lying in the ranch guest room with June as his nurse. That she was very anxious about her patient he could see. She had never before had in her care anybody so ill as this claim jumper. He was delirious and had a high fever. They had dressed the wound as well as they could, and from time to time she bathed his burning face with a cold wet cloth, but she was counting the minutes until the doctor came.

Pete drew Runyon from the bedside to the porch and questioned him. Runyon sat on the top step leaning against a post while he rolled and smoked cigarettes nervously as he told the whole story of Rogers as far as he knew it. There was no use to cover up now. In a sparsely settled country news travels like the wind, and soon settlers in the farthest pocket of the hills would be talking about this.

"So he is a bank robber and a killer," Crawford said when his guest had finished.

"I don't know. Looks like it. Sometimes I think he ain't. Might be the way he claims—that he got in a tight and had to light out sudden to save himself."

"His explanation sounds pretty thin to me," the ranchman replied. "By his own admission he was running around with these bandits for several days. He even rode to the bank with them and held their horses. He could not help knowing what they were doing."

"He might. Say a kid just out of the brush country bumps into a pair of smooth crooks. They are good company and all of them are doing a lot of drinking. They need

41

somebody to stay around with their mounts while they are doing the job. He's right handy and they stick him for it."

"I had some words with this man," Crawford differed. "He doesn't look to me like a raw hillbilly. A cool guy tough and hard would be my size-up."

An anxious voice back of them said, "I wish Doctor Burgess would come. This man is awful sick."

June was standing in the doorway. She was watching the road, her eyes searching for a buggy that was not in sight.

"So do I," Runyon agreed. "He's lost a lot of blood. If he hadn't been all grit, I wouldn't have got him far as I did."

"Take it easy, June," her brother advised. "Texans are tough."

"I've got to go back," she said.

Runyon returned to the bedroom with her.

The wounded man looked at the young woman with eyes perplexed and surprised. Temporarily at least he had come out of his delirium.

"Where am I?" he asked weakly and tried to raise his head from the pillow.

June put a gentle hand on his shoulder and held him down. "You must not move. You have been hurt."

"You're the girl who told me I would find trouble," he accused. "Riffraff you called me."

"Please don't talk," she said. "You must save your strength. We have sent for the doctor."

"What's the matter with me?" Howcome I'm here?"

"You had an accident. We brought you here. Now be quiet and just rest."

He lay still recalling the events of the past hours. His gaze shifted to Runyon. "Yont shot me and you pistol-whipped him."

"Right. Now you do like Miss Crawford tells you."

Rogers nodded assent. He had no energy left. His eyes closed and he fell into a doze. June very quietly brought a chair to the bedside and sat down. Runyon tiptoed from the room.

The sick man stirred restlessly. His fingers clawed at the quilt. The girl took his hand in hers and that calmed him. He wriggled deeper into the pillow and relaxed to sleep.

42

The worry was sponged from his face. June had heard from Runyon that he was the bandit Rogers for whose arrest a reward was posted. So innocent and boyish did he look in sleep that it was difficult to conceive of him as a hardened criminal with a price on his head. Word of his being at the ranch would swiftly spread. It was certain that if he recovered he would be arrested and taken back to Texas, where he would probably be put in prison for many years. The thought of this was disturbing. She felt no grudge against him now that he had ceased being Yont's tool. He was just a boy in trouble with no chance of a good life even if he got well.

Doctor Burgess was a tubby pink-faced little man whose bustling ways did not interfere with efficiency in his profession. Fifteen years of practice in this wild country had given him a large experience in the treatment of gunshot wounds. He thought Rogers' chance of recovery not good. The patient had lost a great deal of blood and it was likely the bullet had torn into some vital organ. Though he could promise nothing, he offered a ray of hope. It was amazing, he told June, how these tough young cowboys recovered from injuries that would kill city dwellers.

A week of days passed and Rufe Rogers' life still hung on a thread. It was not until the tenth day that Doctor Burgess felt he had turned the corner.

"You are going to live," he said to the Texan severely. "And it is due to the fine nursing this young lady gave you."

"I don't reckon I'll ever forget what I owe Miss Crawford," Rufe said.

In the days of his great weakness, while he was fighting for his life, June had been a tireless nurse, all womanly kindness and tenderness. But now that she knew he would live, she withdrew her friendliness from him. He was an outlaw wanted for murder, and that fact built a wall between them. She no longer spent hours in the room. The Mexican cook Juan brought in his meals and waited on his needs. He missed her greatly. Many strong men stricken with illness are drawn in their helplessness to the nurse who tends and cheers them, especially if she is young and pretty. It was so with Rufe Rogers. All June's ways were

43

dear to him. When she was in sight he could not keep his eyes from her. Unless she was near time dragged for him. And now he rarely saw her.

Rufe awakened one morning to see Folsom looking down at him. The marshal pulled up the sleeve of his nightshirt and gazed at the scar on the arm.

"I had a hunch from the first day I saw you that you were Rogers," he said.

"That gives you a fifty per cent average, Marshal," the Texan replied. "I'm Rufe Rogers, but I am not a bank robber."

"You'll have a chance to prove that and I don't think you can," Folsom answered. "Far as I can see you have no evidence at all in your favor, nothing but your own word. You were in cahoots with the robbers sure."

"Strange if I was in the holdup with them that I didn't ride out of town with my pals instead of me heading west and them east."

"Maybe it was planned that way."

"When Downs and Wall were captured, was all the money found on them?"

"Every nickel of it."

"Do you think if I had been in on the stickup, I would have left the others before I had got my cut of the loot?"

"If you were frightened enough, you might have."

"I don't scare that bad."

Folsom realized the young man had a point there. It was the marshal's opinion that Rogers was a cool and nervy character, not one to go into a dangerous enterprise and panic before it was finished. There must be some reason why he had left his partners that was not clear. The officer did not believe for a moment he was an innocent lad caught in a trap. In any case, whether guilty or not, it was his duty to take the prisoner back to Texas and he meant to do so.

That Rogers would not be able to travel for several weeks was clear. In the interval the marshal stayed in the bunkhouse at the ranch, and, since he had formerly been a cowboy, helped the Flying W riders work the stock.

There came a day when, with the help of a walking-stick, Rogers hobbled out to the porch. He looked so weak that

June reproached herself for having neglected him of late. She followed him to make sure he had found a comfortable chair, bringing a cushion with her. This she put behind him in the rocking chair.

"Would you like a book to read?" she asked him.

He thought he would, and when she named Scott's *Kenilworth*, he said it would do. His gaze followed her as she walked back into the house. She moved with a graceful rhythm that charmed him. He told himself not to be a fool about her. This exciting girl was not for him, a man whom she regarded as a criminal about to be dragged back to justice. Somebody else would woo and win her, one with no stain on his name. That would be all right with him. When he did not see her any more, he would forget her. She just happened to be the loveliest creature who had touched his life, and he had lost his head a little. The circumstances were to blame for that, his sickness and her great kindness to him. The soft breathing color in her cheeks, the gracious curves of her slender body, the swell of her sweet breasts, were to him a delight that was also a pain.

Her light step sounded as she came back to the porch.

"I couldn't find *Kenilworth*, so I brought *The Mill on the Floss* and *The Lady of the Lake*. Probably you think poetry is sissy stuff, Mr.—Dillard." She hesitated before she spoke the name.

"I like Scott's poetry. It has a swing to it." He took up the question of his name. "Since I have been smoked out, you had better call me Rogers, Miss Crawford. I borrowed the other name. It belonged to my mother before she was married. James I helped myself to because my father is called that. Rufus Rogers is my name from now on."

"Unless you change it again," she suggested, a small whiplash in her voice.

His eyes met hers directly. "I won't. Maybe you won't believe me, Miss Crawford, but I had nothing to do with that bank robbery."

There was a little glad lift in her heart, for in that moment she discovered that she did believe him. His face and his appearance were letters of recommendation. There was a clean pride in the set of the head and shoulders. Regardless of the evidence piled up against him, she felt sure there was good and not evil in this man.

She said, a throb of emotion in her low husky voice, "I think I'm sure of that, but——" She let the sentence die unfinished.

He ended it for her. "But if I hadn't been running with outlaws, I wouldn't have been suspected. Right. I did not know they were bandits, but I guessed they were hard tough characters on the borderline. I've always been a wild coot. There's a streak of recklessness in me that rebels at mealy-mouthed people who are always proper. And, I might as well admit, I was drinking more than I should."

"But you didn't know what they were going to do?"

"No. We had saddled to ride to Dallas, and they stopped, so they told me, to cash a check. Until the guns sounded in the bank and they came running out, I had not an idea anything was wrong. I had got down from my horse and was watching some kids play marbles. One of them was not very good, and I sat on my heels to show him how to hold the marble between the knuckle of his thumb and finger."

"How old were the boys?" she asked.

"Oh, maybe ten or eleven." The question surprised him. "Why?"

"They might help as witnesses. A man waiting with nerves tight for his partners to come out from a bank they were robbing doesn't fool around playing marbles with little boys."

"That's a point," he agreed. "But I had never seen the kids before and don't know who they are."

An idea had come into her mind. She let it germinate.

"There is one thing I want to tell you, Miss Crawford," he continued. "It's about the homesteading. What I am going to say explains but does not excuse it. After I got a job punching for the Quarter Circle F Y, a Fort Worth paper came to Yont with a picture of me in it and a reward offer of five hundred dollars for my capture. Yont put it to me plain. He would have me sent back to Texas and pocket the reward if I didn't file on that one hundred and sixty acres and later deed it to him. I didn't like it a bit. But I was in a trap. The feeling in Fort Worth was very strong against the bandits on account of the killing of the cashier.

When I reached there, I would probably be hanged. Your people were strangers to me. If somebody had made an error of location in his land entry, it was too bad but not my fault. So I threw in with the old devil. Now I am glad I did, for if I hadn't been his stooge, somebody else would have. The filing I made keeps him from getting it."

"I am glad Yont isn't going to have it. Using it as a wedge for his cattle, he could almost ruin our grazing range."

"You are going to get it as soon as I can give you a relinquishment." He grinned cheerfully at the picture in his hand. "The scoundrel's rotten scheme misses fire this time. In picking me to carry it out, he defeated himself."

Charley Runyon rode into the yard and grounded the bridle reins in front of the porch. He lifted his hat to the girl. "Your patient is lookin' real peart, Miss Crawford. Doc says your nursing pulled him through. He was one sick man. Two weeks ago I wouldn't of give a plugged quarter for his chances."

June was embarrassed. A flush ran beneath the tan of her cheeks. "That's nonsense. Doctor Burgess told me his strong constitution saved him."

"Maybe it was planned for him to get well. They say a guy born to be——" Runyon broke off abruptly. "I talk too doggoned much. I ought to be kicked."

"It's all right, Charley," Rogers assured him. "I don't reckon they will hang me. Something will turn up."

"Sure it will. I was just joshing." Runyon shifted to a less ticklish subject. "Heard a good one in town this morning. Yont has applied for the reward on you, claiming he fixed you so the marshal could get you easy. Folsom says he won't get a nickel of it, seeing he knew who you are and kept quiet about it."

"If any reward is going to be paid, seems to me that you ought to get it with a cut going to Miss Crawford, since you two kept me alive for Folsom," Rogers said.

It was June's opinion that nothing would turn up to save Rufe unless somebody took the trouble to turn it up. She took occasion to see Runyon alone before he left for Rifle.

"How would you like to go to Fort Worth?" she asked him.

"Me?" He looked at her with surprise. "What would I

do there? I've got to get me a job right soon, no foolin'."

"Rufe Rogers is your friend, isn't he?"

"Sure."

"There must be evidence in his favor that we don't know about. Somebody should go and round it up before the trial. It may be lost by then if we do nothing."

"That's right. You want me to try it?"

"Yes. There isn't anybody else available. You'll have to be smart to get it."

Runyon's face reddened. "I'd as lief go. Fact is, I'd be glad to. I like the guy. But the truth is I'm scraping the bottom of the barrel. All the mazuma I have left is a quarter and a thin dime."

"I could take care of that. I have some money of my own my mother left me." She interrupted him as he began to protest. "Don't tell me you won't take money from a woman. You're going on my errand. And if you ever tell anybody I gave you the money, I'll never speak to you again."

Charley stared at her in surprise. She read the thought in his mind and repudiated it almost angrily.

"I don't care a thing about him," she protested. "It's his own fault he is in this trouble. But he isn't much more than a boy, and I hate to see him punished for something he didn't do."

"Same here," Runyon replied. "We'd better go in and have a long powwow with him—find out every doggone thing he has to tell us, like where he met them, and if he roomed at the same place they did and kept his horse at the same corral, and if he has any friends in Fort Worth. I'll have to start digging from the ground up."

They found Rogers back in the bedroom. He had grown tired sitting up and was lying down with his clothes on. For an hour the two pumped him. A lot of the questions they asked led nowhere, but before they had finished Runyon had a pretty good picture of his stay in Fort Worth. He had put his horse up at the Frontier Corral and eaten at a Chinese restaurant. He had roomed at the house of a widow named Hastings and there he had met the outlaws Jack Downs and Bill Klem. Both of them were or had been cowboys. With them he had drifted from one gaming

48

house to another. A good deal of their time had been spent at the fabulous White Elephant, the most gaudy sporting place in the West, playing faro and poker and chuckaluck. It did not take him long to discover that his companions were hard tough characters, but so were hundreds of other range riders who had never stepped outside of the law, men who wore this protective harshness as a cover to conceal in a rough occupation any gentleness others might consider weakness.

Runyon started on his long journey that afternoon. June worried about sending him. It might be dangerous for the boy. Bluntly she put a question to him.

"Is it safe for you to go back to Texas?"

He grinned. "I been takin' care of myself a right smart time, Miss June, with nobody to tuck me up at night or anything."

"That's not what I mean. Are you wanted by the rangers? Before you came here did you do anything for which you might be arrested?"

He gave that consideration and decided to tell the truth, "Onct I put the wrong brand on a calf." He added whimsically, "But it was such a little bitty calf I don't reckon it was hardly a misdemeanor."

"You are a rustler then?"

"No, ma'am. The cow had gone off for water and left the calf hidden in the brush the way they do. Looked like a maverick to me, so I ran the brand of my boss on it, which is common practice in our country. A guy happened along and saw me do it and reported it. There was a long time hard feeling between the owner of that calf and our outfit. He started to raise an unholy row, and my boss figured it would be a good idea for me take a leave of absence till the thing was fixed up. So I forked a bronc and lit out with his blessing."

"I don't want to send you back to get into trouble."

"Nothing to that, Miss June. To the rangers I'm just a two-spot not worth foolin' with and Texas is big as all get out. You'd be surprised how far it is from Fort Worth to Uvalde, where I lived."

"Well, be careful. And try hard to find some evidence in Rufe's favor."

"Y'betcha. I'll be Johnny-on-the-job. So long, Miss June."

They shook hands. "*Vaya con Dios*," the girl said.

As she turned back into the house, June thought that to save Rufe Rogers he would need to have God with him.

8 AFTER DAYS OF TRAVEL IN THE SADdle and by stage, Charley Runyon took a Denver, Texas, and Fort Worth train to the latter town. Fort Worth was one of the chief centers of the cattle business. A few years earlier it had been what the trail drivers called a wide place in the road, but it was now bursting with life and showed every indication of becoming a city. The raw youth of its pioneer days was still much in evidence. It was wild and wide open. Whooping cowboys cantered down the main street, but they tied at hitch racks in front of three-story brick houses to go jingling into gambling halls modern and elaborately appointed, though crumbling adobe huts might neighbor the new buildings on both sides.

The trail herds were changing a vast region, that had been inhabited only by buffaloes and Indian tribes, into great grazing pastures upon which millions of cattle fed. To Runyon familiarity with the Texas steer had bred only a kindly contempt for it. He saw a scrubby animal, leggy and bony, with long horns attached to a big head and very little meat on its gaunt frame. He could not read the future to know that this hardy bag of bones in the course of evolution was to be the main factor in building a dozen cities and nearly as many states.

On his way uptown from the depot, Charley stopped at the Frontier Corral ostensibly to inquire about getting a job. The whiskered bowlegged oldtimer who owned the wagon lot was sitting relaxed as a cat in a tiptilted armchair supported by an adobe wall. He was chewing tobacco contentedly while he whittled thin shavings from a stick of soft pine. His soiled shirt was open and showed a tangled mat of hair on the chest. The sign above the wide gate showed the legend, JIM POOR, PROP, below the name of the establishment.

Mr. Poor had no job to offer, but he had plenty of time and was a garrulous soul. Charley hunkered down against the wall beside him and got the old man started talking. Judicious prodding brought him to the recent bank holdup which was still with him a live topic, since one of the bandits had stabled his horse here and so made Mr. Poor an important character in the story. He was glad to get a good listener.

"Had me fooled good, that Rogers guy did. Doggone it, I liked the kid. 'Course I knew he was a reckless devil-may-care bird, but by thunder I was thataway myself onct. Until the blowup came, I hadn't a notion he was one of those slit-eyed killers who have their thumbs on the hammer of their forty-fives while they sleep, though I could see he was corned up considerable."

"Maybe he wasn't a bad man," Runyon suggested. "Maybe you were right in your first size-up of him."

"How the heck could I be right when he went right spang away from here and killed a poor fellow while he was robbing a bank? Nothing to that story of Jack Downs just before they strung him up that Rogers wasn't in it. He was a game devil with plenty of sand in his craw, and when he saw his own goose was cooked, he just tried to lie the kid out of it in case he got caught."

Runyon's eyes came to life swiftly. "Downs said that Rogers wasn't in the holdup?"

"That's right. But it didn't mean a thing."

"What about the other fellow—Klem? Did he back up what Downs said?"

"In a kind of way. Him and Downs were two different breeds of cats. Klem was trying to git down on his knees and beg for mercy, but Downs looked hard and cold at the men who were going to hang him, with a you-be-damned sneer in his eyes."

"But Klem did say Rufe Rogers wasn't their partner?"

"Downs forced him to come through, but Klem's teeth were chattering he was so scared for himself. He didn't know or care what he was saying, so he could get back to pleadin' for his own life."

Charley shook his head. He would accept no such explanation. For the first time he was dead sure his friend was innocent and he felt a glow of happiness at this support. He meant to use it as a toehold to pry loose further evidence.

"I don't think you are lookin' at this right, Mr. Poor," he said. "Jack Downs was a tough character, a real man who had gone bad, one who had the guts to die game. If Rufe Rogers had been a partner in the holdup, he would have let him take his chance. But it wasn't that way. He had tricked the kid into helping them and he wasn't going to die with that on his soul, so he cleared Rogers. It was the one decent thing left him that he could do."

"A reasonable argument if it squared with the facts," Poor answered. "But Rogers was there holding the horses while they robbed the bank. You can't get away from that."

"Did you hear Downs when he cleared young Rogers?"

"No. There was quite a crowd and I was on the edge of it, just eyeballin' you might say. I hadn't a thing to do with the hanging. When the crowd was breakin' up after it was over, a fellow near the front told several of us what Downs and Klem had said."

"Do you remember who it was? I'd like to talk with him."

Poor's gaze traveled up and down him with cold suspicion. "What for? To make trouble. Lynching is against the law and there is talk going around that the leaders in this may be prosecuted. If I knew who told me I wouldn't help you."

"Listen, Mr. Poor, I'm trying to save the life of a young fellow I feel sure is no more guilty of this crime than you or I. Marshal Folsom is going to bring him back here as soon as he is well enough to travel on account of a bad wound he has. You want Rogers to have a square shake, don't you? If there is any evidence in his favor, he has a right to have it heard. It's up to this witness to decide for himself whether he wants to talk. It can't hurt him for me to ask what he heard. He doesn't have to tell me anything unless he feels like it."

"You are a friend of this Rogers?"

"Right. Lemme tell you about him." Runyon narrated the story of all that had occurred since the hour the two young Texans had first met.

Poor shrugged his shoulders. "Might be the way you think, but you haven't sold me on it. Yet I'll go along this far. I'll give you a name—Bob Grattan. Take it and do what you please with it. Only remember that Grattan is a tough mean *hombre* and he's liable to get sore at you."

"I'm obliged." Runyon rose to leave. "I'll keep yore name out of it if you like."

"It's not important, but I'd a little rather you would."

Runyon ate at Hop Lee's restaurant. He had by great good luck struck gold already. If his luck held up, he might follow the vein and hit a jackpot at the end of it. After supper he made inquiries and found the rooming house of the widow Hastings. She had a vacancy and gave him a room, but not before she had put him through a questionnaire as to his respectability. She had, she explained, recently had three outlaws as roomers and she did not intend to take in any more if she could help it.

Mrs. Hastings was a woman who had spent her life in the sun-dried Southwest. Her husband had been drowned in the Canadian River while helping to take a trail herd across the stream when it was bank full. He had left her without means, half a dozen little children dependent on her. Like many another frontier woman, she had brought them up, sent them to school, and turned them out into the world to make good citizens. But the long years of hard scrabbling had toughened her. She had a leathery tanned face and a blunt direct manner of speech.

"I won't have any roomers but honest folks, young man," she told Runyon. "If you are a scalawag, I don't want you."

Charley's boyish grin was a potent and convincing argument. He reminded her of her youngest son who was in

Colorado working for the Santa Fe Railroad as a telegrapher.

"I aim to be a model roomer," he promised.

"See you do," she answered tartly. "No hellin' around or drinkin'. I've had all of that I'll take."

Charley meant after he knew Mrs. Hastings better to appeal to her on behalf of the recent lodger who was now under arrest in Arizona. He guessed that a kind heart beat beneath the exterior rough rind that protected her from a world that had been none too easy on her. But he could not question her about the relationship of the bandits until he had established a more friendly footing with her.

When he had washed away the dust of travel, he wandered out to have a look at the night life of the town. In essentials it was like that of other frontier towns he had known. Hilarious cowboys, just in from months of dry and dusty travel on the trail, tramped the streets on the lookout for amusement. The blare of blended trumpets, fiddles, and pianos beat out from dance halls to the sidewalk. Saddled ponies were tied to every hitch rack. From a place that bore the name, The Jughandle, came a woman's voice hoarse and scratched from constant wear. She was singing what cowboys called a tear-jerker.

"She's more to be pitied than censored,
She's more to be loved than despised,"

her tremolo pleaded.

In the next block a sign hung above the sidewalk, flanked to right and left by street lamps attached to the wall. On the sign was painted a white elephant. Runyon pushed through the door into the big hall. The display of luxury took his breath. A long mahogany bar ran part way down one side of the room behind which was the famous mirror said to have cost twenty-seven thousand dollars. Below the ceiling lights sparkled crystal pendants. Costly paintings of nude women hung on the walls. To be in keeping with their surroundings, the dealers and croupiers wore suits of black broadcloth and frilled shirts of fine linen.

The customers did not harmonize with this elegance. Those who crowded the faro, chuckaluck, monte, and rou-

54

lette tables were the heterogeneous flotation of the frontier, most of them roughly garbed to suit their way of life. Yet the local residents were immensely proud that Fort Worth could support such a palace for entertainment. The White Elephant was an indication of the city's future.

Runyon's excuse for dropping in was that Poor had told him Bob Grattan frequented the place. But he would have visited it anyhow. The house was widely known all over Texas. He drifted from one game to another watching the play. At the roulette table a heavy-shouldered man, with hard eyes set too narrowly in a harsh seamed face, was playing the corners with expensive yellow chips. He was having a run of bad luck and he manifestly did not like it. When he spoke, his voice had the bite of temper in it.

Charley murmured in the ear of a small bearded man standing beside him. "Who is the gent on the prod?"

The little man answered in a whisper. "Name is Bob Grattan. He's gettin' sore as a boil. Liable to be ructions soon."

He turned to leave and Runyon caught up with him near the door. "Just a minute, Mister," he said. "Perhaps you can give me some information about Grattan. I have a little business with him."

The face of the other man set. "No information," he answered.

"What does he do for a living? Where can I find him in the daytime?"

"Ask him, not me."

Charley could see he was determined to say no more, moved probably by timid caution. Grattan must be dangerous, at least in this man's opinion.

"Sorry I bothered you," Runyon said.

"I mind my own affairs and keep out of trouble." The rabbity man pushed through the screen doors and disappeared.

As Runyon returned to the roulette table, Grattan flung back his chair and rose. "Damn this game!" he exploded.

He pushed roughly through the crowd to the bar and ordered a double shot of whisky. The young man had misgivings about approaching him while he was in such a bad mood, but he decided to try to get an appointment for the next day. He moved up to the bar and ordered a beer.

"A run of bad luck tonight," he ventured.

Grattan glanced at him. "Go drown yoreself," he snarled.

Charley realized his opening had been an unfortunate one. He tried again. "Like to have a talk with you tomorrow if you have time, Mr. Grattan."

The big man gulped down his drink and fixed his eyes on the brash young stranger who was bothering him. Grattan was a notorious rough-and-tumble fighter and just now he felt so edgy that nothing would please him more than to beat up this whipper-snapper.

"Talk now," he ordered angrily.

Runyon was aware he had bungled this. "It's a private matter just between you and me," he explained. "Tomorrow——"

Grattan slammed a heavy fist on the bar and made the glasses jump. "Now," he repeated obstinately.

"All right. Outside, where we can be alone." This was not working out right, Charley knew. While the man was in this vile temper, he would not get anywhere with questions. But since he had started he had to go on.

He followed Grattan to the sidewalk. The bully turned on him. "Spill it," he growled.

Charley made one more attempt to postpone the talk. "If you would make an appointment with me——"

"You've got one right damn now."

"It's about Rufe Rogers. I'm a friend of his. I understand you heard Downs say just before he died that Rogers was innocent of helping in the holdup. If we can prove that, it may save Rufe."

Beneath the leathery skin of Grattan's face dark blood beat up. "So you come to me with yore cheap lie of being a friend of Rogers. You never saw him. You're a spy of Andrews who wants to send me to the pen claiming I was the leader of the mob that hanged the two murdering bandits." Rage mounted in the man, but beneath it was the satisfaction of knowing that he could work it off on this victim who came asking for trouble. He straddled forward, crowding Runyon against the wall, gloating over him, the hairy fingers of his hands knotted into iron fists.

"I'm going to give you the whaling of yore life, then you can crawl back to that puling hypocrite of a prosecuting attorney who put you up to this and tell him he'll be next if he don't lay off me."

Runyon knew he was in for it. Against this two hundred twenty pounds of bone and brawn he had no chance in a fight. The fellow was strong as an ox and for his weight light on his feet. Charley could not duck and escape. To his mind came advice his father had once given him: *If you are pushed into a fight remember that the best defense is attack. Hit the other fellow first hard as you can and keep hitting him.*

Charley lashed out at the taunting dish face pushed close to his. Taken by surprise, the big man let out a growl of pain and fury. Before he could get into action, a second blow cut his cheek and a third brought blood from his nose. Grattan came in swinging wildly, too full of temper to direct his flailing fists. Some of them Runyon took on his arms and shoulders. He drove a hard right into the belly of the bully and landed an uppercut under his chin.

After that Charley's fight was all defense. A slashing blow knocked him from his feet, but he was up again before his foe could close with him. Grattan was fighting more carefully now. His blows tore through a weakening resistance, slogging at ribs and face with a force that left Runyon dizzy and made him sick with pain. Charley was pinned to the wall, a target for a cold and savage hammering. A dozen times the fists crashed home before the boy's body sagged down the wall to the sidewalk.

A crowd was beginning to gather. Grattan was pleased that he had a gallery to watch him, though he paid no obvious attention to it. He kicked the unconscious youth three times in the side before he turned and walked away. It was one of his proud moments.

When Charley came to, he was lying on a billiard table in the White Elephant and a man was pouring whisky down his throat. He tried to sit up and his body was racked with pain. A dozen strange faces swam around him in the air.

"He'll be all right now," somebody said.

A lopsided grin showed on Runyon's battered face. "Mr.

Grattan put me through the wringer certain," he told the world at large.

"What started it?" a whitehaired man asked.

Charley did not give specific information. "I don't think he likes me," he said.

With some help he got down from the table aching in every joint. He tried a few steps and decided he could walk.

"Well, gentlemen, the show is over for tonight," he announced jauntily. "No repeat performance, I hope."

The whitehaired man was a lawyer named Bannister. "Can you make it to travel alone, son?" he inquired. "If not, one of us will help you home."

"I'm obliged, sir, but I don't need any help." A flicker of a smile touched his eyes. "A guy ought to be able to absorb a licking in his system. Be seeing you."

He walked out unsteadily, but with his head up. A boy's pride had to be protected at all costs. He wavered up the street, counting the steps until he reached his lodging house. The distance seemed unending. Opening the door, he stood in the hall under a wall light breathing for a moment before he took the stairs. He was a mass of aches and weary as an old man.

Mrs. Hastings opened a door and came into the hall. She looked at him, tight lips set close, and said nothing. His face was covered with bruises and dried blood.

"I had a little trouble," he explained, with a twisted grin that missed jauntiness.

"You had better find another rooming house tomorrow," she told him grimly.

He said meekly, "Yes, ma'am," not attempting to question her decision.

"I don't want drunks in my house."

He shook his head. "I'm not corned up, ma'am. I asked a guy the wrong question. I reckon he didn't like my red haid, so he stomped all over me like a bunch of wild mossyhorns in a stampede. He certainly gave me an elegant sufficiency. I disremember ever absorbin' a licking so thorough. Me, I never got so tired of a fellow in my life."

His naïve boyish grin disarmed her. "Of course you have excuses," she snapped. "They all do. Who was he?"

"Gent named Bob Grattan."

58

"You picked a fine character to tangle with," she said dryly. "That Grattan is big as a bull moose, strong as an ape, and chock full of meanness. Not only that, he is a cold-blooded killer."

"I didn't choose him," he mentioned. "Mr. Grattan chose me."

She made a swift decision. "Get up into your room and take off your coat and shirt. I'll bring a can of hot water and sponge you off."

"For the hot water I'll say thanks, Mrs. Hastings. I'll look after myself fine. But I'm sure obliged."

"Do as you're told," she ordered. "I've got boys of my own."

She brought with her rubbing alcohol and sticking-plaster. He was standing beside the bed, his coat flung on it. Beneath the tan he was blushing deeply.

"We'll have no nonsense," she told him curtly. "Off with that shirt."

Angry red blotches covered his ribs. Before morning they would be turning purple. She bathed his face gently, patted alcohol into the wounds, and applied sticking-plaster to cover the cuts, after which she made him lie down on the bed and treated the hammered body.

"What was it you said that annoyed this Grattan?" she asked. "You're lucky he didn't maim you for life."

"He sure whangs his fists in like the kick of a mule," Charley agreed.

"You didn't answer my question. Come clean, young fellow. Or out you go in the morning."

Runyon told her the story of Rufe Rogers and explained that he had come to gather evidence to support it. She hoped it was true and almost believed. Small points contributing to it came to her mind. Rogers had not known the others when he first came to her house and she had introduced them. They did not keep their mounts at the same corral he used. Once she had noticed Downs and Klem whispering together, and when Rogers appeared they had stopped at once. He had told her he was leaving for the south and was ordering his mail sent to Lampasas. Runyon could inquire from the postmaster if he had done so. She offered to find out who the children were who had been playing marbles across the street from the bank and let him talk with them. Before she left Runyon, she had become a complete convert to the innocence of Rufe Rogers.

She turned at the door. "You'd better stay in bed tomorrow," she told him. "You'll be very stiff and sore."

At that suggestion he rebelled. He had a job to do. What was a licking to write home about? He would get along fine. And he was sure obliged a lot for her kindness in fixing him up.

The widow lifted her shoulders in a shrug. He was, she thought, young and full of vinegar. She liked the indomitable quality in him. When he first applied for a room, she had taken a shine to him. The rich bloom in his cheeks beneath the tan, the line of golden down just above where the blade of his razor had run, brought to mind her own Peter. And she was very glad that other nice boy Rufe Rogers was not a scalawag.

She fired a parting shot at her lodger. "After this, try and keep out of trouble. Just leave alone folks like that Bob Grattan. He would as lief kill you as not."

When Runyon arose after a restless night, he found that soreness had settled into the muscles of his face. In front of the looking glass he tried a grin and discovered that any movement of the lips or cheeks was painful. His ribs protested at every step he took. He thought it would be a good idea to drop in on a doctor and find out if any of them were broken.

On the way to breakfast, he noticed that his appearance attracted a good deal of attention. A face as battered as his was not seen on the streets every day. No doubt the word had spread that Grattan had worked over another victim. Charley took care to walk lightly disregarding the pain.

As Hop Lee took his order, the Oriental made no verbal comment, but his surprised eyes asked a question.

"I met a cyclone and it picked me up and dropped me in a clump of prickly pear," he explained. "Three eggs, sunny side up, and a nice piece of ham, but first a stack of flapjacks and coffee."

Outside the restaurant, he came face to face with the lawyer Bannister who stopped to ask him how he felt.

"Fit as a fiddle, Judge," Runyon assured him, his voice

light and cheerful. "Except feelin' like I'd been run through a meat-grinder."

"Grattan did some talking last night. From what he said, I gather you are here looking for evidence to help Rogers. I suggest you go see Nate Kinsley, who runs a saddle shop on Houston Street. You made a mistake approaching Grattan."

"Thanks, Judge. When I've gathered all the facts I can, may I come and see you?"

"If you wish. At my office."

Nate Kinsley was a small dark men who wore levis thrust into the tops of high-heeled boots, a checked cotton shirt, and a loose bandanna around his neck. His old flat-topped hat was slightly tilted. When he moved from the saddle he was working on, Charley noticed that he was lame. His light blue eyes had the sun-bleached look of one who has lived much in the open air. Plainly the man had spent years in his youth as a cowboy and was proud of it. The clothes of his former calling he could not bear to give up. Even indoors he was wearing the broad-brimmed hat. To himself he was singing a cowboy song.

Dry bones in the valley,
I really do believe.
Dry bones in the valley;
Oh, some of them bones are mine.

Some come a-cripple,
Some come a-lame,
Some of them bones are mine.
Some come a-walking with a hickory cane,
Some of them bones are mine.

"Judge Bannister told me to see you," Runyon said by way of greeting.

"Fine with me. No admission charge." Though Kinsley was gray around the temples, time had not tamed his jauntiness.

"He did not tell me why, but I think it was in his mind that you know something that might help my friend Rufe Rogers."

The saddler took in his battered face. "You're the kid Bob Grattan picked on last night."

Charley grinned. "That's right. What's left of me. He sure lit on me all spraddled out and whaled me proper."

"He's got this town buffaloed, but some day he'll go out in smoke sudden," Kinsley prophesied. "If it's any comfort to you, kid, he's wearing a black eye today and a badly cut cheek."

"I gave him those before he really got going, but when he got busy—gentlemen, hush! He's one wampus cat." Runyon came to the reason why he was present. "Rufe Rogers isn't any more guilty of this holdup than I am. He's just a young buckaroo in a jam, and he needs all the help he can get."

Kinsley's eyes narrowed in thought. "I reckon the Judge has in mind what I heard Downs say before he was hanged, that Rogers was tricked into holding the horses for them."

"Will you testify to that at Rogers' trial?"

"Sure I will. You may be right about him being innocent. Downs knew he would be dead in five minutes. I think he was telling the truth. He was a game guy and wanted to square what he had done to the boy before he died."

"Grattan got the idea the prosecuting attorney had sent me to him. He was sore as a boil. If there is going to be trouble about the lynching, I don't want to get you into it."

"Forget that. I just happened to be there. It was Grattan's party. Sure I'll speak my piece. I would do it even if I had been one of the lynchers. I ain't so stove up that I run away from trouble when it is laid in my lap."

Runyon believed him. He could trust Kinsley's cool steady eyes. He was a man to tie to when you needed him.

9 RUFE ROGERS HAD LIMPED TO THE corral and was watching Cape Crawford break a colt to the saddle. He was feeling low in spirits, for next morning Marshal Folsom was starting with him for Texas. What fortune awaited him there he did not know, but he did not see how it could be anything but bad.

A blithe voice hailed him, and he turned to see June crossing the yard from the house. "A letter from Charley," she called, waving it in her hand. The sight of this proud girl in gay friendly mood was always better to him than good news.

"It's going to be all right, Rufe," she said swiftly. "I'm sure of it."

He read the letter she gave him.

Dear Miss June, I take my pen in hand to let you know things are braking fine. Im having luck in diggin up evidense for that old bank robber Rufe. First off I lerned Downs and Klem come through for him before they was hung. That Downs was some man even if he was a vilin. He said Rufe didnt know they was aimin to rob the bank. A man named Kinsley will swear to that from hell to brekfast. He is an old cowboy who blew a stirup when his bronc acted up and busted his leg so he is lame. But you bet he will do to ride the river with.

Mrs. Hastings is a lady all her life like the Jesse James song says and she has figgered out a lot of things that will help. She found out who the kids playin marbels was and we had a talk with them. It is like Rufe told us.

Judge Bannister will take our old bandit's case. He is a fine lawyer. I think he will get Rufe off. There are some mean fellows here but some of the best folks are on our side. Well, that is all for now.

CHARLEY

P.S. This is some whoopee town, but no cards, no drinkin for me.

Rufe kept out of his voice the glad lift he felt. "Looks like you didn't send a boy to mill, Miss June," he said.

"Did I send him?" she asked stiffly. "Just because I thought somebody ought to go?"

"He did not have four bits. Neither did I."

Rogers could see her drawing away from him. "If I lent him money, I expect it to be paid back," she answered curtly.

Her dark long-lashed eyes dared him to misunderstand. They told him that her interest in him was wholly impersonal. Circumstances had saddled him on the Crawfords and they had to accept the burden of seeing he was treated justly. She wanted him to be sure of that.

Though Rufe did not say so, he refused any such explanation of what she had done. There was in her a vital zest for living that colored everything she did. She had saved his life when he was wounded and now she was saving it again. A warm tide of gratitude swept through him. He did not mean a great deal to her, but this fine lovely girl, clean-limbed as a young racehorse, would stand out in his memory as long as he lived. She could be hard as steel, but he remembered moments of deep tenderness in the hours of his illness.

Marshal Folsom sauntered from the stable. Since Rogers had been able to move about the place, the officer kept a close eye on him.

"We have been a great imposition on your kindness, Miss Crawford," he said. "It must be a relief that we are leaving in the morning."

"My brothers say you have been very helpful with the stock, Marshal. We are in your debt." She passed the letter to him. "Perhaps you would like to read news from Fort Worth."

Folsom glanced over the letter, then read it more carefully. He gave it back to June. "If this is true about Downs's statement, it is a surprise to me. Nate Kinsley wouldn't lie, but maybe Downs may have done so to save his young partner. Runyon has picked a good lawyer. It is still my opinion that our young friend here will need the best he can get."

"I suppose it never occurred to you to think that Rufe may be innocent," June replied tartly. "Some of us feel that a man is not counted guilty until he is proved so in court."

"You're a good friend, Miss Crawford," the marshal said.

"I try to be fair," she differed.

Turning, she walked quickly to the house.

The officer murmured to himself, "Did I say something to annoy her?"

"She wants you to understand that because she does her Christian duty by a scalawag blown here by the winds of chance, she doesn't have to be his friend," Rogers explained.

Yet that evening, because it was the prisoner's last night at the ranch, she came out to the porch where he was sitting and took a chair beside him. Fireflies lit the darkness of the velvet Arizona night.

"We'll want to know how things go with you at Fort Worth," she told him. "Tell Charley to be sure to write us."

"Charley might misspell some words, Miss June. I'll have Rufe write you." Rogers looked at the girl to see how she would take this.

"That will be nice. The boys will want to hear from you."

He was glad that on the shadowy porch it was not light enough for her to see the smoldering fire in his eyes. Since he was under arrest as a criminal, he had to be careful not to let her know what a tumult of the blood her nearness stirred in him. Even if he should be acquitted, he would be forever barred from her. The shadow of a doubt would be enough to keep alive the gulf between them.

"I have to say thanks for all you have done for me." He raised a hand to stop her protest. "I know. You would have done as much for a mangled puppy. And the puppy would have licked your hand in gratitude. But as it happened, you did it for me. You can't keep me from saying that whatever becomes of me, I'll be always grateful to you."

"All right. Be grateful if you like, but don't be humble. You're not a puppy but a man."

"There are times when a man ought to be humble." He spoke slowly, choosing words to make clear what he meant. "This is one of those times for me. My father and mother are fine people, among the best thought of in the country around Lampasas. My brothers and sisters will always be a comfort to them. But me—I had to go wild. I knew it all and couldn't be told anything. My idea was that soon I would pull up and settle down. But before that my foolishness caught up with me. I found myself trapped. Even so, I was my own man until Yont turned the screws on me. I knew he was crooked as a barrel of snakes, that if I threw in with him I was selling my saddle.[1] I should have told the old sidewinder to do his worst and have me sent back to Texas, but I weakened and knuckled under. I said good-bye to my pride and decency then." Scorn of himself etched his voice.

She was moved by the bitterness with which he condemned himself. Her hand slipped across to cover his where it lay on the arm of the chair in which he sat. "Not good-bye," she corrected. "You lost them for a little while, but you found them later and turned on him."

"When he no longer had any power over me," he scoffed.

"You would have broken with him soon anyhow. What you did for him was not so bad, and every day is a new one in which we can make another start."

Her low husky voice was almost a whisper. She was offering him friendship, and his heart jumped with a sudden gladness, yet a gladness infused with pain. The eager parted lips, the beautiful planes of her face, the rise and fall of her breasts, moved him almost to trembling. He had to remind himself that he would never be closer to her, probably never as near as now.

[1] A cowboy sold his saddle only when he had reached the lowest point of self-respect. The words were used to express contempt for a man's degradation.

He said, greatly moved, "God bless you."

Pete Crawford crossed the yard and sat down on the top step of the porch.

"Folsom tells me you start in the morning, Rufe," he said.

"Yes. In a buckboard until we reach the stage."

"About that land of ours you homesteaded?" Pete asked. "What are your plans?"

"To relinquish my claim to one of you. I understand you have used your right and Cape isn't yet twenty-one. The way things are between you and Yont, it would not be safe for Miss June to live there. Maybe one of your riders could take it up?"

"How about Charley?" June asked. "He says he is coming back here to live. We could trust him to turn it over to us."

Her brother agreed. "Yes, I think we could. But he isn't here. This should be done at once. With you away not living on the claim, Yont might fix up some crooked deal with Hagen on the ground you had forfeited your interest. Pink Ball will do. He and I will go to town with you and the marshal tomorrow, and you can stop there long enough to file the papers."

"That will be fine," Rufe assented.

"We are all pulling for you to come out all right at your hearing," Pete said. "I suppose, after you are freed, you will go back to Lampasas."

"If I am freed," the Texan said. "I shall go back to visit my people, but they probably won't kill the fatted calf for the prodigal. When my visit is over, I am coming back to Arizona to grow up with the country."

June heard this with a warm pleasure that dismayed her. A few weeks ago this lean brown man had been a stranger to her and later an annoying interloper. Now she could not conceal a deep interest in him, one she did not intend to let get out of hand. It was ridiculous to assume that her liking for him had anything to do with love. It was not in her plan of life to marry a footloose cowboy under a cloud. Her man must be not only about reproach, but one with ambition to go somewhere in the world.

Folsom strolled forward from the wagon where he had

been enjoying his after-supper pipe, eyes never straying far from his prisoner on the porch. He felt sorry for this young fellow. The marshal's opinion was that he would get a good long stretch in prison. Rogers had probably fallen in love with this young woman who had nursed him back to health. A lot of good it would do him now. Before meeting her he had mortgaged his future.

"Long trip tomorrow," he said. "I reckon we'll turn in now."

Pete Crawford explained that he and Pink Ball would ride with them as far as Rifle to arrange the relinquishment of title. The marshal agreed that would be a good idea.

The marshal and Rogers slept in the same bed, but before Folsom lay down he put a cuff on one of the young man's wrists and fastened to it a chain attached by a padlock to a bedpost.

Rufe lay awake for a long time, his mind running over again the few minutes he had had with June alone. He wondered if all girls were bundles of conflicting impulses. During the past week June had most of the time shown a complete unawareness of him, yet she was doing all she could to help him out of the difficulty he was in. There were magic and glamor in her, he felt, and the mystery of faraway thoughts from which he was excluded. If this was love he was suffering, it was powerful medicine. Strange that one woman out of ten thousand, by her words and her silences, by the delicious graces of her body, warm smiles and cool indifference, could lift a man to elation or drop him into deep despair.

10 AFTER AN EARLY BREAKFAST, FIVE of them took the road to Rifle. Pete Crawford, his sister, and Pink Ball rode horseback. The marshal and Rufe Rogers were in a buckboard. Folsom showed consideration for his prisoner. Since he did not want to humiliate him, he did not handcuff him before his friends. But he had the young man drive and sat beside him prepared to check any attempt to escape.

The excuse June had for joining the party was that she wanted to buy goods for a dress. She knew she was a fraud. The knowledge irritated and disturbed her. Her reason for coming was her concern for this scamp who was being taken back to Texas to be tried for murder. She did not want him to go out of her life. It was ridiculous, she told herself with self-contempt. What was there about him different from a hundred other cowboys she had met?

He was tall, lean, broad-shouldered. So were many of these careless youths. Why should the faint rippling of the muscles in his back move her? Or the meeting of their eyes bring an electric moment intimate and challenging? She was acting like an idiot. Her strong will was set to one decision. As soon as he was gone, she would put him out of her mind.

The noon sun was beating down on Rifle when they reached the huddle of houses that made the town. They tied at a rack fifty feet below the land office.

Two men on the sidewalk were just vanishing into the Acme Palace saloon.

"Fen Yont and Kurt Barlow," the girl said to her brother. "What are they doing here?"

Pete's narrowed eyes had hardened to a cold gun-metal

69

blue. He had a feeling that their presence spelt trouble. These two men rarely came to town at the same time. "Maybe we're going to find out," he answered, his voice tight.

The land office was closed. A hand-printed sign in the window said, *Out for Dinner.*

Pete looked at his watch. "It lacks ten minutes of twelve. Hagen is probably in the Legal Tender. Go bring him, Pink."

Ball was a tall splinter of a youth, bowlegged and wiry. Tight salmon-colored pants outlined the curves of his muscular thighs.

"Do I hogtie him if he doesn't want to come?" he inquired with a grin.

"Tell him I said to come," Pete snapped impatiently. "He's gone in office hours."

Five minutes passed before the two men appeared.

"What's eatin' you, Pete?" Hagen demanded. "Can't a guy take time out to eat his dinner?"

Pink said amiably, "Seemed to me you were drinkin' it, Mr. Hagen."

"Let your boss do the talking," the land agent told him angrily as he unlocked the door. Beneath the man's annoyance ran a current of fear. Crawford was a hard tough citizen. If he discovered what had taken place within the past thirty minutes, he would likely be fighting mad. He walked back of the counter and the tips of his fingers played a nervous tune on the top of it. "Anything I can do for you, Pete?" he asked.

"Rufe Rogers wants to relinquish the quarter he took up in favor of Pink Ball. I suppose there will be a fee."

Hagen rubbed his chin in hesitation. He was wishing that Yont and Barlow were here to take the curse of this situation from his shoulders.

"I don't seem to remember of any Rufe Rogers taking up a claim here," he said slowly.

"You haven't forgotten me," Rogers cut in. "I took the claim under the name Jim Dillard."

"If your name is Rogers, I'm afraid that entry is void," Hagen announced. "The law covers that point explicitly. Sorry."

70

"In that case the quarter is open to entry," Pete said. "Pink will take it up now."

Hagen could not quite keep the smirk from his face. "Now that's too bad, Pete. This very morning Kurt Barlow filed on it."

Angry blood poured into Crawford's face. He caught Hagen's shirt just below the throat and dragged the man halfway across the counter.

"You can't do this to me, you two-timing scoundrel," he cried. "That land has been ours for twenty years. You know that, and you put Fen Yont up to trying to steal it. I'll thrash you within an inch of your life."

The land recorder lay on the counter half-throttled trying to gasp out a protest. The fat man was as helpless as a flapping trout on dry land. Dark blood poured into his face.

June's fingers closed on her brother's wrist. "Be careful, Pete, or you'll kill him," she warned.

Crawford loosened his grip and slapped hard first one and then other of Hagen's fat cheeks. He turned, heading for the door.

"I'll settle this with Yont right now," he stormed.

June barred the way, her arms tightening on his coat sleeves. "No—no—no, Pete. Don't lose your head. Yont can't make this stick. His money paid for Rufe's filing, backing a fraudulent entry. No court will uphold him."

It was not the girl's argument that stopped Pete, but her presence on the scene. He knew her well enough to be sure that if trouble started, she would be in the thick of it. She would not hold back and let him face the Quarter Circle F Y men alone.

"Why couldn't you stay at home instead of coming here to butt into this?" he demanded. "This isn't woman's business."

The marshal backed up June. "She's right, Pete. If Yont paid for Rogers' entry, knowing it was being filed in a false name, he can't take advantage of an illegality to jump in with a second filing, certainly not until some court action has declared the land open for another homesteader."

"Maybe," Crawford conceded, black temper still riding him. He turned on Hagen, who was still gasping like a fish out of water. "Tell that scoundrel who owns you not to let that ugly shadow of his, Kurt Barlow, move on my land unless he and his plug-uglies are ready for war."

"Wouldn't it be a good idea to put on record my relinquishment to Pink in case the matter comes up for a court decision," Rogers suggested.

"Might be you are right," Pete said. "We'll do that."

Still shaken from fear and the manhandling, Hagen produced the papers and made the release official. He knew Yont would not like it, but the more immediate threat was Pete Crawford. Why in Tophet did he have to be in the middle of a feud beween these violent men? All he asked for was peace and an easy life. It did not look as though he was going to get either. If he knew the signs guns would soon be blazing. On account of his position as land registrar, he would be dragged into a private war in which he had no interest whatever.

"We had better eat dinner at Ma Manly's," June said. "She sets a good table."

She had another reason in mind. It would take them to the far end of the street. By the time they had finished, Yont and Barlow might have left Rifle. She did not want her brother to meet them while he was in his present explosive temper. It would have suited her better to start home at once, but she knew Pete would not listen to that. He would do nothing that could be interpreted as running away from the Quarter Circle F Y men.

June's eyes swept up and down the street when they came out of the restaurant. The sun was shining warmly down on a road deserted except for a flop-eared hound busily nosing its flank for fleas. Scarcely a stone's throw from them their horses and the buckboard were tied. She set a rather fast pace toward them.

"What's the hurry, Sis?" Pete drawled. "I don't see the fire."

"Marshal Folsom has a long way to go before night," she answered.

"Why don't you take the stage here?" Pete asked the officer.

"I don't want to go back by the San Simon," he replied. "We can make better connections farther south." To the prisoner he said, "You might untie that rope, Rufe. We'll be on our way."

Something cold clawed at June's stomach. Yont and Barlow were coming out of a store not twenty yards from them.

At sight of the Flying W party the two men stood stock-still. This meeting was a surprise to them. They had not known the Crawfords were in town. Hagen had thought of telling them, but had decided to keep his mouth shut.

Pete Crawford said curtly, "I'm serving notice, Barlow, that if you move on to my land, I'll kill you on sight."

The coffee-colored crook-nosed foreman showed his teeth in a snarl. "Since you're on the prod, why wait?" he jeered. "Now is a good time."

Rogers spoke fast. "There's a lady present."

"Sure," Yont's ramrod mocked. "I see her. The whole mess of you are hiding behind her skirts."

"Get into the store, June," Pete ordered harshly.

"No." The girl moved closer to her brother. "I'm staying here."

"Better go back into Yocum's," the marshal advised Yont. "I won't have any shooting over this matter."

"I like it right where I am," Barlow retorted. "This is a free country. You can't tell me where to go."

"Over what matter?" Yont inquired smoothly. "Are you talking about Kurt's homesteading a vacant quarter section?"

"I don't care what the difficulty is," Folsom said firmly. "I'm the law. There will be no guns fired now."

"That's suits me fine," Yont agreed. "I'm a peaceable citizen."

"You are a weasely murdering crook," Pete broke out. "There's not a man in the penitentiary at Yuma with such a record of villainous crimes as you have. From the time you settled here, you have been a slimy trouble-maker robbing widows and orphans and honest men trying to make a living. What became of Hans Ukena and Tom Claybolt, legal homesteaders who disappeared from their claims and were never seen again? Who owns their land now? The man who had them killed because of the greed in his heart. You've made yourself top dog, you think. I tell you that hell is gaping for you. It won't be long now."

"Get that woman out of the way," Yont cried, white with anger. "I won't take that from any man alive."

Folsom lifted his rifle from the seat of the buckboard where he had laid it and cradled the weapon in his arms.

"I'll blast the first man that fires a gun," he announced.

"All right," Yont retorted, his voice hoarse with rage. "Not now, but soon. You've started something, Crawford, you'll never live to finish."

He turned and walked back into the store. Barlow glared at Pete for a long half-minute, then wheeled and followed his employer.

"You've spoken yore piece, Crawford, and it was a mouthful," Folsom said. "Those fellows are fighting mad. Better get Miss June out of here soon as you can."

"Please, Pete," the girl urged. "Let's go."

"Suits me," her brother agreed, and helped her into the saddle.

Folsom joined Rogers on the seat of the buckboard and the small cavalcade moved down the street. At the fork of the road just outside the town, the buckboard would turn right and the riders left.

June was pushing her mount forward to get abreast of her brother when, through the half-opened swing doors of a saloon, she caught sight of a crook-nosed savage face above a lifted revolver.

"Look out, Pete!" she cried, at the same time touching her pony with the spur.

The crash of the forty-four sounded and the girl swayed, clinging to the horn of the saddle.

"My God, you're hit!" Pete cried.

He swung to the ground to support her, then lifted her from the back of the horse.

Rufe Rogers, too, had seen for an instant the cruel face of Barlow framed in the half-open swing doors. He reached across the body of the officer, dragged his revolver from its holster, and leaped out of the buckboard. He hit the earth already running, raced across the road, and tore into the saloon. His glance swept the room. Barlow was not there. Three cowboys, who had been playing poker, but no longer had any interest in the game, stared at Rogers.

74

"He shot a girl!" the Texan cried. "Where is he?"

One of the cowboys pointed to the back door. "He lit out fast." The man rose. "I'll throw in with you, fellow."

Rufe did not wait to answer. He hurried out of the back door and his eyes swept the alley to right and left. Barlow was freeing the reins of a horse tied to a post and was making a bad job of it because his roughness had frightened the animal and it was pulling back nervously on the bridle. He heard the slap of the Texan's running feet and turned to face him.

"Keep back, lunkhead, or I'll gun you sure," he ordered.

Rufe slowed to a walk to aim more accurately. There was no hurry now. His gaze fastened on the foreman and did not waver.

"You can't stop me," Barlow snarled. "Try it and I'll rub you out certain."

Rogers moved toward the other, wary as a cat on the prowl. The arm holding the forty-five still hung by his side. He had one advantage. The sun was in the eyes of the killer.

The small wind of a bullet whistled past Rufe's shoulder. The Texan's arm came up and threw the revolver to the level like the snap of a whip. He felt the jerk of the weapon as it roared. Barlow staggered and planted his feet wide to keep from falling. The spread fingers of his left hand clutched at his stomach. That he was hurt badly was plain. His next bullet plowed into the ground ten feet in front of him. But his stubborn will kept him fighting. Another slug tore past Rogers.

Rufe fired again, and knew the lead had slammed into the man's side. Barlow tottered and went down, sagging at the knees, the weapon falling from his grasp. The man's body lay still, all the life stricken from it.

The young man stared down at the slack frame which only a minute before had been so full of vital anger and hatred. He had never killed a man before and he felt a sickness run through him. To steady himself he leaned against an adobe wall.

"You sure fixed his clock sudden," a voice said.

For the first time Rogers became aware that the three cowboys who had been playing cards were there. He could see others heading down the alley toward them. One of them was Folsom.

"I had to do it," Rufe heard himself say. "He wouldn't have it any other way."

"Right. He fired first." Another of the cowboys was speaking. "I'll say you were thorough, fellow. He's done sacked his saddle for keeps. We didn't have a chance to get into it."

"You did this?" Folsom asked, speaking to Rogers.

"Sure he did, Marshal," one of the range riders answered. "Saved you the trouble."

Folsom did not disapprove of Barlow's swift punishment, but as the official in charge of the prisoner who had done it, he was annoyed at his own negligence in letting Rogers snatch a weapon from him. He was a man proud of his record as a marshal and this would certainly be a blemish on it.

"You'll wear cuffs from now on, young fellow," he said harshly. "I've been too easy on you."

Rufe cared nothing about that. His mind was filled with anxiety about June. "Is Miss Crawford badly hurt?" he asked.

"I don't know. She was hit in the arm." The marshal turned to a bystander. "Get Sheriff Crane and bring him to Doctor Burgess' office. I want it made official that Rogers is not to blame for this killing. Barlow asked for it if ever a man did."

Yont had come out of the back of a building to the alley. "Once a killer always a killer," he said savagely. "Too bad I didn't finish this bandit when I shot him while he was trying to escape."

Folsom faced the ranchman sternly. "You are trying to talk yourself out of this, Yont. When your ramrod shot the young lady, you were with him."

"Barlow was a hotheaded fool," Yont retorted. "I had nothing to do with that and I won't have anybody saying I had. But he didn't mean to hit the girl, but her brother. Crawford had deviled Kurt till he was crazy mad. It is his fault his sister was hurt." He added defiantly: "What business is it of yours? You've got no authority outside of

76

Texas. Your job is to take this murdering bandit back to Fort Worth and see he is hanged."

"To see he gets a fair trial," the marshal corrected.

Sheriff Crane listened to the evidence and made an immediate decision. He was generally considered a Yont man, since he had been nominated through the influence of the Quarter Circle F Y owner, but at core he was an honest citizen.

"I don't know anything about the Texas record of Rogers, but he did a good job when he snuffed out Barlow," he said. "Kurt has killed three men to my knowledge. He's better dead."

Pete Crawford came out of the doctor's office and reported that his sister had suffered only a flesh wound and not a very serious one. She was going to stay for a few days at the hotel in Rifle, since Doctor Burgess thought she had better not travel immediately.

"That's good news," Folsom said. "We'll take off now."

"My sister would like to see Rufe for a minute," Crawford suggested.

The marshal and his prisoner walked into the office of the doctor. Rogers was wearing handcuffs.

June flinched a little at sight of them. "I hope you haven't got into any trouble for what you did," she told Rogers anxiously.

The girl was paler than usual, but Rufe thought he had never seen her more lovely.

"No trouble," he assured her. "Nobody has any complaint but Yont and what he thinks doesn't matter. . . . I'm worried about you."

"You needn't be. I'll be good as new in a day or two." She was thinking that what he had done had been on her account, but she did not want to talk of that before so many people. "I'm wishing you the best luck in the world, Rufe. I know you'll be acquitted."

No more words were spoken, but the young man read a message in her glowing eyes. He carried away with him a hope that sometimes burned brightly, but as the weeks passed thinned down to a faint flicker that might be illusory as the light of a firefly.

11 THE JAILER UNLOCKED RUFE'S CELL and said, "Someone to see you, Rogers."

The man who walked into the cell was James Rogers, the father of the prisoner. He was tall, thickset, and bearded, in age close to fifty. The upper lip was shaved and showed a straight close-lipped mouth. He was in store clothes, but the mark of the cattleman was written all over him. His direct gray-blue eyes did not shift from those of his son.

"Are you guilty of this crime, Rufe?" he asked bluntly.

"No," Rufe answered. "But I am guilty of having been a wild and profligate fool."

He told the whole story of his adventures, sparing himself not at all. The unexpected sight of his father had moved him greatly.

"It might be worse, a great deal worse," his father said thankfully. "You have done wrong and have suffered, but I can tell your mother that you are not a villain even if you are not cleared in court." He laid an arm across the shoulder of his son. "I did not hear of yore trouble until last Tuesday and I came at once. How far has the trial gone?"

"It began day before yesterday. The prosecution has proved that I was running around with Downs and Klem, that I stayed with the horses while they were robbing the bank, and that I lit out of town fast. Charley Runyon came back from Arizona to dig up evidence for me and he has done right well. Judge Bannister starts putting our witnesses on the stand today."

When Rufe was brought into the courtroom, James Rogers sensed that the sentiment of the public was strongly against his son. There was a ripple of angry resentment at his appearance.

Bannister did not at once disclose the strength of the defense. He proved that the dead outlaws reached Fort Worth three days before Rogers and that his mount was kept at a different corral from the one they used. By Mrs. Hastings he showed that she had introduced him to the two dead outlaws and that she was convinced they had never met before. In cross-examination the prosecution discounted all of this as camouflage to avoid suspicion. But the landlady was a good witness. She was liked and respected in the town. Bannister's questions brought out that she had several times seen Downs and Klem engaged in whispering talk which they broke off when the defendant approached them.

Bannister called Johnny Gaylord to the stand. The ten-year-old youngster was plainly frightened, but the lawyer's gentle friendliness allayed his fear. He explained to the boy the nature of an oath and that all he had to do was to tell what he had seen while he had been playing marbles across the street from the bank.

Three men had stopped close to them, Johnny said, and two of them had gone into the bank. The third had stayed with the horses. He was the man sitting at the table. He watched them play and pretty soon he grounded the bridle reins and came over to them. Jack Cousins was not doing very well, and the man borrowed Jack's agate and showed him how to hold it. He had Jack watch him while he made two or three shots. Then there was a crash from inside the bank and the two men came out and ran across the street to the horses. One of them was holding a sack. This man—Johnny pointed to Rufe Rogers—jumped up and said, "What's the matter?" The fellow with the sack told him there was hell to pay, that they had just killed a man while holding up the bank and for him to beat it fast. The two galloped down the street. The one who had been taking care of the horses stood there a little while like he didn't know what to do, then he got on his horse and rode the other way from the two.

Jack Cousins took the witness stand after his companion and corroborated everything he had said. The attorney for the state tried to show that the boys had been coached to tell this fantastic tale, but he knew the jury was impressed by it.

Nate Kinsley's testimony carried even more weight. To the jury it was news that the lynched men had exonerated Rogers before they were hanged. Only a few in Fort Worth had heard this even as a rumor.

Erastus Andrews, the prosecuting attorney, pounced on Kinsley's admission that he had been present at the hanging and suggested that if he was near enough to hear what the bandits said he must have been implicated in the lynching and was probably a leader. The witness denied this. Questions to him brought out the fact that Bob Grattan seemed to be the prime mover in the hanging. Grattan created a sensation by shouting from the back of the room, "I'll get you for that, you damned liar!" The judge ordered him ejected.

Bannister brought back a state's witness, Marshal Folsom, to inquire about a point Andrews had brought out without developing the circumstances. At the time Bannister had let it go, preferring to use it later. Folsom had mentioned that he had seen the prisoner kill a man in Arizona.

"Will you tell us the story of the killing of this man in Rifle by my client?" Bannister asked.

Folsom gave a clear unemotional account of Kurt Barlow's death. When Andrews listened to it, he knew his case was lost. To the jury and to those present in the courtroom, Rufe Rogers had become a hero instead of a villain. The evidence of the small boys and of Kinsley had weakened greatly the state's case. But this last romantic touch was a clincher. Rogers had snatched the revolver from the marshal's holster, not to escape, but to avenge the shooting of a young lady. He had risked death to destroy the attempted assassin. This had nothing to do with the case on trial, but it carried to a Texas jury a tremendous sentimental wallop. A boy who could do that must be guiltless of the crime with which he was charged.

Judge Bannister realized the case was won. He spoke very briefly. Young Rogers had met these bandits and trailed with them for two or three days. They had used him without his realizing it. He asked the jury if they thought it was reasonable that a young outlaw waiting for his accomplices to come out of the bank, knowing they must be ready to gallop out of town instantly, would leave the horses to sit down and play marbles with some youngsters. Was it likely that a hardened ruffian would separate from his partners without getting his share of the proceeds of the robbery? Did they think that a man about to be hanged would lie to save a confederate who had escaped? Was it not more probable that having brought a boy into dire trouble, with the knowledge that he was going to face his maker, his conscience had driven him to exonerate their dupe? Every damaging fact pointed out by the prosecuting attorney had been explained away. It was true that, after hard months on the trail, the boy on trial had thrown in with his fellow lodgers to take a fling at the gaming houses. That was a custom of young cowboys who relaxed from the rigors of the long drives "to see the elephant," as they expressed it. But Mrs. Hastings, whose testimony none of them could ignore, had shown that the two bandits were concealing some plan from their new associate. Rogers had left town, not because of guilt, but to save his life from an aroused public sentiment outraged at this unnecessary murder of the teller. He concluded by saying that Rufe Rogers did not ask mercy but justice.

The jury filed out of the room and returned after one ballot had been taken. When the clerk of the court read the words, "Not guilty," there was a roar of approval which the trial judge did not attempt to repress.

Charley Runyon leaped over the back of two benches to be the first to congratulate Rufe.

"You son of a gun, I knew you'd make it!" he yelled, pounding his friend on the back.

"Without your help I would have been convicted," Rufe told him. "Fellow, when I'm eighty I'll still be thanking you."

The Rogerses joined Runyon to put up for the night at Mrs. Hastings lodging house. She insisted on making dinner for all of them. Next morning Rufe and his father were leaving for Lampasas, where the acquitted man was going to spend a few days with his family before returning to

Arizona. Rufe was very grateful to all the friendly people who had helped him to establish his innocence. He had passed through the valley of the shadow and had come out a better man than he had been. The wild foolish days of his riotous youth were gone forever. He had turned his back on shame and had come to adult manhood.

Mrs. Hastings' guests were just finishing dinner when a man knocked on the door to bring news of more trouble. He was Jim Poor, owner of the Frontier Corral, one of the defense witnesses at the trial.

"I'm right glad you got outa that tight you were in, boy," he told Rufe. "This here pal of yores"—he laid a hand on Runyon's shoulder—"sure cut the mustard for you."

"I'm aimin' to be a Pinkerton man," Charley grinned, embarrassed at the praise he had been getting.

"Fact is, I didn't come here to gab," Poor explained. "I dunno as there's a thing any of you can do about it, but dog nab it some of us had ought to go to bat for Nate."

"Nate Kinsley?" Runyon asked. "Are you figurin' Bob Grattan will make trouble for him?"

"Certain as you're a foot high. Right now that killer is in the Horse Shoe tankin' up and servin' notice that he aims to kill Nate on sight."

"Don't you think that is just talk?" James Rogers said. "It doesn't make sense that he would shoot Kinsley for a little thing like naming him as the leader of the lynchers when Andrews had him cornered and forced him to say it."

"No, sir. You don't know Grattan. He has killed two men in this town for no more than that. Each time he got himself liquored up before he did it. Grattan is a black-hearted devil sure enough."

"Perhaps we can get Kinsley to leave town till the fellow has cooled off," James Rogers suggested.

"You don't know that little rooster," Runyon cut in. "His legs ain't ever been taught to run away. He'll go out in smoke first."

"Let's go down and talk with him," Rufe proposed. "If he won't go, we can stay and protect him."

"Seeing as I've drug myself into this, I'll rock along with you-all," Poor grumbled. "But don't fool yoreselves. Grattan is plenty game even though he is a bully. Somebody is goin' to be rubbed out before mornin' and it might be any one of us."

"I don't like that," James Rogers said. He thought intently for a moment and came up with a plan. "You three go down to Kinsley's place. Keep him indoors. If Grattan shows up and starts firing, defend yourselves. Don't hesitate to shoot him down from cover. I'm going to see Judge Bannister and ask him to organize hurriedly a citizens' committee that will order Grattan to leave town at once or take the consequences."

"What consequences?" Poor wanted to know.

"If he doesn't go, to be shot down like a wolf. He'll go."

"Hmp! I dunno." Poor shook his head. "But it might work if you get fellows who mean business. If it's just a bluff, it will be no go. Grattan will know."

Nate Kinsley opened the door of his one-room house when he knew who his visitors were. He had a revolver in his hand. At Poor's offer to side him while he got out of town, the lame man scoffed. He had already been warned that Grattan was drinking heavily and sputtering threats, but this had not moved him to flight.

The homely little wrinkled man faced them, his hat tiptilted jauntily, and wanted to know why the hell he should run away from Bob Grattan. "Back of a Colt's I'm as big as he is," he told them, eyes cold and hard.

"They say he's a dead shot," Poor warned. "Why take a risk you don't have to?"

"I do have to. He has made his brags. If I pulled out, I would feel like a whipped cur all my life. Maybe he'll get me and maybe not. Some day that bullypuss gunman will be knocked off. I might be the guy to do it."

"There may not be any trouble with Grattan," Rufe explained. He told Kinsley of his father's plan. "If there is time enough, it may work. Anyhow we are going to stay right here with you till this is settled one way or another."

The saddler protested he did not need any help. Grattan was only one man even if he had a big reputation as a gunman. But when they refused to leave him, he was glad. It was a lonely business to sit by himself waiting for a man to come and kill him. But if it came to a fight, he insisted, it was his job and they were to stay out of it.

83

Runyon winked at Rogers. They could let it ride that way unless guns began to bark in which case they both knew they would be in it.

James Rogers found Bannister at his home. He was in his slippers stretched out on a sofa reading Lytton's *The Last of the Barons*, but at the news the Lampasas man brought, he came to swift attention. He liked Nate Kinsley and promptly translated his liking into action.

"Grattan is a menace and we'll put an end to his bullying tonight," he said. "We'll have to hurry."

On their way to the business section of the town, they stopped at three houses, at each of which they gained a recruit for their posse. Two of them were prominent merchants and the third a retired cattleman. They separated, to comb the streets and houses of entertainment for other influential men who would be ready to serve with them. Half an hour later the group was complete. It included another cattleman, the foreman of a trail herd outfit, a stage driver, an ex-sheriff, a faro dealer employed at the White Elephant, and an itinerant preacher graduated from the cowboy ranks. All of them were armed.

The stage driver, Will Custis, sauntered into the Horse Shoe. Grattan was at the bar with a couple of cronies still drinking, still making threats, evidently working himself into a killing frame of mind.

Custis lined up beside him and murmured in his ear. "Pack Gibson is outside and wants to see you. He has some dope about that little cuss Kinsley. I dunno what it is, but he says it is important."

"Tell him to come in and spill it," Grattan ordered.

"He won't come. You know Pack. Scared he'll get in bad with Kinsley's friends."

"Get him to tell you what's eatin' him."

"Says he won't talk to anybody but you."

"Damn a man with no guts, I say." Grattan poured down his throat the whisky in the glass before him and strode out of the room to the sidewalk.

An irruption of arms laid hold of him. A hand snatched the revolver from the holster at his side. In spite of his struggle to free himself, he was borne to the ground and handcuffed, after which he was dragged to his feet cursing furiously. He strained violently, thrashing to and fro in an attempt to escape, but the mass weight of his captors propelled him to a store, the door of the place already unlocked by its proprietor.

A stream of threats poured from his throat.

Already a crowd was gathering outside, but Custis closed and barred the door.

Judge Bannister said, "It looks as if we'll have to gag this fellow to make him listen."

The foreman of the trail herd took the bandanna from his neck. "This will shut him up," he said.

"All right," Grattan growled. "What in thunder do you think you're doing?"

Bannister did the talking for the group. "This is a law and order posse, Grattan. Fort Worth has had all of you it will stand. You have shot two of our citizens within a year and are threatening to murder another. You hanged two men lately. It's your turn now. You have come to the looped end of your rope."

The drunken rage of the bully died away. He stared at the lawyer defiantly. "I don't scare worth a cent, Bannister. You're throwin' a big bluff and I know it."

The lawyer's eyes, deadly serious, bored into those of the ruffian.

"No, we have talked this over and we mean business," he said gravely. "We hate to do it, but we are going through with it. You are too dangerous to be allowed to live. We value Nate Kinsley's life more than we do yours."

Bannister's manner, the low certainty of his voice, daunted the badman. They were going to kill him. A cold knot tied his stomach and fear sapped the arrogance out of him.

"It was whisky talking," he pleaded. "I didn't really aim to hurt Nate."

"No, we can't trust you. It was whisky talking the other times, but you drank it to bolster your lust for killing."

"I'd leave here—never come back. And I'll quit drinkin'. Don't do this to me. I'm not ready to die."

They did not make it easy for him. They let him sweat in terror while they discussed it back and forth. In the end he signed a paper agreeing to leave Texas and never return. Next morning he was put on the train with a ticket as far as El Paso in his hand. It was known he could not stop in that town. He had outlived his welcome there before he had come to Fort Worth. His journey's end would probably land him in either New Mexico or Arizona.

12 BOB GRATTAN, RECENTLY OF FORT Worth, Texas, but now temporarily of Rifle, Arizona Territory, leaned against the adobe wall of Si Mabry's drygoods store and watched sullenly the slack midday life of the town drift up and down Main Street. A woman carrying a basket went into a grocery store. The rackety wagon of a lank nester, his poke-bonneted wife seated beside him, lurched along the road stirring a cloud of dust. Two riders moved past him at a road gait and disappeared into the land office. Grattan's interest centered on the horsemen. He guessed that the older of the two, the one wearing the stained and ragged clothes, was Fen Yont, whom he hoped to talk into giving him a job.

Grattan's hurried departure from Fort Worth had come unfortunately at a time when his finances were at low ebb. He had not even money enough to take a hand in the cheap poker game at the Legal Tender. In fact he was stony broke. He had a poor opinion of Rifle. It was not his kind of town. Men of his stripe flourished where money was easy and there was a constant flock of pigeons to be plucked. It was his intention to light out as soon as he could get together a grubstake on which to travel.

This was cattle country and the only job offered him was to chouse longhorns through the brush at twenty dollars a month. Since he had often made five times that in a single night, he refused the work sourly. The land office man Hagen had this morning given him a lead that might take care of him temporarily. Before Grattan had been in town two hours, he had learned of a smoldering feud between ranches that had recently reached the stage of violence. The foreman of the Quarter Circle F Y had been killed and the owner of the spread had the reputation of being a tough vindictive character. Yont was expected in town today and Hagen had promised to put the Texan in touch with the ranchman. Very likely he was one of the men who had just gone into the land office.

Grattan watched the government office while he chewed tobacco, but made no move toward it. He wanted the advance to come from Yont. Presently a small Mexican boy brought a message to him from Hagen. Mr. Yont would like to talk with him. Before he sauntered down the street, Grattan rolled and smoked three cigarettes. No use letting the owner of the ranch know that he was on his uppers and wanted a job. Better play it that he was hard to get.

The fat man said, "Mr. Grattan, meet Mr. Yont."

Neither of the men offered to shake hands. They eyed each other with the wariness of two bulldogs meeting for the first time.

"Looking for a job, I hear," Yont said.

"Why, no." Grattan's manner was indifferent. "I'm driftin' through to Tombstone. This town is dead. The men have no git up and the women no jingle." He spat contemptuously a splatter of tobacco juice to the floor.

"My mistake," Yont answered curtly. "Hagen told me you were looking for work."

"What kind of work?" the Texan asked.

"My business is raising cows."

"I graduated from being a cowhand quite some time ago, in fact soon after I started. A puncher swallows too much dust and puts in too many hours and gets nothing for it."

Hagen understood that both of these men were sparring for an opening. They would not come to terms before a third party. He suggested they discuss this over a bottle of beer.

87

"Nothing to discuss, is there?" Yont replied. To the cowboy who had come to town with him, he said, "Red, step down to Fidler's and see if he has got that wagon bolt ready."

"You bet," Red said, and left.

As Yont followed him, he looked at Grattan and gave a slight tilt of his head toward the door. Before he had taken a dozen steps down the sidewalk, Grattan joined him.

"If you can't tail stock what can you do?" Yont inquired.

"I can stomp out rattlesnakes."

The eyes of the men met.

"Any references?" Yont asked gently.

"Quite a few. But my references can't talk. Two are in the cemetery at Fort Worth, one in Boot Hill at Dodge, another laid away nice in an arroyo near Bandera."

"I don't doubt it, but I would like a little confirmation —say from somebody alive, Mr. Grattan."

The Texan took from his pocket a bill-fold and from it drew two newspaper clippings. Each was an account of a street duel in which Grattan had killed his opponent.

"Recommendations of efficiency," Yont admitted dryly.

"When I drop a guy he stays down," the killer replied callously.

"I have a later report on you—in the Fort Worth paper," Yont mentioned maliciously. "It seems you left there kinda sudden, by request. Well, Texas' loss is Arizona's gain, if you look at it that way."

"Don't rub it in," Grattan warned. "Ain't a man alive who wouldn't have pulled out with a dozen guns trained on him."

"Sensible of you," the ranchman agreed. His gaze scrutinized the man who claimed to be a rattlesnake stomper. Maybe he was one of these hotheaded killers with no sense, the kind that went off their rockers and started smoking. "You'd better get this right, Mr. Grattan. When I buy a gunman, he is mine. You can't grind your own corn in my mill. My foreman was killed two weeks ago because he didn't keep that in mind."

Grattan's narrowed gaze rested on the other. "I'm a gun for hire," he corrected. "If the price is right, I'll carry

88

through, but any day I want to quit, I call for my check and walk out."

"Let's understand each other." The bulbous eyes of the cattleman were hard and steady. "While you work for me, I give the orders. After you have done a job and been paid for it, I don't care how soon you go."

"I'm high-priced but thorough."

"We'll talk about the price when and if the time comes. But what you do has to be done slick. It must not backfire on me or on you since you are my man. As a cover-up you'll have to do some riding with the boys, but I'll make it easy on you as I can."

"Fair enough. I think we understand each other, Yont."

The ranchman would not drop the subject without justifying himself. "I'm a peaceable man, but I can be pushed around just so far. This outfit has been crowding me for years. It kept at the ranch a young ruffian who tried to murder me. Finally it killed my foreman. There isn't anything left for me to do but fight or quit like a yellow dog."

Grattan did not take the trouble to hide his sarcasm. "I know what a fine reputation you have, Mr. Yont," he said.

Each of these scoundrels despised the other. Though a common interest bound them in villainy, neither trusted his confederate. Both were warily determined that if one come to trouble, it would not be he.

The manner of Kurt Barlow's death had complicated the situation for Yont. The best citizens were getting tired of the lawlessness that had been prevalent in this section of the territory. That Barlow had shot a young woman and might have killed her had stirred up a lot of resentment which had focused on the owner of the Quarter Circle F Y. Yont felt that he had not been to blame in the least. Barlow's rage had boiled over because Pete Crawford had poured on him scathing words backed by a threat to kill on sight if he moved onto the disputed land. Yont had not even been in the building when the shot was fired.

But since that hour he had made no offensive move. It had been wiser to wait for a few weeks before renewing the attack. He hoped that this time he had got a man who would not blunder. Among his own men were some—two at least he was pretty sure of—who could be hired to do a job of ambushing. But they were amateurs who might leave behind them betraying clues. Grattan was an old hand at the business who ought to know how to protect himself against being caught. There was no loyalty in the fellow, but a hired gun was tied to his employer by the crime in which they had both become implicated. The gunman could not rat on his confederate without putting a rope around his own neck. Yont had that in mind.

"You had better rent a horse at the wagon yard and ride out to the ranch with us," Yont said.

"I'm yore hired man," Grattan replied. "When I ride you supply the mount." Already he felt edgy toward his employer.

While they were passing the stage station, a Concord swung around a bend into the main street raising a cloud of dust as it moved. Cad Wallop, in the driver's seat, dragged the galloping horses to a halt.

"All out!" he yelled.

A young man dropped lightly to the ground from the seat beside him. Hagen had waddled down from his office to see the stage arrive.

"Look who's here!" he murmured in the ear of Yont.

The ranchman did not need to have his attention jogged. His bulbous eyes stared angrily at Rufe Rogers.

"It's the bank robber," Grattan snarled. "Bannister got him off. A slick lawyer can make black white."

"After double-crossing me and killing Barlow, nobody but a fool would have come back," Yont said.

Rufe faced them, his manner coolly scornful. "A welcome committee of my friends," he said. His eyes did not reflect the thought that ran swiftly in him. He had made a mistake. The revolver he should have been wearing was lying in the carpetbag Cad Wallop had just dropped at his feet. It might as well have been in Fort Worth.

Words dripped from Yont's thin cruel lips. "A bandit and a killer. He has come back to murder me—if I let him."

Rufe had a minute's grace. A young woman had stepped from the stage. She was a stranger, a cousin of Ma Manly who ran the best restaurant in Rifle, and quite unconscious of how close she was to stark tragedy, she was lingering to make arrangement for her trunk and valise to be delivered at the eating house. The mind of Rogers focused sharply on his peril. Hagen did not count, but it was clear that Grattan had tied up with Yont. Since the man would feel Rufe was responsible for the crisis which had resulted in his flight from Fort Worth, he was no doubt already unfriendly to him. Rufe could not quite believe that his enemies would be unwise enough to shoot him down before a dozen witnesses. They could find a better time than this. Yet as protective insurance he answered the ranchman's charge and added a bit of information.

"If you live till I kill you, Yont, you will cumber the earth for a good many years," he said, his voice cool and almost indifferent. "I'm just an unarmed tenderfoot." He patted his body to show no weapon was concealed.

The men's voices had been low and the young woman was busy with her own affairs. Rogers' words had been the first she had caught. Her startled eyes whipped to his face, then shuttled to first one and then the other of his enemies. A squat man, fat as a tub of lard, was disappearing rapidly into the office of the stage company. If there was going to be any shooting, Hagen did not intend to be among those present.

The color faded from the girl's lips. She forgot about her trunk and valise in her hurry to get into the building.

"Killers don't go around without toting cutters,"[1] Grattan jeered. "If you've got any guts and feel lucky, fellow, why don't you draw?"

The attention of Rogers was wholly directed to these two men and the situation they had created. He was not aware of anything else. But later he was to remember details he must have subconsciously noted. The swift silent movement of men getting out of the line of fire. A rider jogging down the street toward them. A barefoot boy on the other side of the road whistling as he passed, "My bonnie lies over the ocean." The flitting of Hagen and the girl. The drifting apart of his foes to take him at advantage if and when guns smoked.

[1] A forty-four or a forty-five was often called a cutter in the Southwest.

91

Rogers spoke to the stage driver, who had shifted to a position back of the left lead horse, but the young Texan's gaze held fast to his foes. "If I am murdered, Wallop, make sure neither of these scoundrels slips a pistol into my hand afterward. It will be up to you and the other boys present to see they don't live till night. I'm not armed. Keep that in mind."

His voice was level and even, no jumpiness in it. He might have been giving directions about the saddling of a horse.

"He's a liar for sure," Grattan retorted venomously. "Didn't he kill a man right in this town not a month ago?"

"So he did and we thank him for it," the stage driver answered. "Mr. Yont, if this young fellow isn't packing a gun, I advise you to leave him alone."

"When I need your advice, Cad, I'll ask for it," Yont snapped.

"It's good advice, Mr. Yont," a drawling voice warned. "Better take it."

The speaker was the horseman who had been riding down the street. He had been carrying a Winchester rifle across the saddle in front of him and now it was in both hands pointed carelessly in the direction of the Quarter Circle F Y owner, but not aimed at him. He was grinning happily.

A warm wave swept away the cold fear that had settled on Rogers. The man with the rifle was Charley Runyon.

"Hell's bells, it's the squirt I beat up at Fort Worth!" Grattan cried. "Get down off that horse and I'll tear you apart."

"Invitation declined," Runyon told him cheerfully. "I'm right comfortable here."

"For two bits I would drag you out of the saddle," the badman boasted.

Runyon produced a quarter and tossed it into the dust in front of Grattan.

"But don't forget, Mr. Grattan, that I've growed since you whopped me," he suggested. "Back of a gun I'm big as the ringtailed snorter who was kicked out of Fort Worth a couple of weeks ago."

Grattan flung his hat to the ground angrily. "I don't

have to take that from a whipper-snapper like you," he roared. "Next time I see you I'll—I'll——"

"Now don't get excited," Runyon pleaded. "You're liable to bust a hame. But you have the right idea certain. *Next time* you meet me whale me proper, but seeing I am kinda Johnny-in-the-saddle now, what say we adjourn this present meeting *sine die*, which I reckon is a Dutch or a frog word meanin' till you get the drop on me."

Yont had seen red for a brief three minutes after Rogers came down from the stage, but the sly caution that dominated his thinking had already brushed aside the urge for immediate action. He could set the scene for his revenge more safely in his own way and time.

"If I were you I would mind my own business and keep out of trouble," he told Runyon sourly, then turned away and clumped along the sidewalk back to the land office.

Grattan glared at Runyon and at Rogers. "Kids still wet back of the ears," he sneered, and wheeled to follow the ranchman.

Runyon swung from the saddle and shook hands with Rufe. "You're the doggondest son-of-a-sea-cook for gettin' into trouble I ever did meet," he said with a grin. "Me, if I was a guy with a chip on my shoulder like you, I'd have me a forty-four handy just for company in case."

"I was mighty glad to see that red head of yours again," Rogers said. "But don't get me wrong, Charley. There's no chip on my shoulder. All I want is peace for the rest of my life."

"Hmp! You've sure come to a funny place to find it, fellow, though I'll say that until you showed up everything has been quiet along the Potomac. But the pot is simmerin' and will boil over sudden one of these days. When Fen Yont and Bob Grattan start pallin' y'betcha it ain't peace smoke they are powwowing about. Maybe you've turned gentle as Mary's little lamb, but that won't buy you a thing. Far as they are concerned you are right in the middle of this rookus."

"And where are you sitting in it?" Rufe inquired.

"I'm just a two-bit cowpoke. Neither of these gents is gonna lie awake worryin' about me. Grattan gave me the whalin' of my life. He'll figure that ought to hold me. But

93

you fouled up Yont's plans and yore father headed the crowd that made Grattan skedaddle from Fort Worth. They'll both be layin' for you."

"Don't fool yourself, my fine-feathered young friend. All you did was to slam Yont on the head and keep him from bumping me off and then to dig up evidence for me that ended in Grattan's having to say good-bye to Texas."

"Have it yore way." Runyon dismissed the subject. "I drapped into town as a rep[1] of the Crawfords to tell you they are expectin' you at the Flying W. Miss June said for me to say to you, 'Bien venidos, amigo,' which means for you to burn the wind out there muy pronto."

"Much obliged, Professor, for the explanation. Is it a Dutch or a frog expression? You sure stack up fine with the foreign lingo."

Runyon gave him a sidelong grin. "I seen that sine die in a newspaper and figured it would come in handy some time. What the hell does it mean?"

"It is Latin, Professor, and it means at no particular time. You'll be lucky if you are a bad prophet and the next meeting doesn't mean when they get the drop on you."

"You never can tell," Runyon replied light-heartedly. "Let's go feed our faces at Ma Manly's."

"Sounds reasonable," Rufus agreed. "You're going to get a pleasant surprise. A young lady came in with me on the stage. She is Ma Manly's cousin. Pretty as a new painted wagon. Her name is Polly Simmons. She will be nineteen coming fall. When she smiles there is a cute dimple on the left side of her mouth."

"Hmp! She has been smiling at you, has she?"

"At odd moments while we ate breakfast. I was fending off the other lads till she met you."

"Like heck you were. Tell that to Miss June when you see her."

"How is Miss June? Has she entirely recovered from the wound in her arm?"

"There's a small scar still showing." Runyon slanted a

[1]Rep: an abbreviation for representative, the word used for the cowboy sent to the roundup to look after the interests of the ranch owner when he could not personally be present.

derisive glance at his companion. "Doc says it won't go away till Mr. Right comes and heals it with a kiss."

He made ready to duck, but Rogers gave no evidence of a hit. "Maybe Mr. Right may happen along one of these days. It will be some time before Miss June is an old maid," he said placidly.

But his smugness was only on the surface. He knew very well that he had not won the heart of June Crawford. It was more than possible that he never would. She had been forced into a position where she had to be kind to him. His weakness and his dependence on her had made an appeal to the girl and the danger hanging over him had lent a romantic touch to their relationship. But all the factors that had drawn them close were now eliminated. He was of the opinion that he must assume nothing, take for granted no peculiar interest in him, but must start from scratch as a stranger to win her regard. And like Charley he was only a penniless waddy.

Polly Simmons was not in the restaurant when the young men entered, but before they had finished eating she joined her aunt there. She was a blonde, slim but rounded, with dark shy eyes that did not miss much. Her smile at sight of Rogers brought out the dimple he had forecast.

"I guess I ran into the stage station when there wasn't any need," she said after her older cousin had introduced her to him and Runyon. "I reckon you were just foolin'."

Charley thought he had better step in and get his share of future smiles and dimples. Her big eyes were blue as a summer sky seen through the tops of pine trees, he thought, and her cheeks rich with color that came and went with changing moods.

"That's right, Miss," he agreed. "Rufe here ain't hardly growed up. He likes to play like he's a Bill Hickok. Don't mean a thing. All of us make allowance for him."

"He had me frightened for a minute," Polly said.

"What happened?" Mrs. Manly asked.

"Not a thing," Rogers replied. "A couple of fellows were there to welcome me when the stage arrived."

"Who?" she asked bluntly. Her cousin had already reported the incident to her. Molly Manly was a business woman who knew her West.

"Why, Fen Yont and a friend of his," Rogers told her lightly.

"What brought you back here?" the woman demanded. "Didn't you have trouble enough when you were here before?"

Runyon chuckled. "Ask him *who* brought him back, Ma."

"I like this country, ma'am," Rufus said. "I intend to be a permanent resident. Maybe I'll take up a piece of land somewhere and run a few cattle."

Mrs. Manly said no more. She knew trouble was brewing and she thought this young fellow would get into it. Rumors had reached her that he was interested in June Crawford. Several other cowboys in the neighborhood had been but had got nowhere. Her wise eyes regarded this Texan, his slender lean-loined figure, the direct steel-barred eyes, with a touch of gay recklessness in them. There was strength in the set of his shoulders. He looked to be hard and tough and enduring. A girl could not read him at a glance and dismiss him. It was possible that he might disturb June's emotions even if her cool prudence might prevent her from sharing his fortunes.

"It is good for a young man to crowd his luck in some directions, but not in others," she suggested.

Rufe gave her a tilted grin. He was not sure he understood her cryptic remark. She might have in mind both June Crawford and the vengeance of Yont.

"Yes, ma'am," he said meekly. "I sure aim to walk soft and slow."

Polly Simmons turned to Runyon for an explanation. "I don't know what you are all talking about. Can you tell me? Or is it a secret?"

Runyon was eagerly cooperative. "I'd sure like to tell you, Miss Polly. It's quite a long story. Yore cousin and Rufe wouldn't be interested. They have heard it before. How about us strolling down to the creek where it is cool under the cottonwoods? I'll bring you down to date about how this scalawag here robbed a bank and otherwise misdemeaned."

Polly let her soft eyes rest on him a moment. "So kind

96

of you, Mr.—Mr. Rumford." She paused a moment to let him correct her if the name was wrong.

"Runyon," he said. "Better just call me Charley. All my friends do."

The dimple showed again. "I don't think I rate that privilege yet, Mr. Runyon, after only three minutes. And I wouldn't think of troubling you to waste your time on me. But it is very, very kind of you, I'm sure."

Charley grinned ruefully. "I expect Mrs. Manly would say I was crowdin' my luck in the wrong direction. Well, you can't shoot a guy for trying. Later we're goin' to be right well acquainted, Miss Polly. We can take the walk then."

"How nice," Polly answered. "When I get downhearted I'll have that to look forward to and it will cheer me."

"I get in deeper and deeper, don't I?" Runyon said. "All right, I was brash."

On the way to the Flying W, more than once Rufe broke from chuckles into sudden laughter.

His friend looked at him suspiciously and asked, "What's eatin' you, fellow?"

"Just call me Charley," Rogers reminded him laughing.

"Think you're smart, don't you?" Runyon said, aware that it was an inadequate comeback.

"Later we're going to be mighty well acquainted. When you get to feelin' low, you can think of that and it will cheer you up."

"I didn't say that," Charley protested.

"That's right. How come I to get it mixed up? Anyway, it was very very kind of you, Miss Polly said. That shows you made an impression on her."

"You wait and see." Runyon's voice sounded aggrieved. It was not the present ribbing that worried him. He knew that Rufe had him in a tight. Any time he joshed his friend in public, Rogers could broadcast an exaggerated version of the conversation in the restaurant. He could shut him up merely by hinting at it.

13 CHEROKEE BILL, TOP HAND FOR THE Flying W, returned from bog-riding to the home ranch with a story that spelled trouble. He had come out of the willows bordering the Soggy to see two men standing beside a fire branding a calf. A dead cow lay close to them. The Indian knew at once that they were rustlers. The cow had been shot as a precaution, for it would be a give-away if the calf should be seen following a mother with a different brand.

While he stood watching the men, too far away to recognize them, one of the thieves had caught sight of him and had at once flung a shot into the ground a few yards in front of him. He was being waved around, in the language of the range. This was a warning to him not to come near enough to identify them. No doubt they were transferring ownership of a Flying W calf. Cherokee did not stay to argue the point. The revolver he carried was of no use at that distance against a Winchester rifle. He turned, splashed back across the Soggy, and headed for home to report.

The only clue he had as to who the men were was that one of them walked lame. Neither he nor Pete Crawford had any doubt that the man was Limpy, a rider working for the Quarter Circle F Y. A year ago he had drifted down from New Mexico after serving a term for murder in the penitentiary.

Investigation showed that the dead cow belonged to the Crawfords. The calf, of course, had been driven many miles from the scene of the branding. By this time it was grazing with another bunch of stock.

Three days later, Pink Ball discovered that several hundred yards of wire at the back of the big pasture had been cut and the strands clipped into small lengths that made them useless. The Crawfords had no question as to the depredators. They were sure that Fen Yont was back of this. He was beginning an undeclared war for the range. Other outrages would follow in quick order.

The problem was a serious one. Yont had three times as many men in his pay as the Crawfords had, and half a dozen of the Quarter Circle F Y hands were of the outlaw type, commonly known as warriors. Including themselves, Charley Runyon and Rufe Rogers, the Crawfords mustered only ten riders.

"Yont is up to his old tricks," Cape said gloomily. "He is trying again to drive us out. We have to fight or go broke."

They were sitting on the porch after supper. Standing in the doorway back of the men, June got a shuddering vision of one or all of these youths shot dead from ambush. A cold wind of dread blew through her.

"Why don't we sell out to him and leave this terrible place?" she cried.

"And take a fourth of what our holdings are worth," Pete answered. "Because a murderous old scoundrel has got us whipped. Me, I'm going to stay and fight. I've talked this over with our boys—told them to leave if they want to go. They'll stick, every last one of them." He turned to Rogers. "But you and Charley are not in this. No reason for you to stay."

"No reason at all," Rogers assented dryly. "Except that I'd hate to live with myself if I didn't. You-all saved my life twice. For another thing Yont is my enemy as much as he is yours. I'm not running away either. Of course, Charley is in a different position. There is no obligation holding him."

Charley differed testily. "What's eatin' you, fellow? I'm drawing thirty dollars a month from the Flying W, ain't I? I got chips in this game same as you have. And neither Yont nor his side kick Grattan are what you would call buddies of mine. I'll back any play you fellows want to make."

June spoke again. She was in the half-light cast by a

lamp in the hall. Rufe listened to her soft throaty voice and as he watched the lovely planes of her face, the outlines of the small firm pointed breasts, and the grace of figure her dress modeled, a glow ran through his blood. No other woman under heaven could move him so. The heat of resentment was in her cheeks and her eyes were stormy. But back of her protest was fear.

"You are talking like a bunch of fool boys," she chided. "This Yont and his men are killers, ruthless as wolves. They are not like you. Remember Hans Ukena and Tom Claybolt. What chance did they have? He hates every one of you—except maybe Cape—far more than he did those poor homesteaders. They'll lie in wait for you and shoot you down from the brush. This isn't going to be a war. It will be murder."

"We'll go through with this and we'll be careful not to expose ourselves," Pete said. His eyes considered June thoughtfully. "This would be a good time to accept Mollie Bankhead's invitation to visit Denver for a few months, Sis."

"Don't waste your breath, Pete," she answered quickly. "If you boys stay here, so do I. I'll be quite safe. Even Yont's men would not dare harm me."

"If that is settled, where do we go from here?" Runyon asked.

"Any ideas?" Cape inquired of Rogers.

"I have one," Rufe said. "Blanchard, who runs the *Rifle Ramrod*, is a good friend of Pete. Why not write a story for it giving a full account of Yont's outrages both against you and other settlers? I think Blanchard would run it. If he did, public opinion would line up solidly against Yont. This might keep him from going too far."

"Would you accuse him of having murdered Hans Ukena and Tom Claybolt?" Pete queried.

"Not directly. I would say that they disappeared overnight leaving their stock and household goods, that none of their neighbors had seen them go or ever heard of them again, and that their claims were swallowed up by the Quarter Circle F Y. The inference would be plain. It would be a shock to Yont to have this dragged into print, since so far it has only been whispered."

"Will you write the article?" June asked.

"I'll take a whack at it if you will give me all the facts."

"All right," Pete said. "I can't see what harm it would do. Yont would be put on the defensive. He would feel the pressure of public opinion even if he did not let it stop him."

"And while public opinion is getting in its work, do we fold our hands and let Yont kill our stuff and cut our fences?" Cape wanted to know.

"We'll have to retaliate," Pete decided. "It's a foul business and I don't like any part of it, but we have our backs to the wall. Tonight we shoot one of his cows and cut the north line wire of his Soggy pasture."

"Do we have to shoot a cow, Pete?" his sister pleaded. "Couldn't we burn one of his haystacks instead? If we have to do something."

"We could," Pete answered dourly. "But why? Since the hay field is close to the house, it would be riskier. And it is fitting to pay him back in his own coin. An eye for an eye."

"He would miss the hay a good deal more than he would the cow," Rogers reminded Pete. "I don't like to kill cattle except when it is necessary, but I would enjoy firing a haystack."

"I'll side you on that job with pleasure, Rufe," Charley volunteered. "From what I hear Yont has been known to burn hay belonging to this ranch more than once."

"If anybody destroys that hay, I'll be the one," Pete announced firmly. "It will be dark tonight. We'll start for the Soggy pasture in a couple of hours."

There were neither moon nor stars when they started. Clouds scudded across the sky and there was the smell of coming rain in the air.

"Hope it will be a humdinger," Pink Ball said, riding knee to knee with Cherokee. "This country needs a good soaker bad."

The Indian grunted. Like most of his race, he was sparing of words.

It was midnight before they reached the north line of the Soggy pasture and a heavy rain was slanting down. Most of them had not brought slickers with them, but the downpour was so welcome that they did not care. Cape guarded the mounts while the others set to work with their wire clippers. It was unlikely that anybody else would be near, but there was no talk except in low tones. The beating of the rainfall drowned the sound of the snipping of the strands. They worked for an hour before Pete called a halt.

"Head for home, boys," he said. "I'll be along later."

"I'll trail along with you," his brother said.

"No, you won't," Pete snapped. "You'll go with the others."

Cape remonstrated, but Pete rode down his protest almost angrily. He knew his mind, he said, and he did not intend to let anybody interfere with his plan.

Abruptly he swung his horse around and rode into the pasture at a canter. Reluctantly the others watched him go. But they knew that when Pete was in this mood he would have his way.

After he had ridden a quarter of a mile, Crawford drew up to listen. He heard no sound of a following horse. When he started again, it was at a road gait. With most of the night before him, he was in no hurry. There was a good deal of spiny vegetation and in the darkness it was better to let his horse pick his own path. He was making for the irrigated field back of the house where hay was stacked for winter feed.

At the south end of the pasture, he cut the wires of the fence between it and the hay field. As he swung into the saddle again, he heard the clop-clop of a horse's hoofs in the pasture back of him. He sat tense, peering into the gloom out of which the approaching rider was coming. The vague bulk of the man and his mount took shape before Crawford's challenge rang out.

"Stop where you're at," he ordered. "And back-track fast."

A bantering voice answered. "I'm here on strictly illegal business, Mr. Crawford. Thought maybe you had forgotten to bring a match."

"I told you to stay out of this, Rufe," answered Pete. "I can take care of it."

"I must have plumb missed what you said. So here I

am." Rogers rode forward and joined Crawford. His grin disarmed the anger of his friend.

"All right. You can hold the horses while I slip forward and fire the nearest stack." Pete swung from the saddle and handed the bridle rein to the Texan.

It was still raining hard and frequent flashes of lightning lit the sky followed by the heavy sudden roll of thunder. Watching Pete disappear into the night, Rogers thought he would be glad when they were out of enemy territory and pointed for home. Though he was not superstitious, it came to his mind that nature was protesting against what they were doing. Not since his trail days had he been out in so wild a night.

Worry that had no logical reason nagged at him. There was a chance they might have to leave in a hurry. He moved the horses in the same direction Pete had taken. Except when a zigzag fork ripped the clouds, he could not see five feet beyond the pinto's head. A bolt struck a cottonwood and by the momentary light he saw that he was not fifty yards from the cluster of buildings that made up the Quarter Circle F Y steading. It startled him to discover that the ranch was alerted. The furious barking of dogs rose in a crescendo of clamor. Lamps had been lit in both the big house and the men's quarters.

A voice shouted, "Get those young calves into the barn before they are drownded."

Another retorted derisively, "What the hell do you think we've been doing?"

"Those blasted hounds are acting funny," somebody growled. "Like an animal is prowlin' around here, maybe."

Lightning again tore through the darkness. The last speaker screamed a warning. "Goddlemighty, there are riders in the field."

Time to be gone, Rogers knew. These men would break for their weapons. He must find Pete in a hurry. The lighted sky had shown him a haystack a stone's throw from him, but when he reached it, his call, "Pete—Pete," brought no answer. Minutes were lost wandering to and fro over the field before he caught sight of a spark fanned by the breeze to a flame. Wheeling his pinto, Rufe raced to the spot. Already the stack was a sheet of fire. Pete came to meet him.

"Thought I'd never find you," Rogers cried. "Fork your horse and let's get away."

Both of them were in the full glare of the burning stack. Gun flashes from the ranch yard stabbed the darkness there. The crack of a rifle sounded. Crawford stopped for an instant, then moved forward limping.

He caught the saddle horn and swung astride the led horse. Both of them jumped their mounts to a canter that took them out of the light. The hammering of the revolvers and the sharp ping of the Winchester followed them. Not until the riders were out of range did they pull down from a gallop.

"You're hit," Rogers said.

"In the leg. Bullet went through my boot. Can't be too bad."

"We'll take a look at it when we reach the creek," the Texan suggested. "Must have been a bullet from the rifle. At that distance the guys with the forty-fives were wasting their powder. You can make it all right to the creek, can't you?"

"Sure. It hasn't started to hurt yet."

When they reached the creek, they rode along the bank for some hundred yards before they stopped. If there was any pursuit they did not want to be discovered.

Crawford clenched his teeth while Rufe pulled off the boot the inside of which was soggy with blood. The wound was a flesh one and the bullet had plowed through the calf and torn a way out through the other side of the bootleg. Rogers carefully removed the sock and bathed the pierced limb. Pete held the injured leg in the running water to wash away any part of the sock that might have become embedded in the mangled tissue, after which Rufe bound the wound.

"You'll be laid up a few days," the Texan said.

"I've been promising myself for two years to read *Nicholas Nickleby* and haven't found time," Crawford replied. "I won't have any excuse now to put it off." He added grimly: "My own fault for being bull-headed. I could have pulled back when I found out the ranch was awake, but I was hell-bent to fire a stack."

When they reached the Flying W, they found everybody still up. Juan had prepared coffee and food for the riders first returning and the men had been too excited to go to bed without learning the result of Pete's adventure. June was greatly relieved to see her brother and Rogers. She had passed through some bad hours, and in the fact that Pete was wounded lay justification for her worry.

Pete made light of his injury. He would be good as new in a few days. If it had not been for the storm, there would have been no trouble, he told his sister. It happened to be the one night in the year when the Quarter Circle F Y riders were out taking care of the stock.

June saw Rufe for a minute alone on the porch as he was leaving for the bunkhouse. They had not been together without others present since his return. This slim hard man, young in years but weathered hard as steel, stirred in her emotions she had never felt for another.

"You followed Pete to help him if he needed it," she said.

He brushed aside the thanks in the low voice. "Pete isn't the only man that can be stubborn. I didn't figure we would be shot at."

"Or you wouldn't have joined him," she mocked.

"Sometimes I get hunches," he told her. "And if I don't take them, I get restless as a tumbleweed. I just kinda thought Pete ought not to play a lone hand."

She said impulsively, "I think the Crawford family have found a friend."

She showed, he felt, the bright and sparkling face of gallant youth. That he was a romantic man he would have denied, but he saw in her clean beauty an inner loveliness. The grace that flowed in all her movements must be the reflection of a spiritual fineness. Perhaps all lovers get a glimpse of truth that later the dust of time obscures.

Runyon joined them. "It's been quite a night," he said cheerfully. "Me for the hay."

June turned and walked into the house flinging a "Good night" at them.

14 YONT LOOKED SOURLY THROUGH the window at the blackened remains of what had been a haystack. A black temper was riding him. He did not like to be reminded that the foe he had despised was strong enough to fight back. The audacity of this attack angered him. Crawford had struck at him almost in his own yard. None of the sodbusters and small ranchmen he had driven out had dared to make any reprisals against his raids except for sporadic cases of brand-blotting in some faraway gulch.

His campaign to break up the Flying W ranch was not going well. It had taken a turn for the worse from the day he had bullied Rufe Rogers into becoming a tool of his. Barlow's fool play in wounding June Crawford while trying to kill her brother and the swiftness of the man's punishment had been a blow to his prestige. He knew well enough that he was a man generally hated, but he had not minded that so long as fear leashed that hatred from action. But these men associated with the Flying W—Crawford himself and Rogers and even the fiddlefooted cowboy Runyon—had treated his reputation as the big man of the district with scant respect. He was losing face, and all the little men who had moved in awe of him would secretly exult and pick up courage.

At the sound of footsteps on the porch, he turned to see his rider "Red" Cowan come into the room. The cowboy blurted out his news.

"They've done cut to hell an' back the north fence wires of the Soggy pasture."

Yont's bleak eyes were a barometer of his rage. His big fist hammered the table so that the inkwell jumped. "Fine.

And what were the big bunch of lunkheads I hire doing while the wires were being cut?"

"I reckon they must of done it last night during the storm," Red explained.

"While you and Swayback were sound asleep in the line cabin not two hundred yards away."

"A fellow has to sleep onct in a while, Mr. Yont," Red said defensively. His voice was humble, with intent to mitigate the fury of his boss. It would be like Yont to cut loose and give him the whaling of his life.

"You're none of you worth your salt. Blast you, what are you standing there for? Get out and send Grattan to me."

Red left fast. He had escaped more easily than he had expected. Grattan was in the bunkhouse reading a dime novel. No other rider in the outfit would have dared take it so indolently as this fellow lately arrived from Fort Worth.

"Boss wants you, Mr. Grattan," Red said.

Grattan rose and stretched himself. "Did he say what for?"

"No, he didn't." Red added information: "He's sore as a wounded bear with cubs. The Crawfords have cut the Soggy pasture fence."

"Does he expect to have it all his own way?" Grattan inquired with a malicious grin.

"I dunno about that. Looks like he can dish it out, but can't take it." Red regretted a moment later what he had said. Grattan was not really one of the boys. He was mean and vindictive. He might tell Yont just to get a guy into trouble.

Grattan buckled a gun belt around his waist before leaving the bunkhouse. It was a fixed rule with him never to go out of the room without a weapon.

Yont grumbled, "You took your time coming."

"I didn't see any fire," the Texan answered. He brushed aside a litter of letters and papers and sat on the edge of the table.

"Those scoundrels at the Flying W have cut the wires of one of my fences," Yont snarled.

"Gettin' right annoying one way and another, aren't

they?" Grattan mentioned cheerfully to anger his employer.

"They have gone too far. I aim to stop it."

"How?" the gunman asked innocently.

Yont stepped out to the porch, looked right and left to see nobody was near, came back into the room and closed the door.

When he spoke, the words came almost in a murmur from his thin-lipped mouth. "Comes a time when a man has to fight back if he is crowded. I'll take so much and no more."

Grattan looked into the man's flinty bulbous eyes. A malevolent hatred glared out of them. The gunman thought, *There is in this man a frozen egotism which cannot tolerate defeat. He means to be top dog no matter what it costs.*

The Texan waited silently. He guessed what was coming, but he was not going to invite an offer. If Yont had to make his proposition baldly without any help, he would be in a better bargaining position.

"Crawford is asking for trouble and he'll get it." Yont's hard gaze bored into the eyes of the other man. "That's where you come in, Bob."

"Me?" Grattan indicated surprise. "I've never even met the gent."

"Let's get down to brass tacks. You're a gun for hire. I'm using your own words."

"I think I mentioned that I was expensive," Grattan replied.

"This is an easy job. All you have to do is lie in the brush and wait till he comes along. No risk at all."

"If it's easy and no risk you don't want me." The gunman grinned down at the sly cruel face of the bullnecked rancher. "You can't save five hundred dollars any quicker than by pulling the trigger yoreself."

"Five hundred dollars!" Though it was difficult to do, Yont managed to shriek in a whisper. "Don't be crazy, Bob. I'm willing to pay anything in reason. Say a hundred dollars."

Grattan shook his head. "No deal. This guy is a tough *hombre.* I'm not taking on a cut-rate job. Maybe Limpy would do it." He got up from the table. "Well, no hard feelings. I'll be drifting back to Rifle."

"I'll go to two hundred, though it's a holdup price."

"I've given you my figure, and it will be cash on the barrel head half now and the other half after the job is done."

"Have a heart, Bob," Yont pleaded. "I'm not a rich man."

"All you own is a controlling interest in the bank at Rifle and most of the lumberyard there, plus a range covering half the county with about twenty thousand of yore cattle grazing on it, and maybe a few mortgages here and there. I know how you love a dollar, but you can get this dough back by squeezing a widow out of her home."

"You're an insolent scoundrel, Grattan," the rancher said angrily. "Men don't talk that way to me."

Grattan was a cold deadly killer, ruthless as an Apache. He was given to furious but rare gusts of temper. Now he did not resent in the least Yont's outburst. It told him that he had the cattleman in a tight spot. Having broached the subject, Yont had to come to terms with him.

"The difference beween us is that I don't fool myself and you do yoreself," Grattan explained contemptuously. "I've gone bad and I know it. You are worse than I ever could be, but you don't admit it even to Fen Yont. Man, you're a whited sepulcher. To listen to you makes my gorge rise. If I wasn't so hard up, I wouldn't do business with you at all. Wriggle all you please. It's still five hundred."

Yont in sullen rage gave up bargaining. "How would you go about getting this fellow?" he demanded.

"I'd find out all I could about his habits by lying out and watching through glasses from a brushy hilltop. It might take me a week before I got a good chance at him. When I'm scouting a man, I don't mind waiting plenty till conditions are right. Some day his hour will come."

"I want this fellow taken care of without anybody ever finding out who did it."

"That will suit me fine," Grattan agreed. "Soon as it's over, I aim to light a shuck for Tombstone."

Yont paid him two hundred fifty dollars to seal the deal. The gunfighter counted the bills and thrust them into

109

a pocket of his trousers. "I've made more than this at one turn of the wheel," he said scornfully.

"And lost it next day at another turn," Yont retorted tartly.

"Why not? Money is to spend. Even if you could take yours with you to hell, it would burn up there."

Yont's narrowed eyes glared at the man with a cold and deadly hatred in them. He wished too late that he had never had any dealings with this assassin whose arrogance matched his own. An instinct warned him that there would be trouble between them. The ranchman understood Grattan's mind because it was so like his own. The fellow wanted to be top dog. To take orders from another galled him. A born bully, he could not bear to play any hand but his own. To kill gave him a sadistic pleasure, but only at the urge of his own will. Though he was hiring out his gun, he would not take pains to curb his insolent contempt.

"I don't know why I put up with you, Grattan," the rancher replied, his voice an ugly rasp. "Don't think for a moment that I'm scared of you. The man never lived that had me buffaloed. You haven't a lick of sense. You're getting yore own price and there may be other jobs like it coming up. Yet you can't say three sentences without insulting me. No wonder they drove you out of El Paso and Fort Worth. You are your own worst enemy."

"I can get along without any preachin', Yont," the gambler replied, anger riding the shallow eyes that glittered like two dark marbles. "Mealy-mouthed guys let you play God out here and take it. Me, I call a spade a spade. To me you are not Mr. Big, but just a guy who can't do his own rattlesnake stompin' and has to hire a man tough enough to deliver the goods. I'll do it, at my own price, but I don't have to kow-tow to you a damned inch. You can't ride me with spurs."

Grattan flung open the door and straddled across the porch to the steps, self-assertion in his heavy stride. Yont watched him go, his thin lips clamped tight. He had to put up with the fellow till he had done his job.

15 AFTER A BLISTERING DAY, DARKNESS had settled over the land. Runyon and Rogers had come out of the stifling bunkhouse to take advantage of a cool gentle breeze blowing down from the hills. They drifted to the corral and sat on top of the fence while they smoked. Rufe was in a silent mood and responded to his friend's attempts at conversation with grunts and monosyllables.

Charley grumbled, "You talk too much," and took refuge in singing softly a song then having a vogue in the cattle country.

> Henry Ward Beecher, his Sunday school teachers,
> And all his scholars to boot,
> Drink what they call sassafras root;
> But 'twould be all the same if it had its right name,
> 'Tis the juice of the forbidden fruit.

"What have you got against Henry Ward Beecher?" Rufe asked.

"Me? Not a thing. I ain't ever heard of the gent till this song came up. Who was he, teacher?"

"He is the most famous preacher in the country. His sister wrote *Uncle Tom's Cabin*."

"She did? I've seen it played twice. That Simon Legree fellow was a no-good."

A sound of saddle leather creaking came to them. Instinctively Charley reached for a hip gun that was not there. A man's voice came out of the gloom.

"Take it easy, fellows. I'm Hack Weaver."

The rider moved forward and dismounted. The heels

of his dusty boots were run down, his jeans patched, and his shirt faded from its original blue. He had a thin wrinkled face with a look of defeat on it. Life as a homesteader was hard for a man with a wife and five children.

"How is it going on Cherry Creek?" Charley asked.

Weaver thought of his young ones who had eaten only corn-meal mush for supper. "We're kinda scrapin' the bottom of the barrel," he admitted. "But I reckon we'll make out."

"Tough luck," Charley said.

"I read that article Pete put in the Ramrod and I been talkin' with some of the boys in my neighborhood. It scalped Fen Yont for certain. Ontil recently folks didn't talk out loud like that. I've been sent down as a sort of rep for those of us on the creek to talk with Pete."

Rogers took him to the house. Weaver explained to Pete Crawford that he figured it would be better for him to come after dark in order not to be seen. "Yont might do we'uns a meanness if he knew I had drapped in to see you."

June was playing the piano, but she stopped and rose to greet Weaver when the men came into the room.

"How are Mirandy and all the children?" she asked after she had shaken hands.

"Fine, Miss June. Fine. They're all right peart, thank ye."

The girl relieved him of his hat which he was holding in both hands by the rim with a nervous grip.

"Looked like one of us up the branch ought to have a talk with you, Pete, after we read yore piece in the paper. Fen Yont has pestered us a heap, and we had to take it seeing as he had the deadwood on us with that raft of bullyraggers who ride for him. We been underdogs a long time, but since you've read the riot act to him and dragged this into the open, mebbe we-all had ought to throw in with you. I dunno."

"It's the only way to beat him," Pete said.

Weaver had waggoned to Arizona from Arkansas where he had been a tenant farmer. A decade and a half earlier he had been a Confederate soldier serving under Price. "I reckon," he agreed. "But a fellow's hands are plumb tied when he has a wife and a lot of kids. Wasn't for that I'd a-been shootin' long ago."

"We don't want any shooting if we can help it," Pete answered. "There has been too much already. But Yont may force our hands. He wants his spread to be the biggest in the territory. Just now he is sore as a boil at our outfit. If he smashes us, he'll take care of you creek homesteaders one after another. We are lost unless we join forces to stand together."

Rogers agreed, and added his personal opinion that Yont could not win against united opposition. In this country no man operating outside the law, even with a gang of ruffians back of him, could defeat resolute citizens standing up for their rights.

Weaver was not so sure of that. He had seen Yont grow in strength and ruthlessness for a dozen years. But in this room he sensed a knot of fighting force that encouraged him. The Crawfords had evidently decided to make a stand, and siding them were these two young fellows who had already had brushes with Yont and come out on top. This Rogers, who had killed the redoubtable Barlow in a duel, particularly impressed him. He looked like one who would do to ride the river with. The Texan had a strong jaw and the blue eyes looking out of a bronzed face gave warning that there was a dangerous fire in him when aroused. The well-packed shoulders, the light easy stride, the muscular coordination, contributed to the impression that he was a seasoned character hard and flinty.

"I dunno," Weaver repeated, rubbing his unshaven chin uncertainly. "Yont's got a mess of leather-slappin' rapscallions who don't give a cuss how far they go. You-uns could put up quite a fight against them, but with us small fry it's different. Our ranches are miles apart, and if we was raided we couldn't help one another a mite."

"True enough," Pete agreed. "We must organize secretly. You hillmen stay out of the fight until the final showdown comes. Yont won't bother you. He'll be busy with us and won't even know you are our allies."

"I reckon that would be all right," the homesteader assented.

"Talk this over with Webb and Adams and Claycomb. I'll see the ranchers on Pine and Bear Creeks."

The best they could do was to work out a loose organization of cooperation. They were at a disadvantage of position in that their strength was scattered over a wide terrain, whereas Yont's forces were compact and centralized. Pete Crawford realized that he could use the hillmen only as guerrillas except in an emergency.

Weaver carried home with him in a gunny sack back of the saddle a package of cookies for the children and a quarter of beef from a three-year-old steer butchered that day. He had promised to bring down two of the children to spend a few days at the Flying W. This June had insisted on. It had been a long time since Hack had felt as hopeful of the future. He had looked on the Crawfords as proud and distant. It warmed his heart to find them friendly young people.

The Crawfords did not make the mistake of thinking that in their fight against the Quarter Circle F Y they would get much active help from the hillmen, but at least they would be a factor in solidifying public opinion against Yont.

16 KNOWING YONT, THE CRAWFORDS felt sure he would resent the newspaper attack on him as much as he would the night raid on his pastures. It dragged his evil deeds into the open for all to read. He would certainly strike back soon. Pete gave orders for all his men to carry arms when they left the ranch. Those who covered terrain adjoining that of the Quarter Circle F Y rode in pairs to minimize the danger of an ambush. How far Yont's anger would take him none

could guess, but any clump of mesquite or cholla, any crease of the hills, might conceal an assassin.

Cherokee Bill was the first to cut sign of an enemy's presence. He was returning in the late afternoon from line riding when his eyes picked up tracks crossing the sandy floor of a wash. Early in the day there had been a light rain. The hoof marks had been made since the shower. He swung from the saddle and examined them carefully. A horseman had passed here within the hour. The sun had not yet had time to bake dry the crumbling edges of the prints. That no Flying W man had been in this vicinity except himself the Indian knew. His racial cautiousness made him suspicious. He decided to follow the tracks in the direction from which they had come.

More than once he lost them in the brush, but by quartering over the ground he each time picked them up again. They wound in and out among the prickly pear and mesquite, avoiding open country, working closer to the Flying W ranch house. By way of a small gulch they led to the summit of a boulder-strewn hill.

In a hollow between huge rocks a horse had been tied to a young live oak. On the ground was proof that the animal had been there several times for hours at a stretch. From the top of the ridge one could look down on the Crawford steading. A man who chewed tobacco had used this observation post for three or four days at least. Dried tobacco juice was splattered in a circle around the spot where the watcher had evidently crouched, some of the more recent shots still moist. The remains of lunches were scattered around. Beneath a small rock were pinned the papers which had wrapped the food.

That somebody was scouting the Flying W for Yont was clear. No doubt he had powerful glasses and watched the riders come and go, acquainting himself with the habits of the outfit. It was possible that he had a more sinister purpose, to pick off with a rifle one of the boys who wandered near enough.

The Crawford group did not make light of the discovery.

"Listens to me like the fellow might be Bob Grattan," Runyon said. "He's a plumb industrious tobacco chewer."

"Wouldn't it be a good idea to drop around and have a little talk with him while he is getting his sun tan?" Rufe asked, his voice a Texas drawl.

"I reckon we'd have to do our talking with guns," Cape said thoughtfully. "If it's that fellow Grattan and he's as tough as they say."

"We'll set a trap for him," Pete decided. "Fix up a welcome committee. These curly wolves tame down considerably when a couple of guns cover them."

Pete picked Rogers and Cherokee Bill to go with him. They left on foot in early morning before daybreak. There was not even a hint of coming dawn in the sky. Crawford led the way across the pasture and into the rough desert beyond. The vegetation through which they moved was gray with alkali dust. They tramped across a dry wash in which lay the white bones of a cow. By way of an arroyo they moved up to the ridge where the Indian had found plentiful signs of an enemy scout. The chill of an Arizona night still lingered in the air.

Day came, magically as it often does on the desert. The plain was a sea of swirling mist which melted as the sun showed over the far horizon edge. Shimmering rays tipped the vegetation with a silvery sheen. Crotches in the hills became caldrons of color. An opalescent sky rode above the peaks. And in a few minutes the witchery had vanished, to leave a dry parched waste raw and arid. A light breeze was blowing fresh across the wide basin.

Crawford placed his men back of the boulders which formed the rim-rock of the prong.

"If the gent is coming today, he'll be here soon," Pete said. "Don't rush him before he has made himself comfortable. He's dangerous as a cornered wolf. We want to take him alive."

"He'll start his gun smoking if he thinks he has a chance," Rufe warned.

Cherokee Bill said nothing. He was re-coiling the rawhide rope he had brought from the horn of his saddle.

There came to them the faint sound of a horse's hoof striking a stone.

"All right, boys," Pete ordered. "Get back of cover. Let me make the play. No firing unless he asks for it."

116

They heard the creak of saddle leather. After that came a silence that seemed to the tense waiters long. The rider was fastening his horse. The head of Grattan appeared over the brow of the hill. In one hand he carried a Winchester, in the other a paper package of food. A cloth-covered canteen hung over his left forearm. Field glasses were in a leather case suspended from his neck. Though he had no premonition of enemies near, he came forward warily, his body crouched. Since he did not want the sun's rays to heliograph from the barrel of the rifle a warning to the ranch of his presence, he kept the weapon shielded by his body.

He stooped to put down the food parcel and the canteen. The sound of a voice jerked his body up, a voice curt and sharp.

"Drop that gun." Crawford had eased out from back of a boulder and was covering him with a forty-four.

Grattan dropped instead the food and canteen. Without taking time to aim, he flung a shot from the Winchester at Crawford. Before the roar of the rifle had died, so swiftly that Pete had barely time to deflect his aim and fling the bullet from his revolver into the loose rubble at Grattan's feet, a rope had snaked out and the loop dropped over the fellow's shoulders tightening around his arms.

Rogers dropped his forty-five and flung himself on Grattan. Though hampered by the taut rope and by the weight of the young Texan leeched to him, Grattan struggled desperately to free himself. The man's bull strength was handicapped. The taut rope and the steely arms of Rufe pinned to his side those of the heavier more powerful man. His shoulder, driven into the other's midriff by the charge, had pumped the breath out of the spy.

Grattan kept his feet, legs solid as fence posts planted wide. His lungs sucked the air back into them. By a tremendous effort he dragged an arm up from the grips that fastened it to his body. A knotted fist hammered on the back of Rogers' head with piledriver blows. Rufe set his teeth and held fast. His body was swung right and left as they quartered over the ground. The big man tried to get at his revolver, but his opponent's elbow was clamped tightly against the butt. They swayed to and fro, Grattan's feet set to keep from falling.

Cherokee was still at the end of the rope, but Crawford had joined the mêlée. The force of the attack was partially neutralized by lack of coordination. The Flying W men were half the time tugging in different directions.

Pete grunted out the first words that had been spoken since his order to surrender. "Lemme have him, Rufe."

He had got a head lock that garroted Grattan, and using all his strength he spilled him backward, going to the ground with him. Rogers flung himself on the threshing legs of their foe. The strength of the fellow was so great that, though they were on top of him, they had difficulty in keeping him down. The other arm was free now and he was lashing out with both of them.

The Indian dropped the rope and ran forward gun in hand. The barrel of the revolver descended on Grattan's head. The volcanic arms, legs, and body collapsed at once.

When Rogers regained his breath enough to speak, he said, "Some man—mighty near whipped all of us."

Crawford wiped the sweat from his brow with the sleeve of his shirt. "He is as strong as a bull," he commented. "Had two strikes on him before he started and would have been fighting yet if Cherokee hadn't put him to sleep." Pete had another word of praise for the Indian. "Your rope saved somebody's life, maybe two or three. The throw was so swift and sure, it cut out the gun play right then. For my money you are the champion roper of the world, Cherokee."

For him Cherokee made practically an oration. "Man or a steer, what's the difference?" he said with a lift of the shoulders.

When Grattan came back to consciousness, he found his hands tied behind him. His scowl passed from one to another and centered on Rogers.

"I ought to have settled yore hash when I had you that day at Rifle," he said venomously.

"Don't blame yourself," Rufe said dryly. "Not your fault Charley Runyon happened along and spoiled your party."

"You have bad luck, Grattan," Crawford told him.

118

"Was it Rogers you wanted to get this time—or maybe me?"

The bound man did not answer, but his eyes were hot with frustrated rage.

"So you are Yont's new killer," Pete continued. "First Kurt Barlow, now you. There are some sizable live oaks down in the barranca. I understand you think hanging a man without a trial is all right. Have you anything to say?"

Grattan broke into savage profanity. If they would free his hands, he would whip all three of them, he threatened. He got to his feet and glared defiantly at them.

In Crawford's eyes was a hard cold light. "You can't curse yourself out of this. You are a dangerous ruffian, kicked out of Fort Worth a month ago because you are a killer. The safe thing for us to do is to put an end to you now."

"You can't do it," Grattan protested, fear back of his bold front. "I have a right to be here and wasn't doing you any harm. You-all jumped me out of meanness."

"How much is Yont paying you for this job?" Crawford demanded.

"I been lookin' for quail," the gunman told him sourly.

"Oh no, Mr. Grattan. To get quail you go to a water hole in the morning and wait for them to come and you don't take field glasses to find them." The ranchman was smiling grimly.

Now that they had captured him, the Flying W men did not know what to do with the man. They had no proof that he was here for an illegal purpose. Cherokee kept the prisoner covered while the other two moved aside to discuss the problem. Rogers suggested that they take him back to Yont with their compliments. This would be a derisive gesture that exactly suited Pete, especially since there was a considerable element of danger in it.

"By General Jackson, we'll do that," he agreed.

Cherokee Bill returned to the Flying W to bring three saddled horses and the others stayed with their unwilling guest. Assured that no hanging was in prospect for him, Grattan kept a stiff front. He chewed tobacco steadily and maintained a cold silence. Inside he was churning with rage. A man of swaggering effrontery, he could not stand to be bested, and to be taken to the Quarter Circle F Y a shackled prisoner was a galling experience. His insolent contempt for the ranch riders had made him unpopular. Now they could gloat over his humiliation.

The gunman was hoisted to a horse. A rope was flung around his neck, the other end attached to the horn of Cherokee's saddle. Crawford led the way down the barranca to the flats and across the thorny desert to Dead Cow Creek. They splashed through the water, at this time of year no higher than the knees of the horses, and crossed a hill slope sown with saguaros. Over rolling country they came to the mesa from which they could see the windmills of the Quarter Circle F Y. Far to the right was a lift of dust stirred by moving cattle. Yont's riders were probably shifting stock to another feed ground. Just beyond where the mesa dropped to the creek nestled the ranch buildings in front of a small rimrock background.

The steading had a shabby ill-kept look. There was no evidence that the owner had any pride in it. Wornout wagons, hay rakes, and the debris of discarded tools littered the yard left untidily to rot at the spot where they had last been used.

A man, standing at an outdoor blacksmith shop with a hammer in one hand and a horse's hoof between his legs, watched the riders come down from the mesa, then suddenly dropped his work and scuttled to the house.

"Informing Mr. Yont of visitors arriving," Rogers said.

Another appeared at the door of the bunkhouse, a rifle in his hands. He shouted to somebody and a cowboy in plain leather chaps came out of the stable, to disappear into it instantly and return a few moments later carrying a sixshooter.

The riders crossed the yard to the big house and reached it as Yont stepped out to the porch. By this time Limpy was added to the welcoming committee. He stood at the corner of the root house armed with a saddle gun.

"We've brought back your trigger man, Yont," Crawford explained. "Thought you knew better than to send a boy to mill."

Rogers and the Indian had swung their mounts half around to face the ranch hands. They knew that if Yont gave the signal the crash of guns would fill the air. It was lucky that all but a few of the Quarter Circle F Y men were away working the stock. Pete and Rufe had counted on that.

The man who had warned Yont stood back of him, the hammer still in his hand, apparently not armed otherwise. He was the cowboy Red, a good-natured friendly fellow. His gaze was fixed on Grattan, and at Crawford's words he grinned. For this Texas gunman he had no use.

That pleased smile brought a blast from Grattan. "If I had a gun I'd clean up all three of them!" he cried.

"Where is your gun?" Yont snarled.

Rufe answered him. "He loaned it to Cherokee."

"Any way. With a gun or without I'll take 'em all on. They sneaked up on me unexpected." The fury in the killer's face was appalling.

"You talk a good fight," Yont told him scornfully.

His glance swept around the yard. A cold fierce eagerness was shining in Limpy's eyes. He was hoping for the signal. The man with the rifle, Curt Slade, was ready also. The cowboy with the revolver was too far away to be of immediate assistance. Yont made up his mind reluctantly. All of these riders who had come with such rash insolence to beard him in his stronghold were hard desperate men. If he raised a hand some or all of them would be shot down, but not before they had got him. It was not worth the price. His sly caution asserted itself.

"I don't know what has got into you, Pete," he complained, in the tone of one whose patience has been worn thin. "Seems you don't do anything lately but harass me. What was the idea of jumping Mr. Grattan? What did he do?"

"You ought to know," Crawford retorted bluntly. "He is your hired gun, sent to kill one of us, probably me. But he slipped up on the job. You are not dealing with Ukena or Claybolt now. Get this straight, Yont. If any of our men are hurt, we'll gun you certain."

"That's no way to talk, Pete," Yont objected. "I'm a peaceable citizen. If we've got any little differences, we ought to talk them over like sensible folks. But don't think you can bully me. If you want trouble you can find plenty."

"I don't want it, but you are laying it in my lap." Crawford's anger spoke sharply in his voice. "You've gone crazy with love of power and money. Only God could get away with what you're trying to do. Back off while there is still time, Mr. Big."

"You always were a fool, Pete," Yont said with impatient scorn. "You always will be. Get off my land before you are carried off."

Crawford gathered the bridle reins. "I find no pleasure in your company," he mentioned, eyeing his enemy with cold distaste. "Let's go, boys. Take your rope from that wolf's throat, Cherokee. We'll leave him to the loving care of the scoundrel who has bought his gun."

"Just a moment, Pete," Rufe's glance traveled around the yard from one of Yont's men to another, stopping to rest on Limpy. "Me, I wouldn't like to be a sitting duck. Since you're so peaceable, Yont, call off your dogs before we start."

"For so insolent a whelp you're mighty timid," Yont sneered. "Why should I dry-nurse you?"

Rufe smiled impudently. "It's yore friends we are worried about. We wouldn't like to decimate the ranch."

From the root house Limpy's harsh voice beat across the yard. "If you want this guy's clock stopped, give the word, boss."

Yont's answer was instant. "No—no, Limpy. Not now. Let them go. I'll have no bloodshed if I can help it."

The visitors took no chances. Crawford held his ground while the others rode to the edge of the yard. Here they turned and waited for him to join them. They passed into a clump of cottonwoods and from the grove to a twisting arroyo. Not until they were out of sight did they feel safe.

Rogers whistled with relief. "Show-off business, boys," he said. "We'd ought to have had more sense. I'd say we just missed a massacre. Yont couldn't quite bring himself to it, seeing he would have been a gone goose if he had."

"It will be war sure enough from now on," Pete said gravely.

17 WHEN CHARLEY RUNYON, AFTER A night at a line camp, returned to the ranch house and heard the story of the adventure at the Quarter Circle F Y, his reaction was a blend of jubilance and regret.

"You certain showed that damned sidewinder Yont what he's up against. Betcha both he and Grattan wanted to crawl into a hole and pull it in after them. But doggone it you might of took me along, boys. I wouldn't of missed it for six Fourth of July's rolled into one." His protest ended with an ultimatum. "Next time there's any fun going on, I'm in it, see?"

June took no pleasure in this minor defeat of the Yont forces and said so sharply. It was like shooting at a grizzly with a twenty-two, the only effect being to sting and madden it. This was not a game, and the sooner they realized it the better. There might be a tragic end to the road they were traveling. They were acting like children who could not leave a dare unanswered.

Back of her exasperation lay fear. She had not lived on the frontier without understanding the strength and the weakness of its men. She knew that when they jested at danger their words were often a cover for a hard core of anger and bitterness. The courage of these young men might prove their undoing, for the cards were stacked against them. They were opposed by killers who would murder from ambush, a course of action to which they would not stoop.

But she had no plan to offer. They had to fight, or yield to Yont's greed and overbearing arrogance. The girl found it difficult to accept without dejection either alternative.

Her restlessness drove her to action. There were times when she would saddle her buckskin Rambler and gallop across the sunbaked plain until she found peace in its windswept vastness. Returning from such a ride, she met one day Rufe Rogers near the little cabin Yont had built for him.

If she was pleased to see him, she concealed it under a manner of curt indifference. An invisible barrier had risen between them. Rufe was one of the ranch hands and June a joint owner of a valuable property. Recently the son of a wealthy Leadville mine owner had come from Denver to see June and visited at the ranch for a few days. They had known each other when she had been at school in the mile-high town. A rumor had it that they were engaged to be married. Rogers had drawn back within himself. He came to the big house only when business brought him there.

"Have you moved back to the claim?" she inquired politely.

That was a question needing no answer. His eyes raked her coolly. "What are you doing so far from the house?"

"I went for the mail," she explained. "Should I have asked your permission?" The words came with smooth and studied mockery.

"Pete told you to keep close to the place."

"Did he appoint you a guardian for me?"

In her dark eyes there was temper, in her voice an edge. She had done more for him than for any man she knew and he had turned his back on friendship. What right had he to tell her what she could or could not do? Her resentment was partly at herself for her deep interest in this lean brown man who had been flung into her life by some wind of chance.

Watching the blaze of her eyes challenging him, the slim body erect in the saddle with squared shoulders, her loveliness greatly moved him. He did not let this tenderness reach the surface.

"You need a guardian," he said, almost harshly. "You know how much trouble your brothers are facing. Yet you increase the risk."

124

"No," she denied. "In this country men do not war on women."

"One of Yont's men wounded a woman," he reminded her.

"Not meaning to," she flung back at him, and added with malice, "I'm sure Pete will be interested to know you are giving the orders at the Flying W now."

He turned his horse and rode beside her.

She said, after they had ridden a few hundred yards, "Oughtn't you to put handcuffs on me?"

By the stormy eyes glaring at him he could see how deeply she was stirred. This disturbed and puzzled him. He did not want to antagonize her and he did not see why she should resent his warning her of the danger in leaving the ranch without a guard.

"Is it presumptuous for me to ask you to look after your own safety?" he asked.

"I don't take orders from the ranch hands, Mr. Rogers," she said haughtily.

He made no answer in words, but his level eyes met hers steadily. Already June was sorry for what she had blurted out. It had been anger speaking, not the true feeling in her mind, but her pride was too strong and her exasperation too keen to retract the affront. She touched her mount with the spur and put it to a gallop. Rufe made no move to rejoin her. He followed to the ranch fifty yards in the rear. She had set the status of their relationship and he would not make any effort to change it.

June dismounted, tossed the reins to the ground, and hurried to the house. She bolted the door of her bedroom and let unhappiness sweep through her. No tears came to relieve her, yet she was a river of woe inside. Why had she let temper rule her mood when she wanted so much to be friends with him again? That he was a proud man she knew. Now he would be a stranger in spirit to her.

18 THOUGH JUNE HAD BEEN ANGRY AT Rufe's warning, she paid heed to it and did not again leave the ranch without an armed guard beside her. To have her riding curtailed was a hardship, for since her early childhood, except for the years when she was attending school in Denver, she had spent a large part of her life in the saddle. In her early teens she had been a wild young hoyden who scandalized the good women of the neighborhood by helping her brothers work the cattle, clad in chaps as they were, her hair flying wild in the breeze.

Time had tamed her. She was now a young woman aware of conventional obligations, but with the feud active, the only opportunity she had for horseback exercise was to go with the Flying W men covering the range. On a side saddle and wearing a lady's riding costume, it would have been folly to dash into the prickly brush after a bolting cow. Like the men, she rode astride in chaps and boots. Usually her companions were her brother Cape and Charley Runyon. Rufe Rogers was never one of them. As a protection against rattlesnakes she carried a small revolver.

Charley Runyon found it pleasant to have her with them. She was a good cowhand. As they started to comb the Red Rock barrancas one morning, he watched the girl rope and saddle her mount Black Beauty.

"You throw a better loop than I do," he told her.

Before answering she tightened the cinch. "I do pretty well for a girl," she admitted.

Cape joined them and they rode out of the yard three abreast. The air of the early morning was like wine and youth was in the saddle. They cantered across the flats to the rolling country beyond, no prescience of danger in their gay hearts. Their course brought them by devious travel through the low hills to the red rock wall which marked the limit of Flying W range. From a distance it looked like an impassable barrier, but a closer view showed leading down to a small mountain park parallel clefts worn by many years of flash floods. The feed above was poor and scanty bunch grass rooted in stony soil, but cattle persisted in pushing up from the valley to the bad lands above. Every few days ranch riders had to drive these strays back to the better pasturage below.

They set their ponies to clamber up one of these deep breaks to the boulder-strewn ridge overlooking the lowlands. After a long steep climb their winded mounts brought them to the summit. There was no hurry and they rested the animals before scattering to comb the mesa. The few small bunches of stock they would find were likely to be hidden in draws of the rough gashed terrain.

Cape suggested that Runyon work the country to the far left. Any Flying W stuff he found could be taken down a barranca that did not lead into the park. They would join him on the flats beyond it. June was to circle the middle ground and Cape the right section, each of them descending by the most convenient gorge.

To search for cattle in this broken country was like playing a game of hide-and-seek. After an hour's search Cape found a small band of two-year-olds concealed in an arroyo. As he turned them toward the nearest ravine, he heard the flat faint report of a shot. This disturbed him but not unduly. Runyon might have fired at a sidewinder or at a deer. Occasionally a cowboy brought home game he had run into while at work.

Yet Cape decided to get back to the park with the young stuff he had and not look for more. His sister might be there waiting for him and he thought it better to join her.

When he reached the lower entrance to the gulch, his gaze swept the park. There was no sign of human life, but a thin rise of smoke caught his eyes. Near it a calf stood blatting beside a prostrate cow. Somebody must have lit that fire since they had ridden up the barranca. He moved forward cautiously, scanning every clump of vegetation that might conceal an enemy. Yet it was not likely that an ambusher would have warned his victim by starting a fire.

He smelled the pungent odor of burned hair and flesh. The calf had just been branded. In the cow's forehead was a bullet hole. It carried on a flank the Yont F Y. But the brand on the calf was the Crawford W. Even before a bullet slapped into the ground in front of him and flung up a spurt of sand, Cape realized that he was snared in a trap.

He had dismounted to examine the calf, grounding the bridle reins. During that instant of uncertainty a harsh voice warned him.

"Stay put or we'll drill you sure."

Limpy gave the order. He had risen out of a small runway, a saddle gun in his hands. Cape's swift glance around showed him two other men, Grattan and Curt Slade. A heavy growth of prickly pear had concealed them. The weapons of all three were trained on Crawford.

"Caught rustling," Grattan jeered. "Right in the act."

The boy knew he had no chance to escape or to fight it out with them. His heart died under his ribs, but he fought down the fear that flooded him.

"So that's to be the story," he said. "You've been waiting till we came to hunt our strays. This is a fix."

"Get yore hands up," Limpy ordered. "Curt, go collect his hardware."

Curt slouched forward and disarmed their prisoner. "Too bad we got the kid and not his brother, but after all nits grow into lice," he said with a bad-toothed grin.

"What do you think you're going to do with me?" Cape asked, trying to keep a tremor out of his voice.

Grattan flung a rope about his neck. "You know what we do to rustlers. Yore brother had his fun the other day with me. It's the Crawford turn now to sweat. But there's a difference. We're thorough. We go through to a fare-you-well."

The boy looked from one hard cruel face to another and realized there was little hope for him. These men had long since turned their backs on decency and human kindness. They wanted to make an example of him to strike terror into the hearts of his friends.

"You can't do this to me!" he cried. "You are not Apaches or devils. You know I'm not a rustler and I have never done you harm."

"It's the end of the trail for you," Grattan snarled. "Buck up and take it game."

An icy hand inside the boy gripped at his stomach and twisted it. A cold sweat broke out on his forehead. His legs were trembling and shaky. He was going to be strangled.

"I'm not nineteen," he pleaded. "You wouldn't kill me." He turned a white stricken face to Grattan. "Pete let you go the other day."

"His mistake," the Texan said callously. "Different here."

"I don't like it," Limpy cut in. "He's only a kid. We weren't laying for him, but Rogers or Pete Crawford."

"Nits grow to be lice," Grattan repeated brutally. "That live oak in the hollow will do. Let's get going."

"There's no hurry. He'll be a long time dead." Limpy was a small bandy-legged man with narrow shoulders and a thin grizzled beard. His cold slaty eyes avoided looking at the boy they were about to murder. They held fast to those of Grattan. He was not yet sure what he meant to do.

"Turning soft?" sneered Grattan. "Want to run out on the job?"

"If you think I'm soft there's an easy way for you to find out," Limpy said, his voice low and cold.

Cape appealed to the lame man. "Don't let him do this. I'm innocent. You know I am." As the horror of his situation flooded his mind the boy's voice broke.

"So you're gonna play baby," Grattan scoffed at him.

The words were a bracer to Crawford. He slammed a fist into the man's gloating face. Grattan dropped the rope and charged at him, both fists flailing at the boy. Cape stumbled back and went down. The sadistic gunman kicked him in the side.

Limpy pushed the mouth of his forty-four against the back of Grattan's neck. "Stop that or I'll blow yore head off," he said.

Grattan glared at him. "Goddlemighty, what's eatin' you? He hit me first."

"You asked for it, you big bully. Lay off him. Don't act like a crazy man."

With difficulty Grattan controlled his rage. Limpy had him covered and the little fellow had a reputation as a badman. "All right. We'll string him up and get going."

They tied Cape's hands behind him and hoisted the boy to the saddle of his horse. Slade led the animal to the live oak. Cape's sudden anger had done him good. Though he was still weak with fear, he set his teeth to take what he must. The first virtue of the frontier was courage. A man had to play game, no matter how full of terror he was.

Grattan flung the rope over a limb of the tree and laid on the ground the rifle he was carrying. "All aboard for kingdom come!" he shouted.

Limpy had taken hold of the bridle. There was a strong urge in him to interfere.

"Let go," Grattan told him and raised Cape's quirt whip the horse from under their victim.

Young Crawford clamped his teeth to keep from begging for mercy.

"I ain't made up my mind," Limpy said. "This is a damnable thing to do."

"Wait!" Slade called urgently.

A rider had come out of a gulch and was galloping toward them. Grattan snatched up the Winchester and as he fired Slade knocked his arm up.

"It's a woman!" he cried.

The rider was June, her hair flying wildly as she raced across the park. The blood had washed out of her face.

"What—what—?" she gasped.

"They're hanging me," Cape told her.

A surge of hope swept over him. With June present as a witness, they would hardly dare go on with this. "You've spoiled their party, Sis," he continued. "After they took so much trouble. They must have seen us when we came into the park and knew we would come back. But they couldn't have been near enough to check on who we are. They killed a Yont cow and branded the calf with a Flying W."

"Damnation!" Grattan barked at the girl. "What are you doing here?"

June was breathing so deeply she could scarcely speak. "But why?" she asked her brother. "Why brand the calf wrong?"

"As an excuse to hang any of us they caught as rustlers," Cape explained.

Slade spoke up, a sly ingratiating smile on his lips. "He's a rustler all right, but seeing as he is so young we aimed only to give him a scare, Miss."

"That's a lie," Cape retorted. His voice was sharp with anger. He still felt sick from the terrible shock he had been given. "They have been waiting here for days to trap one or two of us when we came to work the Red Rock ridge."

Limpy had been thinking fast to come up with a change of plan to meet the inopportune arrival of the girl. "Yore brother would like to talk himself out of it, Miss Crawford, but he can't do it. Sloan is right. Cape is a rustler. We caught him redhanded. We've got to take him to the ranch for Fen Yont to say what we'd better do with him." He spoke reluctantly, as if he would like to turn young Crawford loose, but could not in duty do so. "He had a good scare coming to him."

"No," June said swiftly. "Cape is no rustler and you know it. His life would not be safe with Yont. You can't take him. And I wouldn't trust him with any of you. Already you have been beating him up."

"Grat is a little impulsive," Limpy admitted, "but I give you my word he won't lay a finger on the boy again."

"He couldn't have branded that calf," June explained scornfully. "We separated on the rim-rock not an hour ago. He wouldn't have had time."

"Oh yes, he would," Grattan differed. "As soon as you separated he lit out for the park—and that's what he did."

June leaned forward and put her hand on the running iron hanging by Cape's saddle. "It's not even warm. How could it have been hot enough to brand with a few minutes ago?"

"You can't talk him outa this, Miss," Slade replied stubbornly. "We aim to take him with us."

She loosened the rope and lifted the loop from Cape's

neck. "You can't take him unless you take me too," she announced firmly.

"It is ridiculous to talk about holding me prisoner," Cape put in. "All of us here know that I didn't kill that cow or brand the calf. This is one of Yont's dirty tricks. You can't persuade decent folks that it is anything else."

"You talk mighty brash now," Grattan gibed. "Five minutes ago you were whinin' for yore life."

Limpy amended promptly the implied admission. "Yore brother didn't know we didn't aim really to hang him."

June was recovering from the horror that had shaken her. She turned angrily on Limpy. "You should train your fellow murderer not to give you away. A fine lot of ruffians you are, to take an innocent boy and kill him because that toad at the Quarter Circle F Y wants all the land within forty miles of his ranch. Scum is the word for you. Riffraff blown in from other places that spewed you out." The girl's stormy eyes challenged them scornfully.

Limpy smiled at her pleasantly. "You're quite a vixen, Miss. I reckon yore mammy didn't paddle you proper when you was growin' up. About Yont, if you're ridin' with us to the ranch, you can tell him off to his face."

"You're not going to take Cape with you," June replied. "Who do you think you are?"

"Just a bunch of cowboys tryin' to get along," Limpy told her, still grinning. "Slade, you better ride alongside of Cape, jest to make sure he doesn't fall off seeing he's kinda hampered not having his hands free."

Cape said to his sister, "You'd better go home and tell Pete what has happened."

She shook her head. "I can't leave you with this bunch of killers. No knowing what they would do. They might shoot you in the back pretending you were trying to escape. If you have to go, I'll go too."

"Please yoreself, Miss." Limpy shrugged his shoulders. "I reckon you always do. It will be nice having you a visitor at the ranch. But understand we're not pressuring you. Yont may act some annoyed."

Out of a small gulch Slade brought three horses.

The lame man swung in at the tail of the procession, just behind June. He had taken note of the weapon she carried, and though he did not make her surrender it, he was taking no chances with this tempestuous young lady. She might have an urgent impulse to help her brother escape by violent action.

Yont was not pleased when he caught sight of the Crawfords in the cavalcade riding into the yard. His trap had not been set to take prisoners, but to rub out those caught in it. Even so he could have found a way to handle Cape, but the presence of his sister complicated the situation. This raw western country was very touchy about the treatment given its women. He thought, *The little devil knew I could not touch her brother if she came along.*

"We're not fixed for lady guests here, Miss Crawford," he explained smoothly. "No accommodations for them. My boys are a bunch of roughnecks who wouldn't please you. I've got to keep your brother till Sheriff Crane comes for him. You had better run on home. I aim to treat Cape right."

She looked at him with cold contempt. "I aim to see you do," she mocked. "When I go home, Cape goes with me."

"I got no place for you to sleep," he snapped.

"A pile of hay will do, just so it is near my brother. I understand I am not welcome. That is why I am going to stay." She added, the flick of a whiplash in her voice, "I know how kind-hearted you are, Mr. Yont, but one of your men might make a mistake."

"You'd better go, Sis," Cape urged. "I don't think he would dare harm me now."

"Don't you?" she differed. "I don't trust one of the whole clanjamfry. I wouldn't think of going. This man has no notion of sending for the sheriff."

"You do me wrong, Miss Crawford," protested Yont. "But the fact is this is no place for a lady. You wouldn't like it."

"I'll take pot luck," June answered, and swung from the saddle. She noticed that several of the ranch hands had appeared and, moved by curiosity, had come closer. Among them was the cowboy Red. Her circling glance raked them contemptuously. "You must be proud to work for a sly murderous schemer, one who lays a plot to trap and hang an innocent boy, a man whose own family left him because he is so vile."

"I don't reckon we know what this is all about, Miss," Red said mildly.

"You don't have to know, Red," his employer said harshly. "I'm running this ranch." Yont turned to June. "When you act like a shrew with all this wild talk, you make it hard for me to be nice to you as I would like to be. I'm afraid you've got the bad blood of yore family in you. My boys caught yore brother branding one of my calves. Naturally I'm going to see he is punished for it. It's not doing you any good to go into a tantrum."

June explained the situation to Red. "If you don't know about this, I'll tell you. These gunmen of Mr. Yont's under orders from him killed one of his cows and branded the calf with a Flying W. When my brother rode down from the Red Rocks pushing a bunch of our stock before him, these scoundrels accused him of rustling. They had a rope around his neck to hang him when I showed up."

"Every word of that is true," Cape confirmed.

"I've been missing stock for some time," Yont said. "Now I know where it has been going and I mean to put a stop to the thieving."

He gave orders to have Cape locked up in an old log cabin close to the house. Slade wanted to know what they were to do with the crazy girl.

"Let her alone, but keep an eye on her," Yont said. "I'll figure out something later. You are all witnesses that we did not bring her here. She came of her own will."

He spoke sourly. In his campaign against the Crawfords everything he tried to do seemed to be frustrated.

19 RUNYON CAME OUT OF A BARRANCA below the park pushing before him a small bunch of Flying W stock. Since he had ridden circle over terrain farther from the appointed meeting ground than the others, he was surprised the Crawfords had not arrived. Loosening the double cinches of his saddle, he grounded the reins and sat down in the shade of a mesquite. Below him lay the saffron-hued desert stretching to the porphyry mountains on the horizon, the floor of the plain sown thinly with parched greasewood, gray-green cholla, ocotilla, and other spiny vegetation. Occasionally he caught sight of dust eddies whirling in inverted cones. But for the barking of a coyote no sound disturbed the wide silence.

The day was warm and drowsy. He lay down and looked up at a sky cloudless except for one thin skein drifting past. His eyes closed, opened, shut again. When he awakened, the clock in the heaven by which he judged time had registered an hour gone. He came to with a start, jumped up, and was puzzled to find himself still alone. A faint alarm stirred in him, and it quickened when he faced the facts. Even if they had found the stock difficult, they should have been here long ago.

He rode up to the park and saw there Flying W cattle which must have been driven down by his companions. Why were they not here? Quartering over the ground, he found a cow belonging to Yont with a bullet hole in its head. A calf newly branded stood beside its dead mother. The brand on its flank was the Flying W of the Crawfords. This did not make sense. His friends were not rustlers.

Beneath a live oak tree he picked up a gauntlet. On the cuff was a red star. It belonged to June. She must have dropped the glove to tell him something. Why had she come to this far corner of the park?

Charley read evidence of more than two horses recently here. The hoofprints of five or six ponies led along a wash leading in the direction of the Quarter Circle F Y. He followed these for a short distance and then pulled up. He was convinced that some of Yont's men had run into the Crawfords and were taking them back to their ranch. He had better get to the Flying W quick as he could and tell Pete what had taken place.

When he reached the steading, his pony's shoulders flecked with sweat foam, he found nobody there but Juan the cook. Pete and Rufe had ridden to Rifle where a beef buyer had an appointment to meet them.

Runyon ran up a horse from the pasture, saddled, and started for Rifle. Never in his life before had he abused a horse as he had done the two he had been astride this day. The lives of his friends might depend on the speed with which he traveled. When he flung himself from the saddle in front of the Acme Palace, his mount's sides were heaving and its head hanging low. Probably it would never be as sound a horse as it had been before this furious ride.

Crawford and Rogers were in Barclay's feed store when Runyan ran in and told the shocking news. To both of them it was a blow. They poured questions at him, trying to find another explanation of the evidence written on the scene of the abduction. But no other reasonable interpretation offered itself. This was one of Fen Yont's crafty schemes with possibilities of tragic harm. They started for home at once, leaving Runyon to follow after he had found a fresh horse.

Though Rogers feared the worst, on the way back to the ranch he tried to comfort Crawford. He put it that Yont could not have intended to include June as a victim of his plot. It was possible that her presence might be the salvation of Cape. No matter how great a villain Yont was, he dared not injure the girl. His own ruffians would not stand for that. Since she was a witness of what had occurred, they could not get away with a story that young Crawford had been killed while trying to escape. In a way the scoundrel's stratagem had misfired.

Unfortunately Rogers was not wholly convinced that his argument was sound. Yont was an unpredictable devil filled with hate.

20 THE COWBOY RED CARRIED CAPE Crawford's supper to the cabin where he was confined, but Yont walked beside him to forestall any attempt at escape. June was sitting on a dilapidated old buggy seat beside the door.

"You'd better go home," the ranchman said angrily. "There will be no food for you at my place. If you weren't a woman, I'd fling you in with your brother. It's my opinion you are as guilty as he is."

"Why don't you get wise?" June told him scornfully. "You laid a trap and it failed. If you don't free my brother, a dozen men will be killed. It will be the end of the Quarter Circle F Y. All the hillmen who hate you will join us."

His bulbous eyes stared at her. This was a possibility that had not occurred to him before. He brushed it aside contemptuously. For years he had bullied the nesters up the creeks and had them cowed.

"Don't try to frighten me, you little fool," he stormed. "I'm going through with this. I've sent for Sheriff Crane. That rustler in there is going to the penitentiary."

He took the cabin key from his pocket, pushed past her, and unlocked the door. Red took the food inside.

Cape said, "So you've changed your plan. Or is that just a stall?"

"Don't get sassy with me or I'll beat you into a rag,"

Yont threatened. "I don't have to take any lip from you if I do from that shrew."

He locked the door and strode away.

Red walked back to the kitchen. Resentment simmered in him. That was no way to treat a lady, especially a girl as pretty as this one. He said to the cook, "Fix me up another plate of grub and some coffee, Monte."

The cowboy knew he was asking for trouble. He was an easygoing young fellow, one who avoided difficulties when he could, but he had the deep respect for women that was the heritage of many outdoor Westerners. Since he had been present when Yont insulted the Crawford girl, he had in a sense been a party to it. He was not going to let that stigma rest on him.

June accepted the plate and the coffee, her eyes warm and bright. She was touched at the kindness of this grinning redheaded boy. She knew he was going over the head of Yont to do this, and if the rancher found it out, he would be furious. He would vent his accumulated anger on Red.

"You ought not to have brought me this food," she reproached. "But it is very good of you. I hope it won't make you trouble."

She was just through eating when Yont strode across the yard from the house. "Who gave you that food?" he demanded.

"Kindness of Mr. Yont," she answered.

"I said, who brought it to you?"

June had no intention of telling him. "I don't know all the Quarter Circle F Y hands," she told him.

In a blazing rage Yont walked to the kitchen. "Who took supper to that woman?" he wanted to know.

Manuel hesitated. Yont grabbed the Mexican's shirt at the throat and hit him in the face. "When I ask a question, answer it."

The cook named Red. It was the cowboy's grief and not his.

"Tell him I want to see him at the house *pronto*," Yont ordered.

Manuel found Red at the stable and delivered the message. The range rider looked at the cook's bruised cheek.

"My fault for getting you into this, Manuel," he said. It was in his mind that his own punishment was going to be far worse.

Limpy was in the office with Yont when the cowboy arrived. His eyes were bright with excitement. This was going to be good. Yont's ferocious rage was about to explode on a victim who had invited trouble.

"So you took it on yoreself to feed that wench from the Flying W," the ranchman blared at him. "After I told her she would get no food here."

Red shifted his weight uneasily from one foot to the other. "I reckoned you wouldn't want a lady to go hungry," he explained.

"You reckoned!" Yont barked. "I do the thinking here. When I hire a man he belongs to me. If he takes my money and eats my grub, he backs every play I make. You're too big for yore boots, you dumb lunkhead, and right now I'm going to cut you down to size."

Red knew he could not escape a beating. A surge of anger swept through him and crowded down the fear. It would do him no good to eat crow. He might as well speak out and save his self-respect.

"In regards to that, Mr. Yont, I hired out to chouse cows. The thirty dollars a month doesn't include doing a meanness to a nice young lady."

"You butted in to keep me from doing that little hell-cat a meanness, did you? I'm going to learn you who is boss." Yont spoke through gritted teeth. His fists were knotted by his side.

"I quit," Red said. "Give me my time and I'll go."

Yont lashed out and drove his victim against the wall. With surprising quickness for his age and weight, the ranchman was across the floor to fling a left and right into the other's face. Red raised his arms as a shield and a heavy fist slammed into his stomach. He clawed at Yont's coat, trying to get inside the blows, and an uppercut to the chin made his head bounce back. A weak blow landed on the big man's cheek. Yont battered the ribs and face of the cowboy.

Red's arms hung helpless. His knees buckled and his body slid down the wall to the floor. Yont dragged him to his feet and propped him in a corner, his fists hammering at the semiconscious man. The range rider went down again, to be kicked savagely in the ribs. He passed out completely.

The fury of Yont subsided. He looked at his skinned and bloody knuckles. "Seems like I always bust them when I beat up a guy," he mentioned.

Limpy went to the water bucket and took out the dipper. He sloshed its contents on the face of the prone man.

"Give him the whole bucketful," Yont growled. "And after he comes to fling him out. Tell him to saddle and beat it. He's through here." The rancher straddled out of the room nursing his abraded knuckles in the palm of the other hand.

Limpy poured the rest of the water over Red's bloody head. The eyes of the cowboy flickered open. Still glazed, they did not focus well. It took him a few moments to realize what had occurred.

"He sure jounced me round a-plenty," the beaten man murmured, with a touch of whimsy to keep up appearances. "The old man give me enough and then some. His big fists most tore me to pieces."

"You fought like an old woman, but I give you good for knowin' how to take a whaling," the lame man said. "Yont left orders for you to fork yore bronc and ride."

"Suits me, after I get my pay check." Red got laboriously to his feet. Waves of nausea swept through him. Every muscle and bone seemed to be a center of pain.

"Better not bother about that," Limpy warned. "He might give an encore performance."

"Think so," the cowboy said quietly. "Well, he'll get the chance certain."

Red walked to the door and leaned against the jamb for a few moments to steady himself. He went down the porch steps carefully and made his way slowly to the bunkhouse. From his roll he took a forty-four and tested it. This he pushed down beneath his trousers belt. Strength was gradually flowing back into his battered body. He packed his blanket roll, took it to the corral, then roped and saddled his horse.

Yont was standing by the outdoor blacksmith shop

watching a man grease a wagon. Red led the bronco toward him. June moved forward from the cabin where her brother was locked up. She was shocked at the distorted face of the cowboy. It was a map of cuts and wheals. One eyes was completely closed.

"You poor man," she said gently. "I'm awf'ly sorry. I suppose he beat you because you gave me supper. If I had known——"

A painful grin showed on the battered face. "Think nothing of it, Miss. I'll be good as new in a day or two."

"You're leaving?" she asked.

"That's right. I'm plumb ashamed I ever worked here."

Her gaze shifted for a moment to Yont, who was watching them angrily. "You had better hurry and go," she warned the cowboy. "Get word to my brother Pete how things are with Cape and me. He would be glad to have you on our ranch if you want a job."

"I'll sure get word to him pronto that Yont has got you." His eyes swept the yard and met the stormy unshifting stare of the man who had whipped him. He had for a moment a wild crazy idea of trying to rescue the Crawfords himself. But he realized it could not be done. Before he could get two horses saddled for them, he would be riddled with bullets.

"Don't be scared, Miss," he said. "Wolf though he is, he dassent lift a finger against you."

"It's Cape I worry about," June told him.

"He can't hurt the boy, not with you a witness against him. He has lost his chance."

Red moved toward the wagon holding the bridle rein in his left hand.

Yont glared at him, his fists balled. "I left word for you to get out of here, you lunkhead," he barked.

The bleached eyes of the cowboy did not waver. "I'm on my way, soon as you've paid me."

"I don't pay scalawags who disobey my orders." The rage in Yont exploded. "I'm going to beat you up so you'll remember it all yore life."

Red made a fast draw and covered the ranchman. "Don't try it," he said with deadly gentleness. "I'll send you to hell sudden."

The worm had turned. Yont was caught flatfooted. It had not occurred to him that a meek soft-spoken rider like Red could be dangerous. He said, playing for time, "Don't be a fool. I'm not armed."

"Don't bank on that," the cowboy gave notice. "I would as lief drill you. Better for everybody you were dead."

"You would never get away from here alive."

"I think different. Anyhow, you would be dead as a stuck shote." Red gave orders. "Put yore hands back of yore neck and lace the fingers. Bill, you step back of him, ram a hand in his pants' pocket, and get out the roll of greenbacks there."

Yont hesitated. He was half of a mind to charge, but the hard cold eyes of the puncher daunted him. He would never get across the fifteen feet between them without being cut down. Yet his arrogance would not let him surrender easily.

"You two-bit cowhand, you are digging yore own grave," he snarled.

The man who had been greasing the wagon remonstrated with Red. "Now, looky here, fellow, no sense in you going loco. Be reasonable and——"

"Cut the gab, Bill," snapped Red. "Do as I tell you. Yont, get yore hands up quick. Last chance."

Yont raised his arms reluctantly and laced his fingers behind the neck.

Bill drew from the trousers' pocket a roll of greenbacks.

"Skin off twenty bucks and lay the bills on that swingle-tree," Red directed.

Red stepped to the wagon, his eyes fixed on both of the men, and took the money. "Start for the house, Yont, hands still up," he said. "Take it easy and don't hurry. I'd love to get an excuse to pump lead into you."

There was murder in the ranchman's face before he moved, but the urge to kill had to be postponed. Slowly he obeyed the order given.

The cowboy's glance swept the yard to make sure that nobody was covering him with a rifle. Limpy sat on the porch steps in front of the house smoking a cigarette. He leaned back relaxed and easy. Plainly he did not intend to make this any of his business.

"I reckon you're not toting a hogleg, are you?" Red said to Bill.

"If I was, fellow, I'd be slammin' bullets at you," the man answered.

Red grinned without annoyance. "That's wouldn't be friendly, Bill." He added cheerfully, "The old man won't like you loafing on that grease job and him payin' you all of thirty plunks a month. Better hop to it."

The redheaded man's muscles were so sore and stiff that he had to try three times before he could pull himself into the saddle. As soon as his foot found the far stirrup, he wheeled the horse and jumped it to a gallop. He was in a hurry to reach the shelter of the cowbacked hills before the pursuit started.

June clapped her hands in approval as he passed her. She liked the spirit of the puncher in humiliating the bully who had hammered him so savagely.

21 UNTIL RED FOUND HIMSELF DEEP IN the huddled hills, his first concern had been for his safety. Yont was not one to take his mortification lightly. The riders of the Quarter Circle F Y would comb the barrancas for him and if found he would be rubbed out. But his flight had taken him in the general direction of the Flying W. He must let Pete Crawford know as soon as possible that his brother and sister had been captured by Yont.

He cut into an arroyo that ran between two slopes sown with yucca. It brought him to a ridge from which he looked down on the rolling country leading to the plain.

A winding silver ribbon edged wtih green marked the course of Dead Cow Creek and the willows bordering it.

From the foothills he emerged to the flats below, a country thick with brush. He could not take time to pick a way carefully and branches of mesquite and prickly pear flogged his legs and hands. His cowpony dropped down the three-foot wall of a wash, plowed across the sandy floor, and scrambled up the opposite bank like a climbing cat. The fear of what Yont might do was driving him. It was not reasonable to suppose that the man would dare to injure his captives, but the savagery of the fellow was unpredictable. He might use some trickery to destroy the boy.

Red came out of a hollow and pulled up abruptly. A rider was moving along the ridge not fifty yards from him. In another minute they would meet. The cowboy whipped out his revolver and shouted a warning. "Get yore hands on the horn and leave 'em there."

His eyes not lifting from the other man, Red rode forward slowly. The young fellow, not much more than twenty-one, was in store clothes. If he carried any weapon, it was not in sight. He had stopped, his fingers clasped around the horn.

"I'm not looking for trouble, Red," he said.

The cowboy stared at him and slowly recognition came. He was Billy Yont, the boy who had been driven from home by his father's cruelty.

"I'll be doggoned," Red exclaimed. "Where did you drap in from?"

"From San Diego, California. I been working in a railroad shop. Came back to see my mother."

"Yore mother? Why, Billy, she died 'most two years ago. Didn't you know that?"

Young Yont's face tightened. He was bracing himself to take the blow. "She quit writing," he said after a moment of silence. "I thought mebbe he wouldn't let her write any more. I hoped that, but I guessed I knew how it was all the time." He swallowed a lump in his throat.

"You aimin' to go to the ranch?" asked Red.

"No, not now. There is nobody there I want to see."

"Good for you. I quit today."

"Have you been in a fight?" Billy inquired.

"Ride along with me. I got no time to lose."

As they rode, Red told by snatches the story of what had occurred. Billy stopped when they came to a wagon trail pointing toward Rifle.

"I reckon this is where we part," he told his companion. "The Crawfords won't want anybody named Yont to side them."

"How do you know that? They need all the help they can get. Mebbe they won't trust me either, but I'll have to take a chance on that."

Billy hesitated. "All right," he decided. "The worst they can do is kick me out."

Pete Crawford and Rufe Rogers returning from Rifle followed them into the Flying W yard almost before they had swung from their saddles.

The surprise in Pete's face turned instantly to hostility. His eyes grew agate-hard.

Red spoke swiftly. "Yont has captured Cape and Miss Crawford."

"So he sent you here to tell me," Pete retorted in a grinding voice. "Only a pair of fools would bring that message to me."

"He doesn't know we're here." Red's level gaze did not fall away. "Billy and I are through with that devil forever."

"Sounds likely." There was a controlled fury in Crawford's set lean face. "Do you deny that you came straight from his ranch?"

"No. I did, not Billy. Listen, Pete, and get this right."

"I've got it right. You're fronting for one of Yont's damnable tricks."

Rogers intervened. There was something here he did not understand. Red's battered face, his urgency, a kindly gentleness in him he had noted while working at the Quarter Circle F Y. These did not tie in with Pete's angry interpretation of his presence.

"I'm not so sure of that, Pete," he protested. "I think Red is a good guy. Let's hear what he has to say."

"All right," Crawford conceded reluctantly. "I don't have to believe him."

"First off, I'll say that just before I left the ranch, Yont gave me the darndest licking I ever had. He was sore at

Miss Crawford for staying there with her brother. He wanted her to get out and she wouldn't go. So he figured he would starve her out. I took her food and he didn't like it. Consequence was he whaled me till I passed out. He had a right enjoyable time."

"Then you saddled up and slipped away," Rogers said.

"After I had collected twenty bucks from him that he owed me."

"I'm surprised he paid you."

"So was he." Red chuckled. "He didn't want to, but he changed his mind when I covered him with my hogleg."

Pete brushed this talk aside. "Are you telling me that June is not a prisoner, that she can leave whenever she wishes?"

"That's how it is. Grattan, Limpy, and another fellow jumped Cape in the park below the red rock wall. They were fixing to hang him as a rustler when Miss Crawford came flying out of a barranca and spoiled their game. They took Cape to the ranch and she went along. It was mighty annoyin' to Yont after he had fixed up a trap so nice, to catch somebody in it he sure could of got along without."

"You think he won't do any harm to Cape while she is there?"

"He can't, Pete. The story they were aimin' to tell wouldn't hold water now. Yont claims he sent one of his men to Rifle to get Sheriff Crane. The play now is to try to send Cape to the pen for rustling. Leastways, that's how it looks to me."

"You don't think Miss June is in any danger?" Rogers asked. With difficulty he kept his voice even and cool.

"Yont ain't plumb crazy," Red said. "He wants to keep on living."

"Howcome this Yont boy to be with you?" Crawford demanded.

"Just happenstance. I met him on the flats on my way here."

Billy Yont explained that he had returned from California to see his mother, had learned from Red of her death, and had at once given up the idea of going to the Quarter Circle F Y.

"Why come here?" Pete wanted to know brusquely.

"Red thought you might need a couple of extra men, so I threw in with him."

"You don't like your father," Rogers suggested gently.

Billy flushed angrily. "Would you like a man who had driven you and your sister from home and treated your mother like a slave?"

Rufe Rogers turned to Crawford. "The boys are on the level, Pete. Red didn't get his face worked over by running into a door. Yont's fists did it because he stood by your sister. As to Billy, everybody knows why he left home."

Pete offered his hand first to Red and then to Billy. "I'm obliged, Red," he said. "What you have told us is good news. We were aiming to rouse the hill nesters and clean up Yont's crew. But if my sister isn't a prisoner and Cape is going to be turned over to Crane, that may not be necessary. I don't want a dozen men killed."

"Fine," Rogers agreed. "The question now is where do we go from here. Crane won't be a party to any of Yont's deviltry. I'd bet heavily on that. But he might be fooled by some trickery. Maybe some of Yont's scoundrels have been given the word to see Cape doesn't reach Rifle alive. And as for Miss June, I am not going to be happy about her until we have her safely in our hands."

Billy Yont made a suggestion. "How about me going to the Quarter Circle F Y to find out what's doing? The old man won't be pleased to see me, but there isn't much that he can do about it except throw me off the place. He would have no reason to suspect that I had any interest in his prisoners. If I had a lot of luck, I might be able to free your brother."

"You wouldn't have that much luck," Rufe said. "But you've got an idea. Three or four of us could go along with you and stay hidden close to the ranch. You might be able to come back and let us know where Cape is locked up. If you saw Miss June, you could tell her where we were and she could slip away and join us. We couldn't make a move until she was out of that villain's hands."

"Unless we could get hold of Yont for a hostage," Red amended. "I would like that."

"How can you get hold of him when he has twenty warriors within call?" Pete asked, irritable because he could see no clear road ahead for him. "The whole thing is crazy, but there's an off chance we can pull it off. About one in a hundred. He'll have guards posted all night. Soon as we're discovered, the whole push will come swarming out like hornets."

"We must not be discovered," Rufe answered. He turned to Red. "Where does Yont sleep?"

"In the south room right off the porch. Limpy has a room opening into it. Yont keeps the door between them locked on his side. The point is for Limpy to be on the job if he needs him."

"You're forgetting the guards," Crawford reminded Rogers.

"Do you have any of that sleep medicine Doc Burgess left for me when I was wounded?"

Crawford's anxiety made his temper edgy, but he had a lot of respect for the judgment of Rogers. "Seems to me I saw the bottle in a closet the other day," he said testily. "What's in your mind?"

"The night guards," Rufe replied. "We brought a pint of whisky from Rifle today for rattlesnake bites. My idea may be cockeyed. Or it might work. We'll dope the whisky with the sleep stuff. There's a chance Billy might be able to feed it to the guards who would jump at a couple of snorts to help them make the hours pass quicker."

Billy said, a little alarmed, "The medicine isn't poisonous?"

Rogers grinned at him. "I'm still here. We'll give the lads just enough to send them off into a nice sleep."

Crawford chose four men to side him in this uncertain night ride. Young Yont and Red he had to have because they knew the locale. The other two were Rogers and Cherokee Bill. While they were saddling, Charley Runyon reached the ranch and insisted he had a right to go along. Crawford let him join the party.

It was a light night of a thousand stars. This made travel easier, but increased the danger at the end of their journey. They crossed some miles of spiny desert before taking to the rolling hills that led them up arroyos into a steep barranca from which they emerged to a pine-strewn ridge. The aromatic scent of the pines filled their nostrils as they waited for a few moments to discuss the best approach to the Quarter Circle F Y lying in the valley below the far edge of the mesa.

From here Red took the lead instead of Crawford. He turned into a dry water run bringing them to a slope of saguaros standing out stark and ghostly in the moonlight. Down this hillside they moved to the blurred outline of the brush-floored gulch below. The clatter of branches violently thrust aside startled them as a buck plunged out of the thicket and bounded into the shadowy night.

At the next small rise, Red pointed to the ranch sleeping in the moonlight. It looked peaceful as a New England Sabbath morning.

22 RED LED THE WAY DOWN INTO A pocket back of the cottonwoods flanking the buildings. All of the party dismounted except Billy Yont.

"Keep your chin up, boy," Crawford said. "We're depending on you."

"Maybe I'll get a break," Billy answered.

He skirted the cottonwoods and rode up the short lane leading to the yard. A dog barked furiously and raced toward him. He swung from the saddle and called, "Down, Rover, down." The dog recognized him and leaped up joyfully to greet its returning master.

From the shadowy darkness of one of the buildings a voice flung out a demand. "Who is it?"

Young Yont gave his name. A man carrying a rifle moved

cautiously into the light. "I'll be doggoned if it ain't Billy!" he exclaimed. "So you came home at last."

"Right, Freckles. What's the idea of the gun at this time of night?"

"The old man has got a prisoner in the root house and we're keepin' tabs on him so he won't get away. One of the Crawford boys. Thought you said you weren't ever coming back."

"A fellow changes his mind," Billy replied. "I want to talk with Father about my mother's death. All I heard was that she had died."

"Two years ago come fall. Fact is she kinda pined away after you and Miss Jeanie left."

"Is Father as rambunctious as ever?"

"You bet. He beat up one of the boys today something fierce. Red. You prob'ly remember him."

"Sure. What's this about one of the Crawfords being a prisoner?"

"Some of the boys caught him rustlin' and yore daddy is fixin' to send him to the pen. Funny thing. His sister is here too. She's scared to leave him and she's sleeping on a cot outside the root house."

"What's she scared of?"

"Two-three of the boys were kinda set to string the kid up on a live oak. Mostly talk, I reckon."

Another man came across the yard to join them. He too had a Winchester. His opaque eyes rested suspiciously on the newcomer.

"Meet Mr. Grattan," Freckles said. "This is Billy Yont."

"Glad to meetcha," Grattan drawled. "Kinda late. You going to wake up the old man?"

"I've waited several years, so I expect I can wait till morning to see him," Billy said sardonically. "He isn't going to kill any fatted calf for me." Apparently moved by an impulse he added: "Maybe I had better celebrate my homecoming now with you boys or there may not be any."

He drew from his hip pocket the bottle of whisky and handed it to Freckles. "Drink hearty, oldtimer."

Freckles' eyes brightened. "You must of reformed since you left here. You didn't drink then."

"I was a kid. Now I'm grown up."

"Down the hatch." Freckles accepted the invitation to drink heartily before he returned the bottle.

Grattan took four or five big swallows and Billy made a pretense of drinking. A second round followed and the third one emptied the bottle.

A young indignant voice cut into their talk. "So you're in on this rotten business," it said, the words directed at Billy.

He turned, to face June Crawford. As small children they had gone to the same country school, but he had not seen her for seven years. For some time before he left, she had been away at Denver and when she was at home during the summers there had been no neighborly meeting.

"I got in from California tonight," he told her.

She had developed from a wild tomboy into a lovely woman. The nostrils in the fine face were delicately fashioned. In every line of her was the look of clean pride. The change from a tousled child was amazing.

She said, scorn etched with anger, "California's loss is Arizona's gain."

Grattan could not take his gaze from her. In his sultry eyes was the look that undressed women. "I'd like to have the job of taming this little vixen," he said in a murmur.

Billy spoke hurriedly in the hope that June had not heard. "You oughtn't to be here, Miss June. This little jam your brother is in will straighten out. I'd be glad to run up your horse and see you get home safely."

"I'm not here in this nest of miscreants because I like it," she answered bitterly. "But I'm not going home until I know my brother is safe."

He could see in her shadowed eyes how worried she was. In the presence of the guards he could say nothing to relieve her mind. He considered whipping out his revolver to cover the men while she ran to join her friends back of the cottonwoods. But that would be to upset the plan agreed upon for trying to rescue Cape. He could not hold the guards quiet if they knew Flying W riders were crouched not more than two hundreds yards distant. They would certainly give the alarm.

The doctored whisky was beginning to affect Freckles. He was yawning and his eyes were dulling. But it did not seem to have reached Grattan. The fellow was not at all sure of Yont. His narrowed eyes shifted with misgiving from him to June and back again.

"Run along to the bunkhouse, kid, and get yore sleep," he told Billy craftily. "We don't need you here. I'm in charge of this situation."

"I'm not a bit sleepy," Billy answered. "Glad to help out if I can."

"Get going," ordered the Texan harshly.

Billy did not know what to do. If he stood his ground, the big fellow would start trouble. In case of a fight some of the men in the bunkhouse would be awakened and come pouring out. After that no surprise would be possible. He did not like to leave June alone with this ruffian and the sleepy Freckles, yet it would be only for a little while. He could bypass the bunkhouse and report to Pete Crawford how things stood.

"Well, I've had a long ride today and I'll turn in," Billy said. "You better go to sleep too, Miss June. Cape will be all right when Sheriff Crane comes and he explains the mistake."

"Sure, if the sheriff comes," Grattan amended, a jeer in his slurred words.

Billy swung to the saddle. "I'll go water my bronc first and turn it into the pasture," he mentioned.

Freckles' drowsy voice reached him as he turned away. "I'm so dadgummed sleepy I can't keep my eyes open," he complained.

Yont passed the bunkhouse and rode into the cotton-wood grove.

The pressure of the dragging minutes crowded on Rufe. They had embarked on this venture as a forlorn hope because they could think of no better plan of action, but he knew that success depended upon a whole bundle of *ifs*. It was all very well to reason that Yont dared not injure June or her brother, yet even if he controlled his anger one of his ruffians might take advantage of the girl's defenseless situation. Two or three of them were abandoned villains who had crossed in vice the point of no return.

Out of the dark grove Billy rode into the moonlit pocket.

The news he brought was both good and bad. Cape and his sister were still unharmed. He had talked with June in the presence of the guards, but had not been able to give her even a hint that her friends were near. There were two watchmen. Between them they had finished the pint of whisky. One was very drowsy, the other apparently not affected at all. From something Grattan had said, he guessed that Yont had not sent for the sheriff. He did not like the Texan's manner toward Miss Crawford. It suggested that ideas were simmering in his twisted mind.

Pete Crawford said harshly, "Time I took a hand."

"Anybody seem to be awake except the watchmen?" Rogers asked.

"No. The buildings are dark."

While they had been waiting for Billy, the Flying W men had decided to divide their force. Rufe and Pete were to make sure that June was protected while the others roused Fen Yont and took from him the key to the log cabin where Cape was imprisoned. Nothing in Billy's report caused them to change the program.

With Rover at the heels of young Yont, the larger party circled on foot the corral and moved into the pasture back of the yard in order to reach the big house without being seen. They crept up to it in the bright moonlight and tiptoed along the porch to the room at the end where Yont slept. The others stood lined close to the wall while Billy knocked on the door lightly. He wanted to awaken his father without arousing Limpy.

It was not until his third knock that a sleepy voice demanded, "Who is it?"

"It's Billy—your son. I just got back from California."

"Why wake me at this time of night? I don't want ever to see you again."

"I've got news—about Pete Crawford. I think you had better hear it."

They could hear Yont's feet hit the floor as he rose. He fumbled around in the darkness for a moment before he came to the door and opened it. He was in his nightgown and his right hand held a revolver.

"Spill your news and then get out," he ordered. Out of the tail of his eye he caught sight of the men pressed against the wall. There was time to recognize only the one nearest—Red.

"You damned traitor!" he cried at his son, and whipped up his weapon to fire.

By a fraction of a second Red beat his time. The cowboy's rifle barrel dropped on his head and the world exploded for him temporarily. He went down like a log.

23 AFTER BILLY YONT DISAPPEARED BEhind the bunkhouse on his way to report to Pete Crawford, the Texan Grattan felt free to deal with June. Freckles had slumped down against the wall of the cabin where Cape was locked up and was already asleep and snoring.

The gambler's smile was meant to be ingratiating. "That kid had a good idea, Miss Crawford, but he isn't the man to carry it out. This is no place for you. Yont isn't to be trusted. I'll saddle horses and take you home. It will be a nice ride in the moonlight."

"And on the way you can tame the vixen," June said, a bite to her voice.

"Sho, that didn't mean a thing," he protested. "You had been cussin' me out and I had to say something. I like my women with ginger. I wouldn't have you different."

"You don't know how to talk to a woman without insulting her," June told him and turned to go.

He caught her by the arm. "You're not leaving me, Miss. I've taken a shine to you."

"Let go my arm!" she ordered stormily. "Are you a complete fool? A few hours ago you had a rope around my brother's neck to hang him."

"We'll forget that. This is between you and me. I'm telling you that we are pulling out from this ranch now."

"No. I would as soon trust Yont as you."

He put an arm around her slender body to draw it close. The barrel of her small pistol pushed against his ribs. He jumped back quickly, sweeping her arm aside.

"Goddlemighty, you little devil!" he cried. "Don't play tricks like that. You might kill me."

"If I must, I'll do just that," she told him. "Don't ever lay a hand on me again."

"You young hellcat, I believe you would." His wolfish eyes lit with desire. The liquor had fired his brain and dulled his prudence so that nothing counted with him but the moment's urge.

From the room where he was locked, Cape called to his sister. "If that scoundrel Grattan is annoying you, shout for help and rouse the men in the bunkhouse."

"I will," she answered. "Don't worry about that."

In the instant while June's attention was diverted to answer, Grattan's hairy fingers wrenched the weapon from her hand and his other fist slammed against her chin. June fell back against the wall and her knees buckled. Before her body reached the ground, he snatched her up and started to the corral, the palm of one hand covering her mouth to prevent a cry.

Before reaching the stable, he discovered she was unconscious. Groping in the darkness, he found a bridle and saddle. Carrying the double load, cinch and bridle reins dragging in the dust, he walked to the corral. After laying the girl down close to the fence, he freed the rawhide rope from the saddle to catch one of the four horses in the corral. He had never been a top-notch cowboy and was a bad roper. The ponies raced around the enclosure to keep from being caught and the loop he threw slid from the sides of the animals as they flew past. He made a half dozen casts before the rope fell true. Angry at the delay, he jerked the rope savagely and the captured horse went into the air in a wild effort to escape. It was two or three minutes be-

155

fore he could get the sorrel to stand still enough to get the saddle adjusted.

Grattan led the skittish horse to the place where he had left June. She was rising slowly to her feet and when he came near he could see the terror in her eyes. Her cry for help rang out in the night.

When Pete Crawford and Rufe Rogers crept up the yard to the cabin where Cape was detained, they found neither June nor Grattan. The other guard was lying beside the cabin snoring lustily. Cape was hammering, evidently with his fists, against the inside wall, crying, "Let me out! Let me out!" When he learned that his friends were outside, he blurted the information that Grattan had taken June with him.

"How long since?" Rogers asked.

"Not five minutes ago. Claimed he is going to take her home, but he was lying. He must have knocked her out. She didn't cry out while he was dragging her away."

"Which way did they go?"

"Toward the stable. I think he means to saddle and take her with him. Hurry—hurry!"

Rogers started on the run. Pete stopped a moment to explain to his brother that the other boys were rousing Yont to get a key to release him.

As Rogers passed the stable, he drew up for a moment to make sure Grattan was not there. He did not expect to find him in the stable. When he and Pete had come out of the cottonwoods fifty yards from the corral, he had heard the sound of racing horses in the enclosure. Something had disturbed the animals. Probably a man trying to rope one of them. The fear was strong in his mind that he might be too late.

He was still a stone's throw from the corral when June's cry for help reached him. He wasted no breath in answering it. There was no need to warn Grattan that her friends were near.

When he tore through the gate, Grattan was lifting the struggling girl to the back of the horse. He did not find it easy. The skittish horse backed away when one of June's feet struck it in the flank.

156

Grattan cursed savagely, threatening to knock her cold if she did not stop fighting him. At sight of the approaching man he dropped June and reached for his revolver. His thought was that the runner was one of the Quarter Circle F Y men.

"Beat it, fellow," he ordered. "I'm taking this girl home."

"That's a lie. He is——" The girl's explanation broke off into a glad cry of recognition. "Rufe—Rufe!"

A bullet whistled past the shoulder of Rogers. In his present position he could not return the fire since June was just behind Grattan. He dived for the shelter of the watering trough at the foot of the windmill.

As June rose from the ground, she picked up from the hoof-chopped earth of the corral a double handful of dust. When she passed Grattan, running along the fence to get out of the line of fire, she flung the powdered soil into the air to blind him. The man's second shot went wild. He tried to brush the dust from his eyes with the sleeve of his coat, the gun in his hand still hammering.

The first shot of Rogers was a miss. The bullet struck the saddle horn above the plunging horse. The next slug plowed into the stomach of the big ruffian. Grattan staggered out of the dust cloud and caught at the fence to steady himself. He slid down, his back against the rails. The shock of the wound showed in his haunted eyes. Though he must have known that he had come to the end of his road, the weapon in his fingers still blazed defiance at the enemy. With two more bullets in him, he kept firing until he had emptied the forty-four. Very slowly his body settled into itself and sagged to the left. Before his head touched the ground he was dead.

Rogers held his gaze on the prone huddled figure, the smoking gun still in his hand. He moved forward slowly a few steps before lifting his eyes to June. Stark fear had not yet been blotted from the girl's face. When she could find words to speak, it was to say in a hushed voice, "You're not hurt?"

"No. Thanks to you. If you hadn't blinded his eyes——" The sentence hung in air. She understood the unspoken conclusion.

157

A small moan of distress broke from her lips and she lifted her hands to him. He pushed the revolver into its holster as he moved quickly to her. His arm went around her waist to steady her.

"It's all over now," he comforted her gently.

The sound of a gun racketed across the yard to them. Voices lifted into the night. The figures of shifting men appeared in the moonlight. The crash of forty-fives beat an angry crescendo.

He caught the saddled horse and lifted her to the hull. "We've got to get out of here into the cottonwoods," he told her. "Our boys are trying to rescue Cape."

His place was with her until she was safely in the pocket back of the grove. The firing was already coming closer. His friends were retreating and soon would join them where the horses were tied.

Rufe led the horse into the grove and through it. The hammering of the guns was slackening. The Flying W men had reached the shelter of the trees, and Yont's men, still in the open, did not care to press the attack with the advantage against them. Roused from sleep by the shooting in the corral, the cowboys from the bunkhouse did not know how many of the enemy they faced. To have driven them from the yard was all the victory they wanted to risk.

The Crawford party came to the rendezvous, not bunched but singly. Cape and Red were the first to arrive. Pete and Cherokee Bill brought up the rear, supporting young Yont, who was slightly wounded in the leg.

Runyon gave a whoop at sight of the girl. "Miss June is here!" he cried.

After Billy Yont had been lifted to the saddle, Pete made his way among the horses to his sister.

"You all right?" he asked.

"Yes. Let's go." She was still weak from the fear that had flooded her.

Pete turned to Rogers. "You had trouble with Grattan?"

"I had to kill him." Rufe had been counting heads. "All here. Anybody hurt but Billy?"

"No. The darkness saved us. Billy will be all right." Pete swung to the saddle. "All up? We'll hit the trail."

On the long ride home, Pete filled in for Rufe the facts

158

about his brother's rescue. After Yont had been knocked out, his son found the key to the log cabin in his father's pocket. As the men tramped down from the porch, they could hear Limpy call to the rancher, "What's wrong, Fen?" The guns in the corral fight were already roaring and men began to pour out of the bunkhouse. Pete had to stay and join in the battle that followed. The men scattered, and in the dim light it was hard to know friend from foe. Undoubtedly this saved lives. Most of the shots were flung out wildly with no deliberate aim.

Pete remained with young Yont while the boy unlocked the door of the log cabin. By that time Limpy had got into action. It was a shot from his pistol that had struck Billy. Crawford and Cherokee Bill turned their fire on the lame man and one of them must have hit him. They had seen the weapon transferred from one hand to the other. To avoid further fire, Pete and the Indian had helped Billy to the pasture behind the cabin and came to the grove by a path back of the bunkhouse.

It was not until the men were rehashing the battle after they reached the Flying W that Runyon reminded his companions of the one humorous feature of the affair. Despite the drumming of the guns, Freckles had continued to snore contentedly all through the fight.

Cape came to the door of the bunkhouse and said, "Can you come up to the house a minute, Rufe?" As they crossed the yard, he explained, "Sis wants wants to see you."

June was waiting on the porch. Her brother asked her if Pete was taking care of Billy Yont.

"Yes," she answered. "Perhaps you can help him."

Alone with Rogers, June did not find it easy to talk. Her hand rested on the porch railing and Rufe noticed that it was trembling.

"You've had a terrible day," he said. "What you need is a good night's sleep."

She stood for a long time looking into the darkness before she turned to him.

"I keep seeing that man trying to kill you," she said, her low husky voice close to a break.

"What I think of is that you prevented it," he answered.

"By half-blinding him so that he couldn't see. That I'll never forget."

June gave that no weight. She was emotionally overwrought. All day she had been keyed up to face one danger after another. The crises past, she was suffering a reaction of jittery nerves.

"If you hadn't come to the corral——"

In her haunted eyes was the horror of what might have been.

"But I did. Put it all out of your mind as if it were a bad dream."

"I don't want to put it out of my mind, not all of it. Of course, you think I am spoiled and willful. It's no wonder you don't like me." A confession, wistful and reluctant, fell from her lips. "I can't go to sleep and leave it that way."

She had never been more lovely, he thought. For the first time he saw her as a young girl humble and unsure of herself, all her self-contained pride swept away. She was like a child pleading for forgiveness.

He told himself he must keep a tight rein on his response. The unconscious wish was in her that he would take her in his arms and kiss her. It was what he very much wanted to do, but he must not take advantage of a girl's weakness reaching for strength.

"But you are wrong," he said guardedly. "I like you very much."

"Then we're friends," she cried softly, and gave him both her hands, gifts in her eyes.

In another moment she was in his arms and he was kissing her.

Pete's voice came to them. "June," it called.

They heard his steps moving toward the porch.

Rufe stepped back from June hurriedly.

24 LIMPY LOOKED ACROSS THE TABLE at the huge figure slumped in a chair opposite him. "You don't have much luck with these brash boys at the Flying W, do you?" he jeered.

"I've got a bunch of numbskulls working for me," Yont blurted out. "Every last one of them blundering fools. And no loyalty in any of them."

"You can't buy loyalty with a whip," Limpy suggested. He had sold his gun to Yont, but he neither respected nor liked him.

A dull color beat into the ranchman's cheeks. "Half of them would sell me out if they dared. Not an hour ago two of them got their time and rode away. I asked the quitters what was eating them. All they would say was that they guessed they would drift up to New Mexico. I told the rats that what ailed them was they had no guts."

"Maybe they don't like to be shot up." Limpy let his eyes drop to the bandage covering his hand. "Not at the price. You're a tightfisted old ranikabo and you squeeze a dollar till it screams. The boys have an idea that thirty bucks a month covers riding the brush twelve or fourteen hours a day, but not carrying on a private war for you."

"The government gets plenty of men to fight for thirteen dollars a month," Yont snarled.

"Yeah, but you're not Uncle Sam, regardless of any ideas you have of being Mr. Cock-a-Doodle-Do out here." Limpy's cold fishy eyes rested on his employer. "And since we're swappin' compliments, they have a gripe at you beatin' up Red because he took grub to the Crawford girl. They are tickled to death that he stuck you up for the wages coming to him."

161

"I'm not through with that two-bit brush-popper." Anger flared in Yont's bulging eyes. "You're a fine one to turn pious—after putting a rope around the kid brother's neck."

"If you want to know I'm glad a dozen-times a day that his sister got there in time. I hated what I was doing. How you and Grattan ever talked me into such a hellish business I don't know. I've gone bad. I'm a killer. But I don't belong in yore class. Another thing you might like to know. Every man on the ranch is glad that the Texas gunman Rogers rubbed out Grattan."

"That suited me fine. The fool had gone crazy. I don't pay my hands to grind their own corn in my mill. If he had got away with the girl, I would have been blamed. Only I'd of liked it better if both him and Rogers had been blasted off the map." Yont pushed that out of his mind to face the sneering insurrection of the lame man. There was rumbling menace in his harsh voice. "If you are trying to pick a row with me, it's waiting for you right damn now. I never sidestepped a fight in my life."

Limpy's vigilant eyes held fast to those of his employer. Not a muscle of his body moved. It was as tense and ready as that of a cat at a rat hole. Yont had flung out a challenge he could take up or leave. A faint derisive smiled lurked at the corners of his thin-lipped mouth. He spoke softly but with no indecision.

"Let's put it this way, Yont. I get double pay from you. That buys my gun up to a certain point. I'll decide what that point is. If that suits you, fine; if it doesn't, why, I am waiting at the gate for any other arrangement that suits you."

Yont choked down his choler. He had need of this man. It would be folly to force the issue he had raised. Sitting as close to each other as they were, if weapons were drawn both of them would probably be killed.

"We're making bad medicine," he said irascibly. "We're on the same side. I sent for you to talk over our next step. There is something in what you say. No sense in working up public sentiment against us. So I'm against any more killing just now. I have another idea in my head." He let his ill-humor show petulantly. "If your conscience won't be shocked at driving up into Lost Park two-three hundred Flying W cows. There will be a nice piece of money in it for you and the others that help with the gather. It will be night work. Practically no danger, so the timid boys do not need to be afraid."

"It can be done if we are lucky," agreed Limpy, ignoring the sneer.

"Not once only but a dozen times. There's more than one way to skin a cat. You boys will rob the Crawfords poor and make a pot of dough doing it. You'll blot the brand and change it to a Box M, a brand I bought up from a nester seven or eight years ago."

"After we have rebranded the stuff you will own the lot," Limpy said. "That will be nice for you."

"Don't talk that way, Limpy," the ranchman reproached. "'All I want is a small cut, say twenty-five per cent of the profit. You get the same for handling the deal and the boys divide the rest. We have to use the Box M brand because it is the only one on record to which the Flying W can be changed without blotching."

Yont's argument was plausible. The **w** could be made into a 🔲 by the addition of a few strokes with a running iron. Later the stock could be driven across the line into New Mexico or sold to settlers in Northern Arizona. For several years rustlers had found it profitable to steal cattle in Mexico, run small herds across the line, and sell to the ranchers in the San Simon and Sulpher Springs valleys. There were outfits farther north which would be glad to buy without inquiring too closely into the legal ownership of stock offered for sale at half price.

"This will have to be worked carefully," Limpy said thoughtfully. "Some of your riders won't go along with rustling. What do you reckon to do with them?"

"Find an excuse to fire them. There aren't more than two or three. Old Diehard, Hank Ketchum, and maybe Santone. I picked my hands right careful."

"I'm sure you did." Limpy's voice carried the sting of obvious sarcasm. "You wanted boys brought up right, with a good shorter catechism background."

"We'll have to wait until the dark of the moon—say about the middle of next week. Quite a bunch of the Flying W stuff will be bedded in the meadows below the creek bed fairly close to water. You will have no trouble at all rounding up all you can handle."

"You wouldn't want to go along with us just to make sure, would you?" Limpy fleered.

"Not with a capable man like you in charge," Yont answered.

"So I'm capable now," Limpy murmured derisively. "Ten minutes ago I was a blundering fool and a numb-skull."

"Now—now, Limpy," Yont chided. "You know I wasn't including you. We got to work together in a friendly way."

"No sentiment," the range rider differed. "We're a pair of scoundrels setting out to steal yore neighbor blind. Let it go at that."

"We are protecting ourselves. That is all."

"Fine," the lesser ruffian amended. "I'm just a crook on the make, but you are an honest thief defending yore-self against a girl and her brothers who have the nerve to hold their own range and tell the world that you are a greedy miscreant."

"Is it necessary for you to make yoreself so damned unpleasant?" Yont demanded angrily.

"It relieves my feelings to admit that I am a no-account villain sold to Satan," the man answered. "Be seeing you in hell."

He waved a mocking hand and limped out of the room.

Yont's gaze followed him, rage in his sultry eyes. A month ago he had his men eating out of his hand. He had been the overlord of this whole district. Everybody except the Crawfords had been cowed and it looked like an easy task to crush them. Now even his own men could stand up and insult him to his face. When he went to Rifle he could see the change in the eyes of those on the street. They gloated over his predicament. One man had done this to him—the Texan Rogers. His audacity and his gun had sparked the smoldering resentment of the entire district. As long as the fellow lived, Yont would have no peace of mind.

25 TWO HORSEMEN SAT THEIR MOUNTS at the edge of the mesa and looked down at the valley through which Dead Cow Creek wound its way. There was a fringe of green willows here and there along the bank, but back of it the terrain was baked and dry. The only vegetation that showed from this height was a thin spread of cactus and greasewood, but the riders knew that close to the ground lay a scatter of alfilerilla, a pin-grass fed by the spring rains and now dried on the stem to make edible forage. Usually a sizable bunch of cattle grazed here, but in the past hour they had seen only two lone steers and a maverick calf.

The sun beat down from a brassy sky on the parched earth. Red took the big hat, shapeless with age, from his head and wiped away sweat beaded on his forehead.

"Hotter than hell with the lid on," he grumbled.

Cherokee grunted. His mind was occupied by something else. A suspicion was beginning to filter into his thoughts.

"Never before saw this range so filled with absentees," Red commented. "The cows must be having a Fourth of July somewheres."

The Indian offered laconic explanation. "Quarter Circle F Y heap busy."

Red slapped a hand on his shiny chaps. "Sure. Rounded up and drove away the whole shebang in this valley. Last night. The stuff was here yesterday."

Cherokee Bill wheeled his horse and jumped it to a gallop. Red did not need to ask him where he was going. They must get the news to the Flying W as quickly as they could.

It was mid-afternoon by the time they reached the

ranch. With the exception of the three men Pete Crawford always left now to guard the homesteading, the others were scattered on the range. Messengers went out to call them in, but the sun was sliding down toward the western hills before Pete and Rufe Rogers arrived to lead a posse of the ranch hands. Meanwhile, June had been busy helping Juan cook and pack food for the party. It might be two or three days before they returned. They baked bread and two hams, filled gunny sacks with flour, bacon, beans, and other necessities, and put out on the porch a large coffee pot, a Dutch oven, skillets, tin plates, cups, knives, and spoons. All of these Cherokee Bill loaded on a pack horse, throwing a diamond hitch to hold them securely.

Before the riders reached the valley where the cattle had been rounded up, darkness blanketed the land. Two of the boys roped dead branches of cottonwoods and dragged them to the camp ground. By the flickering light of the fire they devoured the food Juan cooked, squatted afterward in idle talk for half an hour before its glow speculating about the raid, then rolled up in their blankets for sleep. One man remained on guard, to be relieved later in the night. At the first gleam of dawn they were up.

There was no difficulty in finding the spot where the stock had been rounded up. The trail out of the valley was easy to spot, and for some miles it could be followed into the foothills. But it led into a district torn by earthquakes centuries ago, an uptilted waste of jagged rock-strewn slopes, dizzy scarps, and yawning precipices among which they early lost the sign of driven cattle. In this wild region there was less chance of finding and surprising the rustlers than of being shot down by them from any one of a hundred ledges.

They camped the second night in a walled pocket offsetting a cañon studded with dead blackened trees destroyed by a forest fire. It was a wild lonesome spot. The men were depressed by a day of hard riding that promised no results. In these mountain fastnesses there was little hope of running down those who wanted to remain hidden.

Runyon cheered them by singing snatches of songs in

which one or two of the others joined. Rufe Rogers drew Pete Crawford to one side and made a suggestion.

"We're not going to get anywhere keeping together in a bunch. It looks as if these fellows aimed to hole up in the hills for a spell, but we can't even be sure of that. They may be pushing through the mountains to unload the stuff to some ranchers around the Tonto Basin. You ought to send a man up one of the trails to find out if your cattle are being sold up there."

Crawford nodded. "Couldn't do any harm, except to the man I sent scouting if they caught him." He thought this over for a moment. "I would go myself, but I can't leave here."

"I'll be your rep," Rogers offered. "A careful man won't find it dangerous."

"Are you a careful man?" Pete asked dryly.

"I haven't ever been killed yet."

Runyon's voice drifted to them. He was singing a spiritual.

> Oh! My Lawd's a battle-ax,
>   A battle-ax, a battle-ax,
> Oh! My Lawd's a battle-ax,
>   A shelter in de time ob storm.

"Maybe I had better send Charley," Crawford said with a smile. "He seems sure he has a stand-in above."

"Send both of us. I'm convinced Yont is going to keep driving the herd till he is clear out of this district before he stops to do any re-branding. If we keep our eyes peeled, we ought to cut sign on the rustlers somewhere on the other side of the range. One of us could come back and report to you while the other stays in touch with the drive."

"Sounds reasonable," Crawford agreed. "We'll comb the hills another day while you two go back to the ranch and outfit yourselves for the trip. Tell June we are all right and she need not worry."

It was nearly midnight when the two young men rode into the yard of the Flying W. The bunkhouse was dark but there was a light in the parlor of the big house. Somebody was playing the piano.

Rogers swung from the saddle. "Looks like you are elected to feed and water my bronc, Charley," he said.

"I get it," Runyon grinned. "You're so crazy about music you've got to go listen to that piano. Me, I like music too."

"Pete told me to report to his sister."

"That's right. I onct read somewhere how music soothes the savage breast. You go in and get yores soothed. And don't forget what Doc said about that leetle bitsy scar on Miss June's arm, how it would heal when Mr. Right kissed it."

"You go hit the hay and dream about Miss Polly Simmons," Rufe advised.

"There must be something in this here telepatology business. Here's Miss June sittin' in the parlor playin' soft music in the middle of the night and you drappin' in like you was what the doctor ordered. Be lucky, fellow." Runyon headed for the stable with the horses.

Rufe did not feel very lucky. He had not seen June alone since the night when he had kissed her on the porch. He guessed that she was avoiding him except when others were present. Probably she regretted her impetuous friendliness and blamed him for taking advantage of it. Instead of breaking down the wall between them, it seemed to have built a higher one.

She looked around when he came into the room, stopped playing, and rose from the piano stool. He answered her startled look swiftly.

"Everything is all right. Pete told me to report to you."

"He did not come back with you?"

"No." Rufe explained the proposed strategy, to try cutting sign on the drive at the other end.

After he had finished telling her, apparently neither of them had anything more to say. June broke an embarrassed silence.

"I couldn't sleep, so I put on this house dress and was trying to play myself drowsy."

"I am glad. There is something I want to tell you." His eyes looked steadily into hers. "Something I want to get off my chest. I owe you an apology for what I did the other night. I took advantage of the fact that you were wrought up and shocked."

Anger flared into her eyes. "After you have kissed a girl, do you always go around and tell her what a fool she has made of herself?" she asked tartly.

He had not told her at all what he had wanted to say. His blundering attempt to reinstate their friendship had been worse than none. He could do better by telling the truth, by making it clear how greatly he had been moved. A woman does not blame herself for letting a man who loves her hold her in his arms a moment. She is justified by his deep interest in her.

Rufe felt excitement pounding in his veins. Between him and this slim girl with the low throaty voice there had always been some drag that drew them together even when they fought against it. He was going to fling away prudence and shock her back into self-respect.

"All right," he told her. "I'll give it to you straight. Ever since the days when you nursed me back to life, I've been crazy about you. There has never been another woman I wanted to marry. I didn't intend to tell you, but there it is." He flung it out as a challenge. "How do you like that, June Crawford?"

Her eyes came to shining life. "Do you mean it? You're not just trying to be nice to me, to save my wounded pride?"

"I take you with me day and night, your laughter and loveliness, your temper and your sweetness."

An exultant gladness flooded her. Looking at this man, so hard and tough and yet so gentle, she knew that he was the one of all the men she had ever known whom she would have chosen as a mate to walk the years with.

"I like it very much," she said. "I wanted not to care for you, Rufe, but it's no use. I love you—awf'ly much."

Many minutes later he put a question. "What about that young fellow from Denver?"

She lifted her head from the place where it nestled against his shoulder. "I've forgotten what he looked like," she murmured happily.

"Were you engaged to him?" he asked.

"Kind of, when I was at Wolcott School. They call it puppy love, don't they?"

They were both very sure that the love they had found

was very different. But in the back of his mind was a lurking doubt as to his right to marry a girl like June Crawford. Until a few months ago he had been so wild that his folly had dragged him into a trial for murder and bank robbery. Since that time he had been living in the midst of violence and had been forced to kill two men. As a husband for a fine clean girl he was no bargain, he told June. All their lifetime his past would be remembered.

Her starry eyes mocked his doubts. "Maybe you were a foolish boy, but that is past. I'm marrying you for your future. And there is nothing in your past that is disgraceful. You weren't in the bank robbery. The two men you had to kill were villains and you shot them both for me. I have been brought up in a rough country and I know a bad man when I see him. You are good and brave. If you were the kind that ran away from danger, I wouldn't want to marry you." Her smile for him was warm and tender. "Maybe I'm a little wild myself—or was until you tamed me. But I know what I want out of life. We're going to have a lot of lovely years, my dear."

"That settles it," he said, and drew her close to kiss her again.

After all, the important thing about a man was not his reputation, but his character. It did not matter what people said of him if he was four-square and true.

26 RUFE AND CHARLEY REACHED RIFLE in time for dinner.

As they rode down the dusty main street, Runyon said, "We'll eat at Ma Manly's."

"I figured you would think of that," Rogers said. "Too bad we won't have time for you to give Polly Simmons the treat of a walk with you down along the creek, the one you promised her the first time you met her."

"Since you're interested, fellow, I'll bring you up to date. Miss Polly has had that walk with me and several more. We're right good friends. 'Course if you had been around she prob'ly wouldn't have give me a look, you being such a heart-smasher. But with you off the market other guys get a chance."

"I reckon she is right popular," Rufe opined. "Has she told you yet whether she favors red heads?"

"Lemme worry about that," Charley retorted, swinging from the saddle. "And don't you go to making any cracks you think are funny."

When Polly came in from the kitchen to wait on them and saw who they were, her eyes brightened and a pretty blush ran into her cheeks. Since she was aware of this, most of her attention centered on Rogers. Presently Charley protested plaintively:

"No use wasting yore time on this fellow, Polly. He's done roped and branded—doesn't know there's but one girl in the world. Me, I'm a live prospect. Cheer me up some."

She slanted a look at him, fond but derisive. "You don't need any cheering up. What you need is to be stood in a corner and put in your place."

He nodded his head meekly. "Maybe that's right. The influence of a good woman——"

"Oh you!" Polly broke in, her severity somewhat offset by a dimpled smile. "Make him behave, Mr. Rogers."

"If that is going to be your permanent job, Miss Polly, you had better start training him now," Rufe said.

Polly blushed again. "'You're as bad as he is, Mr. Rogers. I declare I wouldn't have him for a Christmas gift."

"She talks nicer to me when we are alone," Charley mentioned reproachfully.

"I do not," she denied promptly.

But Rogers noticed that when she left the room she was smiling. He observed too that she gave Charley the opportunity for a few private words before they departed. His guess was that a romance was in the making.

As they freed their ponies from the hitch rack, two cowboys sauntered down the street, Ketchum and Santone. Rogers waited for them.

"You boys didn't go with that drive into the hills?" he said.

"What drive?" asked Santone.

"The one taking stolen Flying W cattle."

"News to us," Ketchum drawled. "We got fired by Yont five days ago."

"Why?"

"Damfino." Ketchum's face lit up. An explanation had just occurred to him. "Heck, he must of been planning that raid and figured he couldn't trust us. Sure, that's why he gave us our time."

That might be true, or it might be that the men had been planted here to pick up any information they could as to what the Flying W meant to do about the theft. Rogers could not be certain. Both of them had good reputations prior to the time they had started to work for Yont a year earlier.

"You didn't know he was going to make the raid?" he quizzed.

"Nobody knows ahead of time what that old crook aims to do," Santone answered. "He lives under his own hat."

"We were getting ready to quit anyhow," Ketchum explained. "I dunno why we ever went to work for the old skunk, and from the day he played that rotten trick on that kid Cape Crawford we had more than we could take."

Runyon had played around with both of them on their days off. He believed their story. "They are giving us straight goods, Rufe," he said. "They were thinking of quitting Yont a month ago."

"Have you any idea where he would take our cattle?" Rogers asked.

Santone shook his head. "He'd aim to sell the stock, of course. Wouldn't dare keep it. Likely he would hole up long enough to change the brand."

"Talk of the devil," Runyon interrupted. "Here he is in person. We can go to headquarters for information."

Yont and Slade were jogging along the street and drew up to dismount. The ranchman's gaze traveled over the four at the hitch rack. He swung from the saddle and faced them. When he spoke, it was to the men he had discharged.

"So now you are tied up with a bunch of rustlers," he said harshly.

Santone's laugh was a jeer. "You're a little mixed up, Mr. Yont. We've just cut loose from a rustler's outfit."

"Don't talk that way to me," Yont ordered. "I won't take it from trash like you. Get out of the country before you're tagged as partners of this three-time killer and rubbed out with him."

"Better cut yore stick and light out, boys," Runyon drawled. "Mr. Yont says for you to go, and of course he has a monopoly on rustling and killing. He's a fine character and knows what is best for you."

"You go too far, you whelp," Yont threatened. "Some day soon——"

"You'll have yore warriors hang me like they meant to do with Cape Crawford," Runyon cut in. "After they've come back from marketing that bunch of cattle you've just stolen from us."

The ranchman's face mapped the lust to kill. He had been top dog so long that it was hard for him to accept opposition calmly. He let out a long slow breath while his native cunning reasserted itself.

"Not now, Slade." He spaced the words reluctantly as if they hurt him, then turned away and tied at another hitching rack.

27 THE RIDERS LOOKED DOWN FROM the rim of the Mogollon Mesa into the tangled country from which they had just emerged. They had come north by way of Globe, keeping the Pinal Mountains on their right, to the Salado River. Here they had turned westward into the Tonto Basin, scene of the bloodiest feud Arizona had ever known, and north from there to Payson. It had been the hardest week of travel any of the four had ever endured. One range after another had faced them. There had been defiles almost impossible to thread. Now at last they had reached country less forbidding.

Since Santone and Ketchum were headed for the ranch country around Holbrook, they had companied the Flying W men on the trip. At every ranch and settlement Rogers left word that a stolen herd was coming through the mountains and might pass that way. The drive, of course, would not get as far as this for some time. The stock had to be rebranded and the trail herd would not average more than eight or at most ten miles a day through the mountains. There was a chance, too, that the cattle might be deflected eastward by way of Springerville and into New Mexico. But Rogers did not think that likely. The market just now was better in the new ranches of Northern Arizona along the Santa Fe line. Settlers were stocking up the range.

At Holbrook they turned their tired mounts out to pasture. After several days of idleness Santone and Ketchum picked up ranch jobs and departed. Rogers put notices in the Winslow and Holbrook papers that a rustled herd might soon arrive and warned ranchmen not to buy cattle unless they were sure the title was good. He and Runyon talked with the sheriffs of two counties and covered on horseback as much of the district as they could.

It was at St. Johns two weeks later that the first news of the rustled herd reached them. A cowboy dusty with travel rode into the wagon yard where the Flying W men had left their mounts. Runyon dropped in to water their animals. He fell into talk with the newcomer and learned that the puncher had come up from Springerville. A weary trail herd had just reached that town and was pointing north.

"Notice the brand?" Runyon asked carelessly.

The stranger was surprised at the question from another range rider. No cowhand ever looked at cattle without reading the brand.

"Sure. The Box M."

"Don't recollect that one. Wonder who was the trail boss."

"They called him Limpy."

"Heading this way, you said?"

"So I heard, but I don't guarantee it. You interested in the herd?"

Runyon grinned. "A guy on the chuck line gets to figurin' every time he hears of an outfit whether there might be a job there for him."

"Come uptown with me," the late arrival invited. "If you are scraping the bottom of the barrel, I'll stand you a beer."

Runyon and his new acquaintance found Rogers talking with the town marshal Applegate. There was no doubt whatever that this was the stolen Flying W herd, but the marshal raised a legal point. There was nothing the law could do about it until the owner appeared in person, showed these were his cattle, and proved he had not sold them to the trail driver.

On the first eastbound train Runyon left to make the

long roundabout trip to the Flying W. Since the time element was important, he could not afford to waste several days in riding back through the mountains by the route they had come. He had to let the Crawfords know that the rustled stock had been located.

Rogers saddled his pinto and rode south to meet the drive coming up. Long before the cattle came in sight, he heard the bawling of the tired stock. He rode up an arroyo, tied the horse in a brushy hollow, and lay down on a ledge behind a mesquite bush where he could watch the gut below through which the drive must pass.

Limpy was in the lead, a Winchester across the saddle in front of him. Flank riders kept the steers from wandering. A fourth man brought up the drag. Rogers counted the herd and made it two hundred seventeen. Not until the dust had died away did he swing into the saddle and follow. There was nothing he could do for the present but keep an eye on Limpy's movements. The trail boss was due for a surprise. When he began to talk with ranchmen about a sale, he would meet with an unexpected difficulty. They were going to be fussy regarding the title. It would be interesting to see what he would do. If crowded too much he might throw up the sponge and light out for parts unknown. He had been in one penitentiary and would not relish being sent to another. But Limpy was one hard tough hombre. Rogers did not expect him to scare easily.

28 LIMPY AND ONE OF HIS RIDERS, "Toughnut," were relaxing at the Oldtimers' Rest after a bath and shave at the barber shop when a heavy-set man with a long-jawed face ranged up beside them and ordered a beer.

"Expect you find a cool beer refreshing," the big man suggested. "Must of been hot on the trail."

Limpy's narrowed eyes swept the man's rangy figure from the big worn Stetson and the rumpled suit to the expensive custom-made boots.

"Hot everywhere," he said shortly.

"Yeah, but cooler in this altitude than on the desert farther south." The addition to the two at the bar sipped at his drink.

"Sounds reasonable." Limpy's voice discouraged curiosity, but the newcomer did not seem to sense it.

"A nice bunch you have on the mesa but sure travelworn," he said.

Limpy gave him his shoulder and turned to Toughnut. "Reckon we got to get back and relieve the other boys."

"Been a long drive?" the persistent questioner asked.

"They'll be rarin' to get to town to see the elephant," Toughnut agreed, taking his leader's cue and ignoring the third man.

"That's right."

The lame man turned to go, but found the rumpled suit in his way. "I understand you were bossing the drive," its owner said. "Ought to have no trouble selling to ranchers stocking up."

"Good. You a buyer?"

"No. The herd belong to you?"

"What the hell business is it of yours?" The drawling words seemed almost to drip from Limpy's thin lips.

"I'm sheriff of this county and also cattle inspector. My name is George Thorn." The officer's voice was a little harder.

"So? Why pick on me, Mr. Thorn? I don't like yore manner."

"Sorry. You haven't answered my question."

"It's a mixed bunch. The four of us own it."

"You won't object to me inspecting it?"

"Why should I? Hop to it." Limpy's cold hard stare was hostile.

"The brand is the Box M, isn't it?"

"That's the road brand. What's eatin' you, Mr. Sheriff? Do you figure yore office gives you the right to play Mr. Big and annoy every trail driver who comes into the county by snoopin' around?"

"Just a matter of routine I have to go through," Thorn answered. "No offense meant."

Limpy shrugged his shoulders. "All right. Maybe I'm a mite touchy. Have another beer with me and we'll ride out and look the herd over."

"I'll go saddle. Meet you in front right away."

Limpy watched the sheriff disappear through the swing doors. "I wonder if that guy has had notice to look out for us," he said to his companion. "He acts damn funny."

"Maybe we better make a night drive sudden," Toughnut replied.

"We'll see."

They had another beer and jingled out of the saloon to the hitch rack in front of it. In a few minutes the sheriff joined them. After they had swung to their saddles Limpy cried sharply, "Wait." He was watching a man sauntering down the sidewalk. The man was Rufe Rogers.

"So that's it," he said, scowling. "You've been talking with that bandit Rogers, a bank robber, a three-time killer, crooked as a dog's hind leg."

"Can you prove all that?" Thorn asked.

"Ask Toughnut here. The fellow killed a cashier while he was robbing a Fort Worth bank. Since then he has shot down two men in this territory. I dunno how many he rubbed out before that. A few weeks ago he and his gang raided the Quarter Circle F Y ranch. He is in trouble up to his neck all the time."

"That's whatever," corroborated Toughnut. "A sure enough bad man. Lit out from Texas and came here. Hadn't been in the territory two days before somebody had to fill him full of lead."

"But not full enough," Limpy added. "He got well."

The sheriff spoke to Rogers, now only a few yards away. "Let us clear this up. These men claim you are a bad character—a bank robber, notorious killer, and all-round troublemaker. What about it?"

A smile flashed on the lean brown face of the Texan. "It's a long story, Sheriff. Did they tell you I was proved innocent of the bank robbery? I reckon they forgot to mention that one of the ruffians I killed had just shot a young lady and that the other was starting to kidnap a girl."

"The fellow has got the gift of the gab, Mr. Thorn," Limpy said. "If a man doesn't know he is a blackguard, he can talk himself out of anything. But we know him and we stand pat. He's a rotten egg."

It had been the sheriff's business to know men. A long experience told him that first impressions might be wrong. He had met gay and likable lads who were outside the law and had little regard for human life, and he had been acquainted with cross-grained ugly old customers who were dependable in any emergency. His instinct was to distrust these slit-eyed unfriendly trail men with thin-lipped cruel mouths, just as it was to trust the cobalt blue eyes of the young Texan who carried himself wih such negligent ease. The face of the younger man was a letter of recommendation and one look at the others stirred suspicion. But Thorn could not afford to make a mistake. He had read of a prisoner being taken back to Fort Worth for trial on the bank robbery charge, but he had never heard how the case had come out.

"I'll hold the herd here for a few days until I get the right of this," the sheriff said. "The cattle are gaunted from the drive. Grass is good out on the mesa where they are. They will put on tallow and bring a better price when sold."

Limpy barked an angry protest. This did not suit him at all. An investigation was the last thing in the world he wanted. "You got no right to do that. We're poor folks. All the money we had has been spent on this drive. Among the four of us we haven't got six bits left. We have to make a sale right away."

"I'll let you sell one beef to the butcher in this town," the sheriff conceded. "That will give you enough to live high on the hog till we get this straightened out."

The leader of the rustlers grumbled, but appeared to accept the decision. He did not want to increase the suspicion of the sheriff. A night drive would take them into New Mexico out of Thorn's jurisdiction. There an Arizona sheriff would have no authority.

"You're stretching yore right a hell of a long way, but seeing as I am a law-abiding man I'll stand for it," Limpy said. He pointed his index finger at Rogers. "If you are so doggoned bent on doing yore duty, why don't you arrest that rapscallion? Probably you'd get a big reward for him." He added, by way of insult, "If you're scared to do it, make me a deputy and I'll get him for you certain, alive or dead."

Thorn flushed angrily. "When I think it's time to arrest a man, I won't need your help. And another thing, I'll pick the man. Just now I'm busy inspecting a herd."

He rode down the street, the rustlers at his heels.

Two hours later he met Rogers on the street and they went in together to a Chinese restaurant to eat dinner. Whoever had road-branded the bunch had done a good job, the sheriff reported. He thought it likely that the original brand had been a Flying W, but he could not be sure without killing an animal and examining the hide. Limpy's story fell down at one point. He claimed that the four men making the drive had each put in a number of the cattle. If so, their individual brands ought to be on the stock they had flung into the pool. It was not reasonable to suppose that four different brands could be worked over into a Box M without signs of blotching.

"If they are selling a steer to a butcher the hide would tell what the original brand was," Rogers suggested.

"They have sidestepped that chance," the sheriff answered dryly. "They are not selling one, even though they claim they are down to their last dollar. I put a deputy, Jim Dayton, in charge of the herd until Crawford gets here. If your story doesn't hold water, young fellow, I'll be in a jam certain."

"It will stand up," Rogers told him. "Don't worry about that."

The sheriff became sure it would when his deputy Dayton burst into his office next day at noon angry and disheveled with the news that the herd had vanished. Soon after dark he had been held up by armed men, taken to a distant arroyo, and bound hands and feet. Unable to free himself, he had lain there helpless all night. The morning was half-spent before a nester on his way to town had heard his cries and released him. His assailants had worn bandannas for masks, but he was sure they were the men who had been driving the herd.

Thorn at once got in touch with Rogers, appointed him a deputy, and with two others in the posse started in pursuit. That the rustlers were headed for the New Mexico line was almost sure. If they could reach it, they would be for the time safe. They had a long start and no doubt would drive the stock hard. The chance of cutting them off before they got out of the territory was slight.

The outlaws won by a half-hour. When the sheriff reached the line, he could see the dust of the herd in the valley below and could hear faintly the bawling of the fretted cattle. Thorn was annoyed. He did not like to be made a monkey of, as he phrased it.

"Might as well go on and free my mind to them," he decided. "Maybe we can pick up a hint of where they are aiming for."

The drivers saw them as they rode down into the valley and gathered together while the stock drifted. Limpy sat relaxed and easy in the saddle, a Winchester in his hands.

"Nice to see you again, Sheriff," he drawled. "This just a friendly call or have you got business in New Mexico?"

"You assaulted my deputy and took these cattle unlawfully," Thorn charged.

Limpy shook his head reproachfully. "You must be thinking of somebody else, Sheriff. We didn't assault anybody. Fact is, we found our stock wandering all over the county so we rounded them up and moved to another feed ground. In this hot weather they lose tallow less when driven at night. We hated to wake you up and just moseyed along."

"You can't get away with this," Thorn retorted angrily. "I'll notify the New Mexico authorities to arrest you."

"You might tell them, too, that you are thick as three in a bed with the most notorious killer in Arizona," Limpy jeered.

Rogers had no intention of playing more than second fiddle to the sheriff. He suggested mildly, "With so many candidates in the field, aren't you ranking me a little high?"

"Everybody in that part of Arizona knows you are the Flying W gunman." Limpy turned from Rogers to the sheriff. "Better call it a day, my friend. We're out of yore jurisdiction. I wouldn't push on the reins if I were you."

"I still think it's a stolen herd," Thorn said shortly, and turned his mount to ride back to St. Johns.

29 BEFORE THE POSSE REACHED THE territorial line, Rogers stopped and said goodbye to the others. He intended to follow unseen the progress of the trail herd into New Mexico. With him he had brought a sack of food tied to the saddle strings back of the seat.

To keep in touch with the drive well back in the rear offered no difficulty. The dust of the moving herd pointed the way. He skirted the mountains from Salt Lake to Quemado through a desolate country rough and uninhabited, a waste spaced with ridges, washes, and hogbacks strewn with rubble and boulders. Here and there on the uplands grew zacaton and bunch grass on which cattle could feed.

He spent the night at Quemado, the herd only a few miles in front of him. From here by a migrant wagoning west he sent to Sheriff Thorn a letter promising to leave at Datil a message for Pete Crawford, since that village was evidently the immediate destination of Limpy. Two days later he bypassed the drivers by swinging into the foothills, crossed the continental divide, and dropped down into Datil. While waiting for the arrival of the herd later in the week, he camped in a small park west of the village where pine trees clustered on the slope and native grass beside a small stream gave good grazing for his pinto. Each morning he rode into Datil to renew his supplies and make sure no word from Crawford had come.

It was on his third visit that he ran into a surprise. He tied in front of the small store which was also the post office and sauntered into the building, apparently a cowboy on the loose. Within five minutes he heard a voice outside that startled him.

"Hi, Yont! Take a gander at that paint hoss," it said excitedly. "That guy Rogers must be right here in town."

A moment later Yont answered—Rufe would have known that harsh snarl among a hundred: "It's his bronc certain. No gunplay right now, Limpy, not till we've got rid of the stock. Soon as we get the law off our necks, we'll gun him."

The herd, Rogers guessed, must still be fifteen or twenty miles back on the trail. Evidently Limpy had sent for Yont to straighten out the tangle of ownership and had ridden in to meet him. It must be a blow to them to find Rufe already on the scene prepared to raise a cloud on the title.

"Any law against us beating him up good?" That was Toughnut's suggestion, Rufe felt sure.

"I don't know of any, if you run across him and feel

like it." Yont's nasty croak again. "He's been asking for it since the first day I met the double-crosser. But I can't afford to have him killed right now."

Three men walked into the store, Yont, Limpy, and Toughnut.

Toughnut was the first to speak. "Well, look who is here," he gibed, showing yellow teeth in a wide grin. He was a big muscle-bound man, wide-shouldered and deep-chested, probably in the middle thirties.

"Too bad you didn't bring yore friend the sheriff with you," Limpy said. "You being so damned legal these days."

The storekeeper, a small pink-cheeked man with gray whiskers, interposed hurriedly. "Now gents, please. No trouble in here."

The Quarter Circle F Y men paid not the least heed to him. Their whole attention was focused on the man they meant to beat into a pulp. The cold cruel eyes of Yont held a gloating enjoyment.

"I reckon, boys, we'll have to cut this interfering fool down to size. He's been a pain in the neck ever since that first day when he came begging me for a job. This is it." Yont added sharply: "Take yore hand off that gun, you damned killer, or we'll blast you to hell."

Rogers knew that if the guns began to smoke, he would be killed. He had to take a beating and hoped that he would come out of it alive.

"Let's get this straight," he said, his voice cool and even. "Do all of us hand our sixshooters over to Slocum for him to hang on the rack? If it's to be that way, I'll rock along with you."

"That will suit us fine," Toughnut said. "Though I'd as lief have it the other way."

"Gentlemen—gentlemen!" the storekeeper pleaded. "If you've got to settle a difficulty please go outside."

"We lay our guns down all at the same time and wait till Slocum clears them off the counter," Yont said, still mindless of the merchant.

"Your store is going to be wrecked certain, Mr. Slocum," Rogers said. "Not my fault. You'll have to look to Yont for damages."

"Cut the gab and put that hogleg on the counter,"

Toughnut ordered. "We're eyeing you, fellow. Don't make a false move."

The four men laid down their revolvers, watching with catlike wariness before releasing their weapons. Still protesting anxiously, Slocum hung the guns on the nail-studded board prepared for cowboys' weapons.

As Toughnut made a dive for their victim, Rogers snatched an ax handle from a rack of them. There was no room for a full swing, but the helve beat down the cowboy's lifted arm and landed on his head. He staggered against the counter, for the moment dazed. Yont and Limpy closed with Rufe. To defend himself he dropped the club and lashed out with his fist hard to Limpy's jaw. The lame man was flung back, lost his footing against a box of apples, and crashed down into a half-bushel basket of eggs. He pushed himself out of it to his feet, streams of yellow viscous semi-fluid dripping from his hands, face, and clothes.

Toughnut had recovered and was moving around Yont to get at Rogers, who was trying to beat off his former employer's attack. The big man was hammering into Rufe's body and face savage blows regardless of the jabs landing on his eyes and nose. He knew he was more powerful than his slender opponent. Fighting back Yont, Rufe was jarred to his heels by a looping right from Toughnut.

If the attackers had not got into each other's way, the fight would not have lasted three minutes, but in their eagerness to get at their foe they crowded one another aside. Some of their blows were deflected. Rufe tried to keep his back to the counter in an effort to protect him from a rear assault. The tide of battle swept him to and fro. Heavy fists beat against his ribs, his head, his stomach. They lashed at him from all sides. His boxing skill was of no use here. Toughnut was a notorious barroom brawler with the awkwardness and power of a bear. His employer was even more dangerous because his muscular coordination was better.

Limpy snatched up from the floor the ax helve and skirted the outside of the mêlée looking for a chance to rap Rogers on the skull with it. Rufe's face was a map of blood and wheals. One eye was closing fast. A dozen hammers beat dizzily in his head. His arms carried heavy weights and his legs were rubbery. When the ax handle descended on him, his whole body caved in and he went down as a sack of meal.

Toughnut crowded forward. "Lemme get at him. He's playin' dead on us."

Yont barred the way, flinging him back. "Leave him lay. He's had all he can take. I can't have him killed and have a pack of sheriffs on my back. All I need is twenty-four hours to put through a deal for the sale of our stuff. I've got a buyer interested."

The store looked as if a cyclone had wrecked it. A flour barrel had been upset and its contents scattered all over the floor. The glass case containing cigars was shattered. Bottles of patent medicine, swept from a shelf in the struggle, lay broken on the counter, the contents dripping over a cheese and flowing into a butter tub.

Slocum emerged timidly from where he had been crouching behind the counter. He looked woefully at the havoc created.

"Gentlemen, I'm ruined," he moaned. "Who will pay for the damage? It's terrible."

Toughnut grinned. "Mr. Rogers will be glad to pay," he said. "It was his party."

The storekeeper's troubled gaze shifted to the unconscious man. "Do you reckon he's—alive?"

There was a slight flicker of Rogers' eyelids.

"You bet," Toughnut assured him. "Maybe we ought to rough the guy up some more."

"No," Limpy cut in sharply. "He's had a bellyful. I won't stand for it." He looked with disgust at his yellow sticky clothes. "I could be fried for an omelette."

Yont glared down with savage satisfaction at the prone man. "He won't bother us for a while. Let's go."

The ranchman led the others out of the store.

Slocum said plaintively, "With all New Mexico wide open before them they had to come in here and bust up my store. I'll never get a nickel out of them."

Rufe murmured weakly, the one eye that was still partially in commission half-open, "Correct."

"They gave you an awful beating." The storekeeper

extended part of his sympathy to the battered cause of his financial trouble. "I'd better get Doc Ford."

The bleeding head of Rogers rested on a bolt of muslin that had been dragged down from a counter where a half-hour earlier Slocum had been showing it to a potential buyer. He tried to raise himself and found he could not do it.

"I need a doc—to put the pieces together," he admitted. "The boys jolted me up considerable."

Doctor Ford was a gaunt middle-aged man who had lived most of his life on the frontier. He did a good deal of drinking in his spare time, but a wide experience had made him a competent surgeon in patching up wounded cowboys. Rogers was sore in every joint and muscle above the waist, but he endured the ministrations of the physician with the usual stoicism of the outdoors plainsman. Two of his ribs appeared to be fractured and his head had been worked over into something gruesome to behold. One sure thing was that he had to be put to bed and kept quiet.

"Better run around to Mrs. Watts and ask her if she will take him in and nurse him," the doctor said to Slocum.

Rogers started to protest and Ford shut him up decisively. "You don't have a thing to say about this. That is, if you have money enough to pay her."

The patient assured him that he had.

He was carried in a buckboard to the cottage of Mrs. Watts and fainted as he was being lifted into the spare bedroom. For a time he was semi-delirious. Fever ran high in him. During the small hours of early morning he fell into a troubled sleep.

When he awoke, it was to hear Doctor Ford say, "The fever is dying in him and he'll get well fast."

A low husky voice answered, "They might have killed him."

Rufe thought, *I'm still out of my mind.* That voice could not be in the room with him. The girl to whom it belonged was far away in Southern Arizona.

Even when a cool soft hand brushed his cheek and rested on his forehead, he did not believe it. Yet this could not be the work-roughened hand of Mrs. Watts. He squinted out of one half-opened eye. June Crawford was standing by the bedside looking down at him.

"I'm plumb crazy in the head," he told her. "You're not here."

"Yes, I'm here. We got in ten minutes ago, Charley and Cape and I. Pete had to stay and protect the ranch." June knelt beside the bed and kissed softly his swollen cut lips. "You poor boy, alone against all of them."

He was not alone any longer. His body was weak and battered, but his heart lifted. He thought, *She is so slim and lovely, but so silken strong.* Her eyes were shining with the tender light of one who is both a lover and, for the hour at least, a mother. He had come home, as a child does, where the wicked cease from troubling and the weary are at rest.

It hurt him to smile, but he managed one. "I'm the luckiest guy that ever lived," he told her.

When Cape and Charley came into the room, he gave them directions what to do. The stolen herd was west of town somewhere on the trail, probably not more than ten or twelve miles out. They must get the sheriff, prove they owned the Flying W brand, and ride out to the herd. One of the steers must be killed and the hide examined. The evidence it showed would be convincing. It would be the sheriff's job, not theirs, to arrest the rustlers. That officer had been alerted and was prepared to act.

"He'd better take an armed posse with him," Runyon said. "That bunch of rustlers ain't any gentler than a passle of wampus cats."

"You and Cape will have to go along to identify the stock, but neither of you must serve on the posse. This has got to look right, not like a fuss between feuders. If Yont or his men ride you with rough tongues, take it like lambs."

"There won't be any shooting, will there?" June asked anxiously.

"Not likely. The law will be handling this."

Runyon grinned down at his friend on the bed. "You've sure turned gentle in yore old age, considerin' you have the rep of a fighting fool. But don't worry. We'll let the sheriff make the play."

"I heard Yont say he had a buyer," Rogers said. "Better move fast."

June followed her brother and Runyon out of the room to urge them to keep out of any trouble there might be.

30 YONT WALKED INTO THE POST OF-fice and leaned against the counter while Slo-cum waited on a customer. He was implicated in serious trouble and felt it would be wise to placate the storekeeper before taking up with the sheriff the more vital charge of rustling. There were several others in the room when he opened the matter of damages. He wanted it broadcast through the village that he was a responsible cattleman willing to pay for any loss Slocum had sustained even though the killer and bank robber had been the one to blame.

"My boys are a fine bunch, but when they caught sight of that trouble-maker they went a little haywire," he explained.

Slocum had an opinion on who had started the fight, but he accepted the version Yont offered. He had figured out the amount of loss without expecting to be paid for it, and it was a pleasant surprise to have Yont pay him the sum without protest.

From the post office Yont went to the office of Sheriff McDonnell. That officer gave him a frosty reception. Like many of the sheriffs of this Western country, he had for-merly been a cattleman himself and took a dim view of rustlers. It was his opinion that any found guilty should go to the penitentiary.

189

"You claim this herd belongs to you?" McDonnell snapped.

"That's right." Yont went on to mention that he had the largest spread in the Rifle district and shipped more cattle to market than any other three owners combined.

"The drivers of this herd say they made it up by throwing in stuff from their own small ranches." The cool gray eyes of the sheriff fastened on those of his visitor.

Yont was taken aback by this, but did not show it. "I reckon the boys were doing a little bragging over their drinks—trying to seem important."

"We'll go take a look at the herd," McDonnell said stiffly. He had just had a talk with the three young people from the Flying W and he believed their story. Though he had never met Yont before, he had several times heard the man discussed unfavorably by ranchmen of Southern Arizona. There was no doubt in his mind as to which party in this controversy was right.

Yont had seen June and her brother on the street and he was disturbed at the way events were shaping. It might be well to prepare a defense by putting the blame on his men if the theft of the stock should be proved. Pushed to the wall, it would be his word against Limpy's.

"I wasn't at home when the stuff was picked for the drive, but I feel sure my men can't be trying to pull a fast trick by rounding up somebody else's cattle to sell for their own pockets. I haven't yet had a look at the herd."

It might be that way, McDonnell reflected. Certainly the drivers had claimed the herd as their own. Ordinarily a big operator like Yont did not get mixed up in deals of this sort.

"Would you know when you see this herd whether it belongs to you?" the sheriff asked.

Yont hedged. "I might and then again I might not. I'm running more than thirty thousand head. It would be difficult to point to a steer and say it was mine."

"We'll kill one, skin it, and see how the brand looks," McDonnell said.

"Probably that won't be necessary," Yont told the officer quickly. "I reckon I'll know my animals." The one thing he did not want was to have the brand on a hide inspected closely.

"I'll get young Crawford and the three of us will ride out to the feed ground," the sheriff decided.

"There is a nasty wind blowing. It would be pleasanter to go tomorrow morning than now." Yont was playing for time. His men were moving the stock into the hills and an extra day would be useful.

"We'll go now and get it over with," McDonnell answered.

Two deputies went with the party. If an arrest had to be made, they would be needed. Cape Crawford was the fifth member of it. Runyon reluctantly decided he had better stay with Rogers for fear the Quarter Circle F Y men might make another attack on him.

Young Crawford and Yont glared at each other, but exchanged no verbal greeting. Cape took pains not to ride beside his enemy. He was afraid his temper would flare up and cause trouble. This was now in the hands of the law and the less he said the better it would be.

They found no cattle grazing on the mesa. Yont showed voluble surprise. He suggested that Limpy must have driven them to water. The sheriff looked hard at him and said that they would check that possibility. Just below the mesa a small creek ran. After an examination, McDonnell was convinced that no herd had watered there within twelve hours.

"We'll comb the hills," he announced. "No bunch as big as that can just vanish."

At the edge of the foothills, they ran into an old mossyhorn steer carrying the Box M brand.

"Must have slipped away from the herd in the darkness and not been noticed," a deputy guessed.

"You have hit it on the nose, Monte," the sheriff agreed.

He swung from the saddle, rifle in hand, and shot the steer. Monte helped him skin the animal. The hide showed plainly that the brand beneath the new one had been a Flying W.

"A few strays belonging to other outfits get into every trail herd," Yont mentioned.

"And we by chance happened to find one," Cape said, with pointed sarcasm.

"Don't even look as if you thought I am rustling your stock," Yont warned angrily. "I still think this herd is mine, but if the boys have turned thieves, I'm through with them. It's on their own heads."

The boss of the Quarter Circle F Y had made up his mind. He had little doubt that the driven cattle would be found and the theft proved. Fortunately there were no witnesses against him except Limpy. He had stayed in the background and let the lame man handle the rustling. It was time to get indignant at the guilt of his men and throw in with the sheriff to help arrest them. McDonnell might continue to suspect him, but there would be no evidence to support this but the word of a rustler caught in the act.

"They can't have gone very far," the sheriff said. "Probably they are going to cut over the pass through Box Cañon. Monte, you ride back to town and pick up a couple of good men. Load a pack horse with grub and meet us at Two Forks. We'll camp there tonight. Mr. Yont, you had better go with Monte."

"No, sir," Yont answered sharply. "I aim to see this thing through. If my men have turned bad, I want to know it. If this is my herd—and I'm sure it is—I don't aim to have this slick thief Crawford steal it."

McDonnell looked hard at him, then shrugged his shoulders. "All right. But get this, I'm wagon boss here and I won't have you interfering."

"I'm standing with the law," Yont said virtuously.

Cape's glance whipped to him. There was unveiled contempt on his face. "A rat and a sinking ship," he jeered.

As it chanced, Monte's horse was at the moment jammed close to Yont's sorrel. When the furious ranchman whipped out his forty-five the deputy's fist slammed down on the man's wrist. The bullet tore into the ground a few inches from the hoof of the sorrel. The animal went into the air and came down bucking wildly. By the time Yont had quieted his mount, three guns covered him.

"Hit the trail for town," McDonnell ordered. "I don't want yore company."

Yont glowered at him a long moment, making up his mind. He thrust the revolver back into its holster, swung the horse around, and rode away, his flat back straight and defiant. Monte turned and followed him.

The sheriff's anger turned on Cape. "Haven't you a lick of sense?" he rasped. "Hadn't been for Monte you would have been dead as a stuck shote. If it wasn't that Yont would probably bump you off, I would send you too back to town."

"I'd ought to of kept my mouth shut," Cape said, apology in his voice. "But I hate the ground that fellow walks on. Some of his gunmen had a rope around my neck once ready to hang me."

They rode into a cañon enclosed by high perpendicular precipices, the floor of it sand and rubble gashed with boulders that had fallen from the edge of the cliffs above. Though the gorge was dry as a lime kiln now, its walls were marked with high water lines where flash floods had roared down in wild fury.

Even a tenderfoot could have read the signs of many cattle having passed up Box Cañon a few hours earlier, but by the time they had ridden through the pass and dropped down into the park below the rim darkness had fallen and stars were pricking the sky. A mountain creek watered the valley and the grass was fetlock deep to the horses. McDonnell led the way along the stream to a point where a smaller brook joined it.

Here he swung from the saddle. "No supper till Monte gets here," he announced, and picketed his horse.

"My belly is flat as an empty mail sack," the deputy reported cheerfully. "I never did know before how fond I am of Monte. I'm plumb anxious to see him."

They lit a fire and crouched before it while the darkness deepened, glad of its comfort against the night wind blowing down from the mountains.

It was three hours later when Monte and two other men arrived driving a pack horse. All of them attacked the food like famished castaways.

They were in the saddle as soon as the first faint streaks of light were in the sky. Later mists filled the valleys and lifted into the crotches of the hills. Then the sun came over a ridge, scattered the mists, and took the night chill out of the air.

31 WITHIN THE HOUR THEY HAD picked up again the trail of the herd. The drive had passed this way late the evening before. McDonnell warned his deputies to be on the alert. Back of every depression or every clump of brush might lie an ambush. He did not think it likely. The rustlers were probably scurrying for cover as fast as they could push the stock.

Far across the undulating plain, near the foot of a low ridge, Cape caught sight of a small flat-roofed adobe building. He pointed it out to the sheriff.

"Smoke rising from the chimney and a horse standing in front of the door," Crawford said.

"Old man Bissell's store," McDonnell told him. "Used by the Dry Creek ranchers and nesters in the hills. So small you couldn't swing a cat in it."

"Believe I'll run over and buy some smoking," Cape suggested. "I'll ask if they've seen anything of the fellows we're trailing."

The officer's grin was sardonic. "Go if you like. You won't get anything out of old Bissell. Half his customers are gents on the dodge."

As Cape drew up at the adobe and flung himself from the saddle, a man came to the door, a half-filled gunny sack hanging from his left hand. He had evidently been buying provisions. The man was Limpy.

His pale blue eyes narrowed. "Don't you know better than to crowd me, you fool?" he said, in a low chill voice. The fingers of his right hand crept toward the butt of the forty-five at his hip.

"Wrong guess," the boy said quickly. "I'm not lookin' for you."

The man's gaze swept the terrain. It chanced that the posse had dipped into an arroyo and could not be seen. "How come you here—alone?" he demanded.

"Listen, Limpy," Cape answered urgently. "I'm a two-spot in this trouble. I've got bad news for you. Yont knows the game is up and he has thrown you boys down. He is siding with the law figuring to protect his own hide. By his way of it, he's shocked to discover you are rustlers and is all for sending you to the pen."

Limpy had spent some bad moments fearing this, since Yont had not showed up to join them as he had promised. This boy might be telling the truth.

"How do you know?" he snarled. "When did you see him?"

Cape told the story of what has occurred—the skinning of the stray steer, Yont's swift change of front so as to leave his employees holding the sack.

The lean muscles of the outlaw's face tightened and his washed-out eyes searched the boy's countenance. Limpy had the look of a cornered wolf ready to leap.

"So you came here to save me?" he jeered.

"I wouldn't lift a finger for you. I'm riding with Mc-Donnell to prove you are driving our stock. But Yont is the one I want to cinch. He's aiming to slide out of this. He is in it up to his neck certain."

Bitter anger surged up in the lame man and drove the dark blood into his face.

"If Yont has done this to me—if he has dared—I'll get him if it's the last thing I ever do."

"You ought to know him by this time," Cape said.

Limpy's mind shifted to the immediate danger. "You haven't told me yet howcome you are here alone. Where's McDonnell's posse?"

"It's moving up that arroyo back of the hill."

The lame man thought fast. There was no chance to save the herd now. He and his partners must make a get-away in a hurry. But first they had a job to do.

"Where is Yont now?" he asked.

"He went back to Datil last night."

The pressure of Limpy's thoughts broke into a murmur just audible. The words Cape heard were, "He's lived too long."

32 IT WAS ONE OF THOSE PLEASANT days when the sun shone on red New Mexico with a genial warmth, the heat moderated by a cool breeze from the hills. Charley Runyon squatted in front of an adobe wall and rolled a smoke. From the corral pasture across the street a meadowlark flung out its full-throated joyous note. It did not take much to move Charley to song. He was relaxed and at ease with the world. He would be going back to his girl soon. His lips started to hum a bit of night-herding doggerel.

Two young people had just come out to the porch of Mrs. Watts' house. At sight of Rufe Rogers and June Crawford, the cowboy's eyes warmed. They were his best friends. He could see that they were absorbed in each other to the exclusion of the outside world. They had come through danger and near disaster to safety. The law was closing in on their enemies. The years ahead for them promised only happiness.

Rufe was still a little shaky from the terrible beating he had been given, and Charley noticed that he and his girl were taking advantage of it. As they started up the street, she tucked her arm under his with a shy proprietary air ostensibly for support. Runyon guessed the real reason was that the close contact filled them both with delight.

He slanted an impish grin at them as they approached. He had shifted to an old folk song of trail driving days.

> Eyes like a morning star, cheeks like a rose,
> Laura was a pretty girl, God Almighty knows;
> Weep all ye little rains, wail, winds, wail,
> All along, along, along the Colorado Trail.

Rufe laughed. "All this scrumptious morning, and a sere-nade thrown in for free," he said.

"If you're headin' for the post office, ask if there's any-thing for me," Charley suggested. "Fellow owes me two dollars. Might be he has sent it."

At the office they were handed a letter for Charles Run-yon postmarked Rifle. When they reachd the cowboy on their way back to the house, he was still intoning the old trail song:

Keep the herds a-rollin' on, rollin' on their way.

Rufe stopped and felt the letter over carefully. "Says it's for Mr. Charles Runyon, but I don't reckon it has any two dollars in it. Looks more like one of these billet-doux from a lady."

June took the letter from Rufe and examined it. "What lady at Rifle could be writing to Charley?" she inquired.

"Couldn't be Polly Simmons, could it?" Rufe ventured. "Charley claims she likes redheads."

"Maybe you better read it, then you won't have to do any more guessing," the owner of the letter said.

June nodded her head and dropped the letter into Charley's outstretched hand. "I think it's from Polly," she decided. "Let us know when to congratulate you."

Charley grinned and waved them on their way. "Vaya con Dios," he told them, using the Spanish salutation that is almost a benediction.

Their light-hearted foolery stopped abruptly, vanished swiftly like the flame from a blown candle. A man had come out of a saloon and moved toward a horse tied to a rack in front of the place. The man was Fen Yont. His casual glance picked up Rogers and there was an instant deadly tensity in his body. The bulbous eyes narrowed to points of light with a glaring intentness in them. All his sultry hatred, his frustrated rage, had at last come to the moment of explosion. The man moved forward slowly, the feral urge to kill stamped on his savage face.

To June, Rogers said sharply, "Back to the house quick."

She made no move, her terror-filled eyes were fixed on Yont.

A cold wind blew through Rufe. He had come to the final hour of reckoning and was unprepared for it.

"Take your time, Yont," he said. "There's no hurry. I'm not armed. Wait till Miss Crawford has gone."

She said in a voice hushed by fear, "I'm not going."

"Hiding behind a woman again," Yont snarled.

Charley Runyon came up from his lounging position in one lithe movement. "Don't forget me, Yont," he warned. "I'm heeled, and my iron is out too."

Yont seemed to pay him not the least attention. His words were for Rogers. "You're a liar. I know you are packing a gun."

"No!" June cried. "He isn't."

Long seconds slipped away while Yont thought it out. The unwritten law of the time and place was that a man could kill another with no penalty attached, but he could not shoot him if his foe was unarmed. Four or five men were watching the scene from doors and windows. He came to an urgent wild decision, helped to it by another suggestion from Runyon.

"Better put up that hogleg, Yont. This isn't your day."

Yont whirled and fired. Runyon stumbled back against the wall. His knees gave way and he slid down. The revolver slipped from his grip.

The beat of horses' hoofs came down the road, but nobody paid any attention to them. June was paralyzed by fear. Rufe was sure his turn would be next. His enemy had gone mad with the lust to kill.

Yont pointed to the weapon in the dust. "There's yore gun," he yelped. "Go get it and start smoking."

June's arms went around her lover and she clung to him convulsively. "No. No. He means to kill you before you can fire."

The leading horseman jerked his mount to a halt and leaped from the saddle. He stood crouched, his legs wide apart, a forty-five in his hand.

"So you threw us down, you damned double-crosser," he snarled.

"What fool notion is eatin' you, Limpy?" Yont demanded. His eyes whipped from Limpy to Toughnut and from him to Sorrel and Black. They too had their weapons out. The cowboys had set themselves in a semicircle backing him against the wall. A chill fear ran down his backbone. He knew that he had come to the end of his road. But no sign of this showed on his craggy face. His voice sounded even and undisturbed, the bite of scorn in it. "Never knew a cowpoke with a lick of sense. I come hundreds of miles to pull you out of a jam and this is the thanks I get."

Toughnut's cruel laugh sounded. "Go on, Yont. Make it good. See if you can talk yoreself out of this one."

The trapped man's hard gaze settled on Toughnut. "You've always claimed you are the best two-fisted fighter in Arizona. Say we put our guns down and see about that right now."

"No go, Yont," Limpy answered. "There's a man lying against the wall you've just killed. If we had been ten seconds later, you would have got another. Time's up for you—was long ago. You're better dead."

Rogers had pushed June swiftly into the alcove entry to a saddler's shop. "Don't look," he said, and put his body between her and the street.

The words were hardly out of his mouth before the crash of Yont's weapon sounded. Instantly the answering guns roared. The noise of the explosions filled the street. Shifting figures moved back of the films of smoke. A man's voice cried, "God, I'm hit!" Bullets plowed into the adobe wall and flung spatters of dirt.

Then, suddenly as it had started, the fusillade ended. Toughnut was on the ground, the spread fingers of both hands clutching at his stomach. Yont too was down, trying desperately to raise his pistol arm for another shot. Limpy moved slowly forward, not lifting his eyes from the mortally wounded man. A moment later a slug from his revolver tore into Yont's heart.

Rogers supported June into the saddler's shop and seated her in a chair. He told the storekeeper to get her a dipper of water and went back to the street. Limpy and Sorrel were hoisting Toughnut into a saddle. The wounded man clung with a tight grip to the horn, his body bent forward.

Limpy called to Rogers, "We've done a job for you, fellow."

He and Sorrel rode with Toughnut between them, supporting his sagging body. They were heading for the safety of the San Andres Mountain fastnesses. Three of them reached the gorges where only men outside the law nested. Before the outlaws were a mile out of Datil, Toughnut died in the saddle.

Rufe knelt beside his friend, desperately unhappy at his loss. What he saw lifted his heart greatly. The bullet had creased Runyon's scalp and knocked him senseless, just as wild horses were creased by their hunters and knocked out for a short time.

Charley's eyelids fluttered open. He lifted a hand to his head and looked with surprise at the blood on his fingers. "Howcome?" he asked, puzzled.

"Yont's compliments," Rogers explained. "Luck was riding on your shoulder this time, boy. All he did was give you a haircut."

Charley's roving glance took in the dead body of their enemy. "Thought you weren't heeled," he said.

Rogers told him of the timely arrival of the men Yont was betraying.

"Looks like the war is over," Runyon commented.

He was right. The man who had poisoned the life of a whole district had come to the end of his evil crooked trail. Since Billy Yont and his sister were his heirs, there was nobody left who wanted to carry on the feud.

When the two friends walked back into the saddler's shop, June stared in astonishment at Charley Runyon.

"I thought—I thought——" she began.

"Only a scalp crease," Rufe explained. He added, after a moment, "Yont is dead."

June stood up, white and trembling. Her lover took her into his arms and peace flowed into her soul. The anxious days were over and all through her life he would be near to comfort her.

William MacLeod Raine, hailed in his later years by reviewers and contemporaries alike to be the "greatest living practitioner" of the genre and the "dean of Westerns," was born in London, England in 1871. Upon the death of his mother, Raine emigrated with his father to Arkansas in the United States where he was raised. He attended Sarcey College in Arkansas and received his Bachelor's degree from Oberlin College in 1894. After graduation, Raine traveled throughout the American West, taking odd jobs on ranches. He was troubled in his early years by a lung ailment that was eventually diagnosed as tuberculosis. He moved to Denver, Colorado in hopes that his health would improve, and worked as a reporter and editorial writer for a number of newspapers. He began writing Western short stories for the magazine market. His first Western novel was *Wyoming* (Dillingham, 1908), that proved so popular with readers that it was serialized in the first issues of Street & Smith's Western Story Magazine when that publication was launched in 1919. During World War I, Raine's Western fiction was so popular among British readers that 500,000 copies of his books were distributed among British troops. By his own admission, Raine concentrated on character in his Westerns. "I'm not very strong on plot. Some of my writing friends say you have to have the plot all laid out before you start. I don't see it that way. If you have it all laid out, your characters can't develop naturally as the story unfolds. Sometimes there's someone you start out as a minor character. By the time you're through, he's the major character of the book. I like to preside over it all, but to let the book do its own growing." It would appear that because of this focus on character Raine's stories have stood the test of time better than those of some of his contemporaries. It was his intimate knowledge of the American West that provides verisimilitude to all of his stories, whether in a large sense such as the booming industries of the West or the cruelties of nature—a flood in *Ironheart* (1923), blizzards in *Ridgway of Montana* (1909) and *The Yukon Trail* (1917), a fire in *Gunsight Pass* (1921). It is perhaps Raine's love of the West of his youth, the place and the people where there existed the "fine free feeling of man as an individual," glimmering in the pages of his books that will warrant the attention of readers always.